The Wife Swap

ALSO BY LISA HALL

The Day She Disappeared
Eight Years of Lies
The Wife Swap

THE WIFE SWAP

LISA HALL

JOFFE BOOKS

Joffe Books, London
www.joffebooks.com

First published in Great Britain in 2026

Cover art by Nick Castle

ISBN: 978-1-80573-430-7

This one is for the Tedds.

CHAPTER 1

'It looks like a body,' I say into the phone as I peer out of the living room window, peeking around the edge of the blinds so as to stay out of sight.

'Don't be daft,' Nate tuts on the other end of the line. I can picture him sitting on the edge of his hotel bed, his blond hair flopping over his forehead the way it always does after a long day on the road, flogging his big pharma drugs to hospitals and surgeries up and down the country. His hair always starts the day neatly slicked back, but by lunchtime, meetings with GPs, hospital doctors and pharmacists mean it hangs into his eyes the way it used to when we first met, twelve years ago.

'It could be. You don't know.' I peer out again, as the man hefts the rolled item from the removal van onto his shoulder with an almost audible grunt. The way he looks over his shoulder as if checking to see if he's being observed makes my spine tingle. 'It's the right length and shape.'

'You watch too much Netflix, Hayley. Why on earth would our new neighbours be moving a body into a house they just bought? Surely you'd leave it buried in the previous back garden?' Nate sounds amused, but I can hear a familiar undertone of annoyance as he speaks.

The man drops the package, and it unrolls across the path.

'It's a rug,' I say, half disappointed, half relieved. 'A nice one though.' It looks Persian and expensive, in deep hues of amber and camel. I take a long swig of my wine, the crisp Sauvignon rolling over my tongue.

'Like I said, too much Netflix.' There is a pause. 'Are you drinking?'

I look down at my glass, at the half inch of wine left in the bottom. 'No.'

Nate sighs. 'I thought you were giving it up for Lent.'

'Lent was over ages ago.' I sip again and turn my attention back to the window. 'You should see some of the stuff coming out of the removal van.'

'Hayley . . .'

A spurt of irritation floods my veins. I know what Nate is about to say. That I should step away from the window. That next door is none of my business. But he's away all the time and I am here, alone and lonely. If Nate would agree to starting a family, instead of stalling for time, then I'd be too busy to watch the neighbours. And besides, the house next door has been empty for six months, ever since the last couple moved out. Of course I'm intrigued by whoever has bought it.

'Nate, come on. Let me have some fun while you're not here. Oh . . .' I breathe out, as the man reappears from the house. He's tall, a good two or three inches taller than Nate, and he isn't exactly short at six foot. He has a thick head of dark hair, with salt and pepper threaded through it, and as he turns to look back at his own house, I catch a glimpse of his face properly. He is *handsome*, for want of a better word. A proper looker, my Gran would have said.

'They have a hundred-inch TV,' I say, watching as the man leans the box against the removal van.

Nate sucks in a breath. 'They'll never get that in the sitting room,' he says, envy turning his words a bright, vivid green.

'They're going to be renovating,' I say, 'at least, that's what the estate agent told me when I saw her outside. Knocking down walls and expanding things. Building an extension just for the telly, probably.'

The house previously belonged to a pair of young professionals who didn't stay long enough to make improvements, after buying from an elderly couple who died. Our street, leafy and quiet, far enough out on the outskirts of London to feel properly suburban but close enough for the commute into town to be bearable, is full of freshly renovated, old Victorian houses that sell for ridiculous money once there's a lick of Farrow and Ball paint on the walls. Thankfully I inherited this place when my grandmother died, because Nate and I could never have bought it on a pharma rep and an office manager's salary.

'Just get away from the window, before they see you,' Nate says, his irritation leaching through enough to be obvious now. 'Please, Hayls. Go and get some dinner or something. They're going to think you're a peeper, or worse, neighbourhood watch. Neighbourhood watch, or pervert? You decide.' He lets out a bark of laughter.

I neck the last of the wine in my glass, but don't move. 'Sure, OK,' I say brightly, not taking my eyes from the man outside as I hear Nate exhale on the other end of the phone.

'I'm going to go down to the restaurant and get some dinner myself,' Nate says. 'And a beer. God knows, I need a beer after the day I've had. I'll be back Friday, OK? I'll call you tomorrow.'

He's gone before I can say goodbye, before I can tell him I love him and I miss him, and I wonder if he's going to be eating alone in the hotel restaurant at the other end of the country tonight. He'll tell me he is, but the last time I took his work jacket to the dry cleaners I found a receipt. A bottle of Malbec — an expensive one — fillet steak and seabass. A slice of cheesecake and a frozen berry parfait. Even Nate doesn't eat that much, and he doesn't like parfait.

Hurrying to the kitchen, I pour myself another glass of wine and move back to the window, less bothered now about whether I am noticed or not by the new neighbours. Maybe I'll catch the man's eye and he'll lift a hand in a wave, and then I'll trot out and introduce myself, welcome them to the neighbourhood. The man has moved the TV inside while I was in the kitchen, and now I see he is joined by a woman, her arms full of a box with *books* scrawled across the side. She grins, tossing her head as a breeze whips her blonde hair across her eyes. She has the kind of hairstyle that you see in magazines, or in Instagram adverts for clothes that normal people can't afford. It's a soft, beachy wave style, and her skin is a smooth tanned brown to match. Silver bangles rattle on one arm as she hoists the box of books up to stop it from slipping, and my hand goes to my head.

Shoulder-length, mousy brown, straight as a die and too slippery to curl, my own hair hangs in my eyes as I reach up to tuck it behind my ear. It's in desperate need of a dye kit, but I just haven't had the time and I make a mental note to pick one up next time I'm in the supermarket. I wish I could wear jangly silver bangles, but the one time I wore jewellery to the office — a beautiful, bright gold bracelet studded with ruby paste stones that I picked up at Portobello Market — Kev in Sales, a fat, old racist who nobody likes and who looks as if he could play an extra in *The Walking Dead*, asked if I was auditioning for a Bollywood film, and then when I went to get it out of my desk drawer at the end of the day it was gone.

The man comes up behind the woman, wrapping an arm around her waist, making her jump. The box of books slides out of her grasp and I gasp alongside her, as she presses her hand to her mouth, before turning to the man and swatting him on the arm.

'Seb! You idiot!' Her voice rings out in the warm, June evening air, high-pitched and full of laughter, with no trace of a discernible accent.

The man — *Seb* — laughs aloud, and then moves towards her, taking her into his arms and kissing her. The kiss is long and slow, not the kind of kiss that should be taking place on a public street at all, and definitely not next to a removal van, on a Wednesday evening at the beginning of summer. I turn away as my cheeks blaze. There is a kernel of something in my stomach that I think might be envy. I can't remember the last time Nate kissed me like that. On our wedding day, seven years ago? Surely not. Surely my husband must have kissed me like that at some point since we tied the knot. Only I really couldn't tell you when. Unable to resist, I turn back, but the kiss is over and the two of them are disappearing up the tiled pathway into the house.

I watch as they take in lamps (ornate, Tiffany style), another rug (smaller, for the bedroom, maybe?) and a battered red leather Chesterfield armchair that they struggle to manage between them, the woman breathless with laughter as Seb trips on the split tarmac outside the house where the tree roots poke through. As the last box is taken inside, I move to the sofa, but keep the blinds open as I watch them lock the van. Seb wraps an arm around the woman's shoulder, dropping a kiss on her hair, and I feel that bolt of envy again. There is something familiar about him, and I pause, my glass halfway to my mouth. I feel sure I have seen him somewhere before, but I shake the feeling away when I can't place him. There is a muted murmuring as they pass by my front window, and then the slam of their front door and I reach for my phone.

'Goodnight,' I text to Nate, picturing him sitting down to another steak dinner, a faceless woman sitting opposite him, a bangle sliding down her arm as she reaches for the expensive red wine my husband is paying for. 'I love you.'

Nate doesn't reply.

* * *

The next morning, I am hurriedly running a lip gloss over my mouth in the mirror in the hallway, when I hear the slam of the front door next door, and then a cheery voice calling out a good-bye on the path. Grabbing my handbag, I yank open the door and hurry outside, rummaging in my bag for my phone.

'Oh, hey!' The man, Seb, stands at the driver's door of the removal van, keys in his hand. 'You must be our new neighbour. Sorry if we *disturbed* you yesterday — I did try to tell Tamsin that Wednesday is a weird and disruptive day to move in, but she wouldn't wait until the weekend.' He beams at me, showing even, white teeth.

'Oh, no problem at all,' I flap a hand and grin back, hoping I don't have chia seeds from my breakfast stuck in my teeth. 'It's nice to meet you. Lovely to have neighbours our own age to be honest. The last ones were pretty old.'

A frown crosses Seb's face. 'I thought—'

'The ones before them,' I say with a laugh. 'The last lot weren't really here long enough to get to know. Anyway,' I take a deep breath, 'what I meant to say is, welcome to the neighbourhood. I'm Hayley, and my husband is Nate. He's away at the moment.'

'Seb.' He holds out a hand, and I take it. His palm is dry, rough with slight calluses that scratch my skin. 'My wife, Tamsin . . . she's inside, but I'm sure you'll meet her soon.' With that he turns back to the removal van. 'Nice to meet you, Hayley.'

'Nice to meet you,' I echo as he climbs into the van and starts it with a roar, flashing me a quick grin as he pulls away. I turn back to the house, to the closed curtains at the window on the top floor, where presumably Tamsin is still in bed, and feel a lurch of excitement in my stomach. I can't wait to introduce Nate to our glamorous new neighbours.

CHAPTER 2

The air is stifling in the sitting room and I push the window open even further, desperately hoping for some sort of breeze. Thursday and Friday might have dragged at the office while I chased people for timesheets and took endless minutes for mind-numbing KPI meetings, but at least there was air conditioning there. It's the hottest Saturday of the year so far — twenty-five degrees — and it's not even ten thirty yet.

'We could go to the beach?' I turn to face Nate, who is dressed in running shorts and a vest as he hunts under the stairs for something. 'You wouldn't even need to get changed.'

Nate pulls his squash racket out of the cupboard with a triumphant grin. 'I'm going to play squash with Paul for a bit, and then I was hoping to drag the deckchairs out later, maybe grab a snooze in the sun. I'm shattered, I didn't get back until nearly midnight last night and then I swear I kept hearing a dog bark.'

Not too shattered to play squash. I am fully aware of what time Nate got back, even though I was in bed, covers pulled up to my chin despite the heat. I'd thrown his dinner in the bin at ten o'clock, when he'd finally texted with some excuse about a crash on the M25. I'd resisted the urge to google whether there really was a crash on the motorway, but even so, I didn't want to have to listen to him make his excuses to my face. Who knows, maybe there really was an accident that held him up for hours.

'Come on . . . who knows how long this weather will last?' I pull the racket out of his hand and press myself against him, lifting my face to kiss him, feeling more forgiving now he's actually at home, with me. 'You play squash with Paul every week. We could go for a dip, then the pub for chips and cider?'

'After sitting in traffic for three hours?' Nate pecks me on the lips and scoops me up, tossing me in a heap on the sofa cushions. 'Much as I'd love to, I can't let Paul down, and you've been nagging me for weeks about sorting the garden furniture out. Maybe next week.'

That's what he always says. He's always too busy to go anywhere or do anything with me at the weekends, and I fight the sting of tears as he goes to the kitchen. I hear ice rattle into his sports bottle, and then the kettle go on and sigh. That's Nate's way of apologising, but I don't want a cup of tea. I want cold rosé and Scampi Fries in a pub garden. I want chips on the beach. I want a cocktail on the rooftop of a bar on the Thames. I want anything that actually involves us doing something together. The slam of the front door next door breaks into my thoughts and I slide off the sofa, pulling my hair up off my sweaty neck. Stepping towards the window, I scoop up the magazines on the coffee table as if tidying and glance outside, watching as Seb strides down the path. He pauses at the end, turning back to his own front door, running his fingers over the rose bushes that grow between our houses. The elderly couple planted them, but neither the last couple, nor Nate and I, have bothered to prune them and their deadly thorns are wreaking havoc, plucking at our clothes every time we leave the house.

'That him, is it?' Nate appears beside me, a cup of hot tea in one hand, his sports bottle in the other, as he looks out on to the path.

'That's Seb,' I say, taking the cup. At least it's mint tea — ever so slightly more exotic than PG Tips. 'And that's his wife.'

Tamsin appears on the path in a brightly coloured maxi dress, her blonde waves pinned up on top of her head. Silver earrings dangle from her ears, and her sandals are a pair that I eyed up longingly in Kurt Geiger on my way home from work last week. She carries a Mulberry Bayswater over one arm, exclaiming as she rummages through it, before turning and hurrying back up the path towards the house. Seb sighs and leans in to sniff the roses, but he doesn't seem irritated. Not the way Nate would be if I had forgotten something just as we were leaving to go out.

'Don't you think he looks familiar?' I say, inclining my head in Seb's direction. Nate looks up, casting his eyes quickly over Seb's form.

'No,' he says, turning abruptly away from the window. 'Not really.'

'Don't you think?' I move closer to the window, my feet seeming to move of their own accord. 'I swear I've seen him somewhere before. Have a proper look.'

Nate shakes his head, pulling back out of sight. 'No, Hayls, I really don't think he's familiar. I reckon he's just got one of those faces. Or maybe you've just been spying on him out of the window a bit too much.'

'Hey!' I whirl away from the window, straight into Nate's chest. He locks his arms around me, pulling me tight towards him, and I melt a little as he leans down and drops a kiss on my lips. 'I don't spy out the window,' I say against his lips, failing to stop the grin that tugs at my own mouth. 'Maybe we should invite them over.'

'You're spending too much time ogling the new neighbour for my liking,' Nate says, pressing against me in a way that makes me gasp. Maybe that's all that was needed, was to catch sight of our handsome new neighbour and a glimpse of the green-eyed monster to make Nate remember who I am. He kisses me now, long and hard like he used to, as Tamsin's voice floats down the garden path next door and out onto the street.

'Maybe you could skip the game, *and* we could skip the beach,' I murmur as Tamsin's voice gets fainter and fainter, but Nate lets me go as abruptly as he took hold of me.

'Nah, come on. Get your beach bag while I text Paul and tell him the game's off. Let's go. You can ogle me on the beach, instead of the new neighbour.' With a wink, Nate taps me on the bum and I hurry upstairs to change into a bikini before he can change his mind.

* * *

We get back from Margate late in the evening, so late that all the lights are off next door, bar a faint glow from the top window. I would have wondered what Seb and Tamsin were up to, whether they were still awake or if they had fallen asleep wrapped in each other's arms, but my mind is full of Nate. He held my hand all the way along the beach, listened to me rabbiting on about work while we drank cider and ate fish and chips and even jumped in the tidal pool with me for a quick swim. It felt like it did in the beginning, when there was only room for the two of us. If living next door to fit Seb means Nate is going to give me his undivided attention then I am all for it.

Nate's good mood only lasts until Sunday morning, when the sound of drilling wakes us both up before nine o'clock.

'What the actual fuck?' Nate gropes on the bedside table for his glasses, as I push myself into a sitting position. It sounds as though the neighbours are drilling directly into our bedroom.

'It's Sunday morning!' Nate growls. 'Has that chap got no consideration? Pass me that shoe, Hayls, I'm going to hammer on the wall back at him. Who the fuck does DIY on a Sunday?'

'No, Nate, don't.' Shoving the duvet back, I swing my legs out of bed and pull on a T-shirt. *Everybody does DIY on a Sunday, don't they?* But it's rare that Nate sleeps in and I don't want someone hammering and drilling to spoil it. 'I'll go and knock. They just moved in . . .' Remembering the way Nate behaved towards the young professionals who lived in the house before, the night they held a leaving party for some friends, I shove my legs into my shorts from the previous day and slide my feet into flip flops. 'You stay there. I'll deal with it. I'll even bring you up a cup of coffee when I get back.'

Hurrying out of the bedroom before Nate can respond, I run lightly down the stairs, pausing for only the briefest moment to check my hair in the hallway mirror, before I step out into the warm Sunday morning. The fragrance of the roses on the path between the houses assaults my senses, and despite Nate's poor mood, mine is buoyant as I press my finger against the doorbell.

The drilling continues and I press the bell again, rising up on to my tiptoes to try and peer through the stained glass at the top of the door, when it breaks off suddenly and footsteps thud down the stairs. Seconds later, a breathless Seb opens the door, in running shorts and little else.

'Oh! Sorry . . .' I try for a smile, but it's difficult when I'm staring straight at his sweaty chest. 'I mean, I didn't want to disturb you, but . . .'

'The drilling?' Seb thumps a hand against his forehead. 'Shit, I'm so sorry . . . Hayley, isn't it?'

I nod, absurdly pleased for some stupid reason that he's remembered my name. 'Sorry, we were just . . . it's a little early on a Sunday, that's all, and Nate, my husband, he has to be up early tomorrow, he works away you see, and . . .' I trail off, aware that I'm rambling.

'No, *I'm* sorry,' Seb apologises again, and we are at the very real risk of this becoming a never-ending loop of apologies. 'I should have thought, but Tamsin wanted some bits putting up, and you know . . . happy wife, happy life.' He grins, and it's like the sun is shining even more brightly overhead.

11

There is movement behind him and Tamsin appears on the stairs, hurrying down them two at a time as she clips her blonde hair up, pausing at the bottom to snatch up her bag.

'Seb, darling,' she leans in and kisses him, 'that mirror isn't straight up there, you know that?' She pauses as she notices me on the doorstep and then gives me a beaming smile, her teeth even brighter and whiter than Seb's. 'Hey.'

'Hi. I, err . . . I live next door,' I say. My cheeks flush as I hold out a hand, and I get the unnerving sensation of being the new kid in the playground on the first day of school, which is ridiculous because I was here first.

'This is Hayley,' Seb says. 'Hayley, this is Tamsin. My wife.'

'Lovely to meet you.'

'Likewise.' Tamsin runs her eyes over me as she shakes my hand, but not in a way that makes me feel self-conscious. 'Those shorts — are they Mint Velvet?'

I run my hands over my pink pleated denim shorts. 'Yes.' They're not. They're from Shein.

'God, you lucky thing!' Tamsin says, reaching out to rub her thumb and forefinger over the fabric. 'They sold out almost immediately! And they look *gorgeous* on you. Sorry, I would really love to stop and chat but I have to dash, I'm late as it is. It's been lovely to meet you. See you tonight, Seb.' With a full kiss on his mouth, Tamsin squeezes past me and she's gone before I've even managed to process what she's said.

'Sorry, she's a bit of a whirlwind,' Seb laughs, as Tamsin disappears down the street towards the tube station. 'She's working this morning — she's a voice actor, and usually she wouldn't work on the weekend, but it's some rush job. I don't know, I just make sure the wine is open when she gets home.' He laughs, pushing a hand through his thick hair.

'Well . . .' I shift awkwardly on the balls of my feet. 'I should get back . . . if you wouldn't mind just holding fire on the drilling until lunchtime, maybe?'

'Sure, no problem!' Seb steps back, holding the door open so I can see into the house. The hallway walls still have the horrid old-fashioned flowery wallpaper I remember the elderly couple having, but the carpet is gone, revealing a stunning original tiled floor. 'Listen, if Tamsin is out and I can't drill, why don't you stop for a coffee? Unless you have to rush back next door?'

I pause for a fraction of a second. I should go back and take Nate a coffee in bed, but then I think of his furrowed brow and the way he grumbled about the noise and I realise I don't want to. 'That sounds lovely.'

* * *

The house is more modern than I imagined. My grandmother was friendly with the elderly couple before they all died, so I had been in the house next door a few times as a kid and I remembered it being dark and gloomy, with a musty smell in the air, but the previous owners must have done a little bit of work. The kitchen, when I follow Seb along the hallway, is bright and airy now, the window on the back wall transformed into double patio doors. The floor is still patchy old lino, and it contrasts sharply with the gleaming Smeg fridge and the Gaggia espresso machine.

There is a low grumble from somewhere behind me and I turn to see a dog lying in a tattered, well-loved dog bed. A huge rottweiler with a greying muzzle.

'Hey . . .' Crouching down I offer out a hand for him to sniff as Seb looks up.

'Wait, he's not that friendly,' Seb says, before he frowns. The dog is pushing his head against my hand, his dark brown eyes drooping closed as I stroke his head. 'Well, I guess he likes you . . . Usually he's a crotchety old thing.'

'He's a daft thing,' I say, as the dog taps my knee with a paw to urge me to keep stroking him. 'I love dogs, but I work full-time and my husband is away a lot so it wouldn't be fair for us to have one.'

'You're privileged. Tank clearly likes you and believe me when I say he doesn't like anybody usually,' Seb says with a grin. 'So I guess we know who to call to dog sit, huh?'

'Any time.'

'I hope he hasn't disturbed you at all? It's taken him a few days to settle and he keeps barking at night. I think there's a security light in your garden that comes on sometimes . . . He's a bit protective, you know.'

Seeing as it's our security light that seems to have disturbed Tank I can hardly tell Seb that Nate has been kept awake by the barking, so I just shake my head.

'Coffee? Or tea?' Seb takes down two small cups, far too small for a cup of builder's tea.

Straightening up, I wipe my hands over my thighs as Tank settles with a sigh. 'Um, coffee please.' I never drink coffee, but I can't take my eyes off the shiny red espresso machine, and I have a fleeting image of myself sitting in the garden, a tiny cup of freshly ground coffee in my hands, silver bangles gliding down my arm as I raise the cup to my lips.

Moments later Seb places an espresso in front of me, and while it smells incredible — exactly like a Sunday morning should smell — the first taste has me battling not to screw up my nose. 'So,' I say, 'a little bird told me that you're going to be renovating the house.' Seb frowns. 'The estate agent,' I say hastily. 'She told me when I saw her after the Sold sign went up. That's very exciting. I'd love to bring ours more up to date, but it's finding the time.' *And the money.*

Seb lights up as he moves to the patio doors, spreading his arms wide towards the garden. 'Imagine this,' he says. 'These doors are gone, and there's a huge orangery across the back of the house . . .

imagine the light it'll let in! It'll be the perfect space for entertaining, and then I'm thinking upstairs, we can knock the wall down between the two smaller bedrooms and create one large master suite, with an en suite and a dressing room . . . eventually I'll want to convert the attic into a useable space too, and maybe do something special with the garden.'

'Wow.' I grin into my (sadly, disgusting) coffee. 'You really have a vision for this place. Are you an architect or something? You could maybe install some light tubes in this part of the kitchen — that would let even more light in.'

Seb pauses and looks at me. *Really* looks at me. 'Hayley, that's a fantastic idea. God, I wish Tamsin were interested the way you are. She just wants it done, with no mess and no fuss, ha ha!' He reaches out a fist and bumps it gently against mine. 'No, I'm not an architect, but I know where I'm going to come for home improvement ideas.'

Blushing, I get to my feet and set down the espresso cup. 'Any time. And thanks for the coffee, but I should be getting back.' At the front door, I turn back to find Seb standing close enough to touch. 'You could use bi-fold doors for the orangery, you know? Open it right up into the garden in the summer . . . maybe put some solar lights up in the garden and really mesh the two spaces together? It's just a thought.'

'Genius! That's what it is.' Seb grins and then in an unexpected move, leans in and kisses me on the cheek, leaving a waft of his tobacco leaf-and-ginger aftershave in my nose. 'Any more ideas like that, you come and let me know.'

I float back next door, ready to tell Nate about how lovely Seb and Tamsin are, but when I step into the hallway and call his name there is no response. His running shoes aren't in the shoe rack, and his phone isn't charging on the hallway table where he left it last night. Nate has gone out.

CHAPTER 3

He didn't take his AirPods. Nate said he went for a run, that's why he wasn't home when I got back from Seb and Tamsin's, but he didn't take his AirPods, and I know he hates running without listening to his true crime podcasts. I was on too much of a high to challenge him though and while our Sunday passed slowly and without comment, just as it usually does, I didn't mind for once. *Seb thought my ideas were genius!* While Nate spent the rest of the day watching the cricket, tapping out messages to his buddies on WhatsApp and chuckling to himself, I scrolled Pinterest and home décor sites, looking for inspiration that I could offer up to Seb as my own ideas the next time I saw him. Not that I'm bothered as to whether he uses my ideas or not, but it's nice to have someone show an interest.

When Nate wakes me up before dawn on Monday morning, zipping up his suitcase and brushing his teeth with the bathroom door open, I don't roll over and hide my head under the pillow like I would usually do. Instead I watch through half-closed eyes as he buttons his shirt and pulls on his trousers. He still has the ability to make my heart pound, even after all this time. He leans over to kiss me and — remembering the AirPods — I snap my eyes closed, feigning sleep.

I remember the first time I saw him. I was working in a local pub, serving students and contractors in our university town. Nate was there with friends, but he wasn't like the rest of them. When I was swamped by customers he didn't click his fingers in my direction, impatience etched all over his face. He smiled and told me not to worry. He wasn't in a rush. He didn't get black-out drunk and obnoxious or slice the pool cue into the table, tearing the fabric, or pinch me on the arse hard enough to leave a bruise when I did the rounds collecting empty glasses. I'd gone home that first night with his features imprinted on my brain, the small kindness he'd shown me in the middle of what was a hellishly busy shift impacting on my heart.

When did things change? When did Nate's spare time start getting eaten up by squash games and football matches and jet washing the patio? I turn over as I hear the front door snick closed downstairs, and then the roll of the wheels on Nate's little suitcase as he heads to the car. When did we stop trying? Was it when I told him I wanted us to try for a baby for the first time and he dismissed the idea, saying we weren't ready? Was it when I brought it up a second, third, fourth time, and still he said we weren't ready? Or was it when Nate started working away all week? At first, when he came home on the weekends, we'd talk over each other and stay up late into the night catching up, eager to replace the time we'd lost, but as time has gone on it seems as though whatever spark flared between us in the beginning has finally started to dim. Nate's weekends are full of pints with his mates and match scores and mine are spent wondering if I should take up yet another hobby that will fall by the wayside after a matter of weeks. Sometimes, as the door closes behind him on a Monday morning, I feel the sense of relief he leaves in his wake. I think about Tamsin, about the way she breezed out of the front door yesterday with a brief peck on Seb's lips, leaving him staring after her as she flounced off towards the tube station. *Maybe I need to be more like her.* Maybe I need to treat Nate a bit meaner.

* * *

'Nate's on the phone for you,' Wendy, my assistant tells me just after lunch. She looks concerned but she's American, from New Hampshire originally, and she always looks worried about something. I bet Matt, her husband, doesn't give her anything to be concerned about. 'He said he tried your mobile a few times but you didn't answer.'

I sigh and push my blue light blocking glasses up onto my forehead. 'It was on silent,' I lie. 'I've been trying to get these reports done.'

'Can I patch him through? And then I can help with those reports if you like?'

'I can do them, but thanks,' I say, nodding for her to put Nate through. There is a pause before I hear the rush of tyres on the other end of the line, the faint whirl of wind that tells me he has the sunroof open. 'Hello?'

'Where have you been? You haven't been answering my calls.'

I glance at the mobile phone on my desk, at the four missed calls and three texts from him. 'It was on silent.' As if to spite me, the phone pings now with a Facebook notification.

'O . . . K . . .' Nate's voice rises and half of me wants him to question me on why I've been avoiding him all morning, but in typical Nate fashion he doesn't. 'Listen, I wanted to let you know a few of the guys have invited me fishing this weekend. It's up north somewhere, I don't know exactly where, but Lee is going to drive and, well . . . I'm just letting you know, that's all.'

'You're not coming home this weekend?' My throat thickens and I swallow. 'But you're away all week, Nate! I barely see you as it is. And you don't even know how to fish!'

'Hayls, please. It's some team-bonding weekend thing. You know I'd rather be at home with you.' His voice takes on that soft tone that he knows makes me melt. 'I'd much rather be in bed with you on Friday night than sleeping in a fucking tent with Lee and Brad.'

'Can't you get out of it?' The thought of spending the weekend on my own, after a week of girl dinners for one and trash TV makes my heart sink.

'I wish I could.' For a split second I believe him, thinking I can hear the sigh in his voice. 'We can do something next weekend if it's still good weather? Go into town and wander along the South Bank. Try out that new cocktail bar you showed me.'

'I guess.' My gaze falls to the home décor magazines I picked up on my way into work. 'Maybe I'll see if Seb and Tamsin are home. I've got some ideas for their orangery that I thought Seb might like to see.'

'Hayley . . .' Nate sounds wary now. 'Is that a good idea? We don't even know them. You don't want to overstep the mark.' *Like last time* is what he's insinuating.

'I didn't overstep the mark before,' I say, hotly. Movement catches my eye and I glance up to see Wendy hovering at the next desk, her movements a little too stilted to be a coincidence, and I lower my voice. 'I just offered them a bit of advice after I heard them rowing in the garden. You were the one who called the police on them when they threw that party.'

Nate sighs and I can envision him pushing his hand through his hair in frustration. 'Look Hayley, I have to go. I'll see you Sunday, OK? Try and stay out of trouble.'

Pushing my pencil into a wad of Blu Tack, I force a smile onto my face. 'No worries. I'll see you then. I lo—' But he's already hung up.

* * *

Friday evening is hot and sultry and I find myself in the garden with a glass of white wine and the home décor magazines, but I can't concentrate on them. Instead, I swipe up to open my phone for the hundredth time since I got in from work, and pull up the Find My iPhone app, searching for the blue dot that will tell me where Nate is. Half of me almost wants him to be lying about the fishing trip — after all, if I catch him out we'll have a blazing row, and then of course I'll forgive him, for the make-up sex if nothing else — but the other half of me knows I'll be devastated. It takes a moment but then the blue dot that represents Nate updates, and he is whizzing along the M18 towards East Riding. *He really is going on a team-building fishing weekend.*

Closing the app, I sip wine and flick between social media apps, scrolling mindlessly until I hear the buzz of the lawn mower next door. On the pretence of refilling my glass I stand and head towards the patio doors into the kitchen, peering over the fence as I do. Seb is mowing the tiny patch of grass at the back of their house, headphones clamped firmly to his ears. The muscles in his bare back ripple as he pushes the mower back and forth and I find myself wanting to stifle a giggle like a teenage girl before I shake it away. What would Nate think? At the thought of Nate's soft, pale body — not fat, but not muscled, not white but not tanned either — in short, the ultimate dad bod — a wave of longing washes over me and I wish it was Sunday evening already. Pulling out my phone again I tap a quick text to Nate. 'Have fun! For what it's worth, you're the biggest catch of my life!'

Seconds later, I get a reply — two rolling on the floor laughing emojis, a thumbs up and a red heart — and I regret not answering his calls this morning. My wine replenished, I head back out into the garden, where the mowing has ceased. As I step off the patio, I peep over the fence to see Seb kneeling on the edge of the untidy border, plucking out weeds. He doesn't look very confident and when he pulls up something that definitely has something bulb-like at the end of it, I realise he has no clue what he's doing. I open my mouth to call out, to tell him I'll gladly come over and give him a hand in the garden if he wants when a voice splits the air.

'Seb? Darling? Where are you?'

'Out here.' Seb gets to his feet, wiping his hands over his shorts and I slink into my lawn chair, my heart pounding as though I got caught doing something I shouldn't.

I hear Tamsin's heels tap their way out onto the patio, and there is a muted murmuring from the other side of the fence as they greet each other. Moments later there is the pop of a champagne cork, followed by a squeal from Tamsin, and I get to my feet. *Could I pop over there? Tell them I heard the champagne pop and I just wanted to congratulate them on whatever their good news is?* In my head I hear Nate's comment about 'overstepping the mark' and I slide into the house, feeling itchy with loneliness and a resentment that I'm not sure who I am aiming at.

Later, when the sun has disappeared behind the trees but the summer sky is still varying shades of lilac and flamingo pink, I head upstairs to bed, too bored to slump in front of the TV any longer. It's evenings like these that I wish I hadn't dropped my friends so quickly when I met Nate. It wasn't on purpose, we just drifted apart as I cancelled more and more plans to spend time with Nate, until eventually there wasn't anyone left to call any more. I could be friends with Tamsin though, I think. She seems like just the kind of woman I could hang out with. She's bright and beautiful with a glamorous job, and I'd be happy if even a fraction of her charm rubbed off on me. As if I've conjured her out of thin air, a peal of laughter comes from the garden next door, followed by a gasp. Intrigued, I move to the window as if to close the blinds, and peer down into the garden next door.

Oh. Pressing a hand to my mouth I step back, before hurriedly leaning over and switching out the lamp. My gaze goes back to the window, to the scene in the garden below. Tamsin is lying on a sun lounger, her head thrown back, an empty champagne flute overturned on the grass beside her. Seb has already installed solar lights along the garden path and the soft glow catches on her silver bangles, the jewellery jingling as she pushes her hands into Seb's hair, pulling him up her body from where his head rests between her legs. With a barely audible moan, she reaches down to pull off his shorts and then he is on top of her, thrusting deep into her as she sighs, her brightly striped maxi dress yanked up high above her thighs.

My cheeks burn, and there is an almost painful longing in my groin as I struggle to look away, wanting to but unable, as if there is some magnetic force pulling me towards the two of them. Seb gives a strangled moan as Tamsin rakes her nails down his back, and then her eyes open and she stares straight at my bedroom window. Straight at *me*. With a gasp, I stumble back away from the window, my pulse ratcheting and my breath coming loud in my throat. *Nate was right*, I think, shame making my armpits prickle and a bead of sweat roll down my spine. *That was overstepping the mark.*

CHAPTER 4

My legs are tangled in the sheet and my hair sticks to my neck when I wake the next morning, the disturbing remnants of a dream involving myself, Seb and Tamsin vaguely clinging to the back of my mind in a way that makes me feel as though I need to shower. My head pounds, the bedroom air thick and stuffy where I kept the window closed following last night's performance, and my mouth is dry and sour from the wine.

My phone pings with a text, and I smile as Nate's name flashes up on my screen. He's sent a picture of a fish, gold-green and slimy, and I send a love heart back. I was stupid to think he was doing anything other than telling the truth. I am tempted to spill the beans on what I saw last night, but the memory of Seb's head between Tamsin's thighs, and the soft guttural moans she made make my stomach clench and I throw my phone back onto the bedside table. Nate will only tell me I should have stepped away and closed the blinds immediately anyway.

It's another scorcher of a day and I can't bear the thought of sitting in the house on my own, so I shower and dress in a light sundress with thin straps, pack a book, some snacks, sun cream and a bottle of water into a bag and head for the park. I used to spend many a Saturday in the summer sitting in the park with a good book, but since Nate and I got together that's another thing that dropped off my radar. I have forgotten how nice it is to sit under a tree and read, and as I lick at the ice cream that runs down my fingers — I also can't remember the last time I visited the ice cream van — I think that perhaps I am looking at Nate's absences the wrong way. Maybe I should be looking at them as ways to rediscover myself, instead of moping about feeling lonely.

Hours later, with the beginnings of a faint, pink sunburn across my shoulders, an ice-cream-stained copy of Asako Yuzuki's *Butter* in my bag and a rumbling stomach, I walk back up my own front path feeling more rested and relaxed than I have in a long time. I don't even feel concerned that I haven't heard from Nate since this morning.

I don't see the parcel on the front step until I trip over it as I push my key into the front door lock and it's only once I'm inside, the parcel clasped tightly under one arm as I drop my keys and bag on to the table, that I realise it isn't addressed to me. *Sebastian Cooper* is neatly typed across the label, with next door's house number.

Shit. I'm going to have to knock and take it round. My stomach flips at the thought of seeing either Tamsin or Seb, before I remember that they don't know I saw them in the garden last night. Or at least, I don't *think* they did. And besides, I reason with myself, everyone gets a notification via email these days that their parcel has been delivered. They'll know if it's not on their doorstep that it might be on mine.

Tucking the parcel under one arm, I pause in the hallway and smooth my hair down, practising a smile in the mirror. The sun has brought out a light dusting of freckles, the ones Nate calls 'cute', and while my shoulders are a little burnt, my face has a healthy glow. Seconds later, I am pressing my finger against the doorbell next door.

'Hayley!' Tamsin opens the door with a wide smile, seeming genuinely pleased to see me. 'How are you? I'm so sorry I dashed off like that the other day, I felt so rude! Gosh, you look gorgeous, have you been out in the sun all day?'

Momentarily blindsided, I open my mouth and for a second nothing comes out. Tamsin is talking as though we were in the middle of a conversation, as if we are old friends and not new neighbours. 'Err, yeah,' I manage, somewhat awkwardly. 'I went to sit in the park and read. It's so nice out, I felt like I was wasting the day sitting indoors.' I shift the parcel out from under my arm. 'This was delivered to me by mistake.'

Tamsin takes the parcel and inspects the box. 'It'll be Seb's artisan snack subscription. Honestly, I've never seen anyone get so excited over fancy pork scratchings in my life.' She rolls her eyes. 'And a good job you didn't tell him you were off to the park to read, he would have tagged along like a shot. That guy is a bookworm of the highest order.' She beams at me.

I manage a weak smile back, not sure how I would feel about that at all. As Tamsin calls over her shoulder that Seb has a parcel, a waft of garlic-scented air hits me and my stomach gives an audible growl. All I've eaten today is a protein bar, some strawberries and an ice cream. I hadn't thought I was hungry, but the smell wafting out of the Coopers' kitchen is mouth-watering.

'Why don't you come in?' Tamsin stands to one side, holding the door open. 'Is Nate home? Run back and get him, and both of you come in for a drink. It's such a nice evening, and Seb is dying to show off his new solar garden lights to somebody.'

At the mention of the solar garden lights, I feel my breath stop dead in my chest, but Tamsin is smiling, giving no sign that she knows I saw them last night. 'Oh . . . no, it's fine. Nate's away this weekend, so I'm just going to . . .' I trail off, feeling it's too pathetic to say *I'm just going to order a pizza and watch* Real Housewives of Salt Lake City.

'Well, that's even better!' Tamsin grins and reaches out a hand to tug at my arm, leading me into the hallway. 'You're staying for dinner. Seb! Lay the table for one more!' She is already marching towards the kitchen, and not knowing what else to do, I follow.

Seb is standing at what looks like a brand-new range cooker, over a sizzling pan filled with something that smells incredible. There are small earthenware pots all over the counter, all filled with various different things — small green peppers, olives, slices of chorizo in an oozing, thick sauce — and my stomach growls again.

'Hayley!' Seb looks up from the pan, which I can see now holds a thick piece of steak. 'You look lovely . . . and this is a nice surprise. I hope you've got more interior design ideas for me.' He grins and my stomach flips.

'Honestly, guys, you're too kind but I really don't want to disturb your evening. I just stopped by to drop off a parcel.'

'Nonsense.' Tamsin hands me a glass of fruity sangria, and I can smell the brandy in it before I've even taken a sip. 'Seb always cooks too much — he fancies himself as a bit of a chef—'

'Hey,' Seb laughs, 'I don't fancy myself, I *am* a bit of a chef.' He turns to me as Tamsin swats his behind. 'At least I would be if I wasn't a TV producer.'

Oh. Maybe that's why I think his face is familiar. Maybe I've seen him attending one of those TV awards shows that Nate calls crap and I call keeping up with popular culture.

'You can tell when the meat is a good cut,' Seb says as he slides the steak onto a wooden board to rest. 'The knife goes through it like butter.'

'Stay, please,' Tamsin says to me, with a roll of her eyes. 'He is actually really rather good at lots of things, and cooking is definitely one of them. Plus he always makes too much and I'll end up the size of a house.'

I can hardly see that being the case, Tamsin being tiny, but I lift my glass in a toast and give in. 'In that case, I'd love to stay for dinner. Thank you.'

* * *

It's a perfect evening. I've had the most fun I've had in ages, and I didn't even think about Nate and what he might be doing once. Seb really is a good cook, serving up lots of tiny tapas dishes, which at the time looked as though there was no way they'd feed us all, but I am stuffed. The sangria is excellent too, hand mixed by Tamsin, and far boozier than the weak stuff I am used to drinking on package holidays.

'You've done so much with the house already,' I say, the wine loosening my tongue. 'It's gorgeous out here.'

After eating in the dining room — which has already been re-wallpapered in a delicious teal-and-gold paper that looks too expensive to touch — Seb showed me the hand-built bookcases he's installed in the sitting room, the two of us exclaiming over our shared taste in books while Tamsin good-naturedly rolls her eyes.

'Honestly, wouldn't you rather just watch *Gone Girl* than spend hours reading?' she groaned as both Seb and I shake our heads.

'The book is always better,' Seb said, giving me a nudge and I nod enthusiastically, my head spinning slightly from all the sangria.

'Seb can show you his book hauls from now on then,' Tamsin said with a grin. 'Thanks for getting me off the hook there, maybe Nate and I can go to the pictures while you two swoon over dead trees.'

We then headed out to the garden after I promised to lend Seb my copy of the new Wally Lamb novel. Seb has finished his attempts at weeding, and with the cut lawn and the solar lights it's a warm and welcoming space. I try not to look at the sun loungers, still in the positions they were left in last night.

'Seb loves to be outside,' Tamsin coos, linking her little finger through his. 'He'd do everything out here if he could.'

'Only in the summer months,' Seb laughs. 'What about you, Hayley? Are you a gardener?'

'Oh no, not really,' I shake my head, my cheeks burning. 'I like to spend time in the garden, but I mostly just keep on top of the weeds. There is nothing nicer than sitting out after a long day in the office.'

'What is it you do?' Tamsin asks, her head cocked to one side. Her hair is messier than usual, and today's earrings are large teardrop aquamarines that set off her tan perfectly.

'I'm just an office manager. Nothing exciting.'

'Are you kidding?' Tamsin raises her eyebrows. 'People like you are perfection to people like me! You must have to be organised, and dedicated, and . . .'

'On time?' Seb says, with an amused look on his face.

'And on time! Gosh, I can only dream about being that organised . . .' Tamsin sighs. 'That probably explains why you have such impeccable taste. You always look so well put together, while I . . . I just look like I threw on an old rag.'

Is she messing with me? I look down at my sun dress, a cheap one from H&M that's seen better days, before glancing sideways at Tamsin's white linen trousers and orange tank top. OK, her trousers are creased, but they're *linen* for Pete's sake.

'Will you come shopping with me?' Tamsin says suddenly, leaning forward and resting her chin in her hands. 'Will you come to Westfield and we'll spend the day? I really need some good capsule pieces and I love your style so much. Please?'

I hesitate briefly. 'Ermm, yeah. OK. I can do that.'

'Yay!' Tamsin claps her hands together. 'It's going to be so much fun! Maybe the boys can spend the day together too? I know Seb has been dying to meet Nate properly.'

'Tamsin.' Seb's voice carries a low warning and I frown. 'Nate works away, the last thing he probably wants to do is hang around with his new neighbour on the weekend.'

'No, I'm sure it'll be fine,' I say, crossing my fingers mentally. 'It'll be nice to have friends as neighbours.' As I speak I realise it's true. Nate and I don't seem to have any 'couple' friends at all. He goes on his 'team-building weekends' and meets his mates for boozy sports filled afternoons, and I avoid going for drinks with Wendy after work. It'll be good to have friends again.

Later, the rest of the sangria drunk and my head spinning lightly with the booze, the good food and the prospect of shopping with Tamsin in the week, Seb offers to walk me home.

'I'm right next door,' I laugh, stumbling slightly as I reach the front door, the sangria making my head spin.

'We insist,' Tamsin says, planting a sloppy drunken kiss perilously close to my mouth. 'I want you home in one piece, I'm not losing my shopping buddy before we've even got started.'

On my doorstep, I turn to face Seb, wondering if Nate will see us on the Ring camera. I should have texted him, I think through a drunken fog. I left my phone on the table when I went round to drop off the parcel. He might be worried about where I am.

'Thank you for a lovely evening,' I say.

Seb gives me that megawatt grin. 'No, thank you,' he says. 'You really brought Tamsin out of her shell. For a voice actor she's remarkably reserved. I'm sorry if she seemed a little full on . . . she's just excited to meet someone she's really clicked with.'

Warmth spreads through my entire body, and I feel I must be glowing from the inside out. 'No, really, I like her. And I'm looking forward to shopping with her.'

'You're a gem,' Seb says and then he leans in and kisses my cheek, one hand coming up to rest on my shoulder. My stomach flips as he pauses for just a second before pulling away. 'See you later?'

'See you later,' I echo weakly, as he turns and hurries up the path towards his own house, giving me a brief wave as he passes the rose bushes. Once inside, I pour myself a large glass of water and check my phone. Nate hasn't texted.

CHAPTER 5

'Did you enjoy yourself at the weekend?' Wendy is already sitting on the edge of my desk when I arrive at work on Monday morning, juggling my laptop bag in one hand and an iced chai in the other. Her dark hair sits in glossy curls on her shoulders, and she's wearing a blue wrap dress from & Other Stories that I tried on and ditched because it made me look like I was wearing a sack.

'Errr . . . yes?' I pull my laptop out of my bag and open it, punching in my password. 'I didn't do much. Dinner with some friends.' I feel a spurt of something warm flood my veins at the memory of the evening at the Coopers.

'Hardly just dinner,' Wendy scoffs. 'It was Fifty-Two! It's a Michelin-starred restaurant, Hayley, that's not just "dinner".' I keep my gaze on my screen, but something in her tone makes my fingers slow on the keyboard. 'I wish you'd said you were going to be in Harrogate on Saturday night, we could have travelled up together . . . although I'm sure Fifty-Two was more exciting than my parents' wedding anniversary dinner.'

I blink at her, confused. 'I'm not sure what you mean.'

'Harrogate? Fifty-Two, the restaurant? I saw you guys there.'

'I didn't go to Harrogate this weekend,' I say, my mouth suddenly dry.

'Really? Are you sure? I'm certain I saw Nate in the carpark at Rudding Park,' Wendy says blithely, before she sees the look on my face.

'I'm sure,' I say through gritted teeth, as my heart crashes against my rib cage. 'I know where I ate at the weekend.'

Wendy's cheeks pale and she tucks her hair behind her ear in a gesture that I know means she's nervous. 'I mean . . . it looked like him, although he didn't turn around when I called his name so . . . maybe I was mistaken. I mean, I *am* mistaken. I must have been.' She slides off the edge of my desk with an uncertain smile and slopes off to her own desk, her head down. I open up my email, my mind whirring.

Of course she didn't see Nate, she got it wrong, it was someone who looked like him, that's all. Nate was on a fishing trip, I tell myself as I force myself to sip at my iced chai. *But he* was *in Yorkshire on this fishing trip.* Saliva fills my mouth and Wendy looks up in surprise as I shove my chair back and head for the Ladies, my stomach a washing machine on a spin cycle.

'Hayley?' Wendy's voice filters through the door of the stall in the Ladies moments later. 'Are you all right?'

Resisting the urge to lay my head on the cold porcelain of the toilet, I sigh and wipe my mouth. 'Yes,' I manage. 'Just a bit of a . . . I felt a bit light-headed and nauseous, that's all.'

'I got you a bottle of water.' Wendy's voice is low, and there is no movement outside the stall, so I haul myself to my feet and open the door.

'Thanks.' I take the water and snap the lid open. It's icy cold and I feel better after the first sip.

Wendy looks at me, her brow creasing. 'Are you sure you feel OK to go back to your desk? I could speak to Harry if you want to go home . . . . I can finish up the expense claims for you, I don't mind.'

I shake my head and grip the water bottle so tightly my fingers slide over the plastic as I head back to my desk. Wendy scurries along behind me, discreetly slipping a packet of extra-strong mints on to the desk as she passes. It's a good job I didn't eat at Wendy's fancy restaurant at the weekend. It would have been a horrible waste.

* * *

By Friday, I am exhausted from overthinking the whole thing. I swing between imagining Nate holed up in a swanky hotel (and it is swanky, I've googled it) with another woman, and wanting to throttle Wendy for even mentioning it to me. She's only met Nate twice, I doubt she could pick him out in a line-up. Ten minutes before I leave the office on Friday evening, I cave in and call the restaurant, and the relief that washes over me when they tell they have no reservations at all, past or future, in the name of Nate Turner is like a balm to my soul.

Now, as Nate steps out of the car, miraculously managing to find a space outside the house, I fly down the garden path and into his arms, pressing my mouth to his. He briefly returns the kiss before he pulls away, frowning.

'All right?' he asks as he turns to the boot to lift out his suitcase. 'What's up with you? Did something happen? Am I dying?'

'Oh, stop.' I swat at him, before linking my arm through his as we walk back into the house. 'I missed you, that's all.' Seeing Tamsin and Seb together last weekend, the way they casually touched each other and finished each other's sentences made me realise that perhaps Nate isn't entirely the problem. Maybe I don't make enough of an effort either. I can't be that great a wife if I'd let Wendy's comments make me doubt Nate without any proof. 'I'm making your favourite for dinner. I've got a big, fat rib-eye waiting for you.' I give him a lewd wink and relief courses through my veins when he laughs back. *Wendy was mistaken.*

'Let me get showered and changed and I'll be right back.' Nate leans in and pecks me on the cheek. It's not quite the home-coming smooch I was hoping for, but it's more than I got on Sunday evening when he returned from the fishing trip. 'Get the grill fired up.'

Half an hour later I've lit the gas barbecue, poured some drinks — gin and tonic for me, beer for Nate — and Nate is standing over the grill, having taken over the cooking of the meat, just the way I knew he would. He smells of something woody, his damp hair falling over his forehead and I feel a squeeze of affection towards him. The resentment I'd felt all week at not seeing him, at the thought of him having dinner with another woman with lies tripping off his tongue eating away at me as I prepared reports, filed invoices and listened to Wendy rabbit on about her kids and her mother-in-law, has faded to leave me feeling content to have him home. Although that might partly be the wine.

'Here you go, my lady.' Nate slides the smaller piece of steak onto a plate, and I add some salad before sitting at the garden table. 'Cheers.' Nate joins me, lifting his beer bottle. 'It's nice to be home.'

It's on the tip of my tongue to say something about the fishing trip, to ask if they stopped in Harrogate at all, but I try to swallow it down and sip my wine.

'So . . . good week?' I take a tiny bite of steak, readying myself for the real thing I want to talk about.

'Excellent,' Nate nods. 'Made a killing. You?'

'Oh, you know. Same old, same old. I think Wendy is angling for a pay rise but the directors won't have it. She's offered to take on some of my jobs more than once this week. She thought she saw you last Saturday.' I pause, watching him closely. 'In Harrogate.'

'Harrogate?' Nate coughs, as if beer has gone down the wrong way. 'She needs to get her eyes tested.'

'So, you weren't in Harrogate? At Fifty-Two?' I don't want to ask him, but I can't help it. I have to know if Wendy was mistaken or not.

'Fifty-Two? What the fuck is that? It sounds well poncy. Whatever it is, I wasn't there. I was stuck in a tent with slimy fishing gear and Lee's farts.' Nate's smile fades as he looks at me. 'Hayls? You don't actually think . . . oh, you daft thing.' He scoots across to sit beside me, wrapping his arms around me.

'I didn't really think it,' I say into his chest, 'but I didn't actually know what to think.'

Nate's chin digs into my hair as he speaks. 'I can call Lee now if you want? And I took pictures on my phone . . .' he rummages in his pocket but I put a hand out to stop him.

'No, it's OK. I just freaked out a bit, I guess. Bloody Wendy.' Pulling away I swipe a hand over my face. 'It's fine, honestly.' And it is. Nate sent me a picture of the fish he caught. His location showed him in East Riding. I don't know why I let Wendy get in my head so much.

Nate moves back to his seat, picking up his fork. 'You didn't tell me what you got up to at the weekend?' I'm not sure if it's just me or if there is a palpable sense of relief in the air.

'I went out,' I say, 'and I had a good time.'

'Oh?' Nate's fork pauses halfway to his mouth. 'What did you do? I thought you just . . . stayed in.'

'Well,' I force a smile, still feeling unsettled despite his reassurances. 'You didn't ask. I spent Saturday in the park, and then I went for dinner next door.'

Nate's eyebrows shoot up and disappear under his floppy fringe. 'Yeah? How was that?'

I put my fork down and reach for my wine, aware that we are sitting only feet from the neighbours back garden and there's every chance that they'll decide to eat outside tonight too. 'Really, really nice. They're lovely people, Nate,' I say, catching the expression on his face. 'Come on, you should get to know them too. It's nice to have people our own age next door.' I reach for his hand, but he wraps his fingers around his beer bottle, raising it to his lips. 'In fact, they've invited us for a BBQ tomorrow night.'

Nate takes a long drink, pulling a face as he swallows. 'Hayley, I've got a busy weekend. I need to pop in on my mum and put some shelves up for her, and then Paul and I need to get that squash game in that I cancelled the other day. Work has been mental this week too, and to be honest, I'd rather stay home tomorrow night, just the two of us.'

Something ugly flares in my chest. 'But I wouldn't, Nate. I go to work and come home to an empty house on repeat all week, because you're never here. I want to do something with my weekends.'

'I work away!' Nate says indignantly, the soft, apologetic Nate of a few moments ago firmly hidden again. 'It's not that I don't want to be here, I don't have a choice. It's my job. And I'm sorry things are busy on the weekends, but you know football and squash and stuff is the only way I can relax.'

'This *is* relaxing,' I press on, tears of frustration scorching my eyes. 'That's what normal people do, Nate. They hang out with their friends on the weekend.' I blink, and Nate sighs as a single tear tracks its way down my cheek. 'Please? Tamsin and Seb are really nice people — they really made me feel welcome last weekend, and this . . . this is important to me. If you really don't like them, we won't see them again, but please can we just go tomorrow?'

There is a thick silence for a moment, and it crosses my mind that maybe I should just tell Nate I'm going anyway, with or without him, and then he gives a slow nod. 'OK. If it's that important to you.'

'Thank you!' I squeal, thrilled at the thought of a proper grown-up evening, out of the house, with *friends* that I've made myself. 'I promise you'll have a good time.'

Nate huffs non-committally and gets up from the table, clearing our dirty plates. For the rest of the evening, I sneak glances at him, trying to figure out if he really is OK with going tomorrow, but he keeps his eyes on the telly and when I reach for him in bed, he rolls over, leaving me staring at his back.

CHAPTER 6

On Saturday afternoon I spend a ridiculous amount of time in front of the mirror, trying to pick out the perfect outfit for the BBQ, Tamsin's words ringing in my head about how I look 'so well put together'. Eventually I settle on the first outfit I tried — a slouchy white vest teamed with green pin-striped linen trousers and a pair of wedges — when Nate threatens to change his mind about going at all if I don't hurry up.

'I'm ready.' I hurry down the stairs, pausing at the bottom to check my hair looks OK. I've curled it, but the mousy brown curls have drooped already, and I think again about how I need to dye it. 'Have you got the wine?' Nate holds up a bottle of white and a bottle of rosé. 'Is that . . . I mean, are you wearing that?'

Nate looks down at his weekend uniform of shorts and a T-shirt that has been washed approximately 117 times. It's Ralph Lauren, but he bought it when we first met for goodness sakes. 'What's wrong with this?'

'Well, we are going out.' I suppose I should be grateful he's not in his running gear, and he does still look good, despite the T-shirt.

Nate sighs. 'We're going *next door*. This is fine. It's a BBQ, not a fashion show.'

I nod, defeated, although part of me wants to mention that he wouldn't be caught dead going out in that T-shirt if he was meeting his mates. If we argue now, there'll only be tension between us at the BBQ, or Nate will flat-out refuse to come at all. Instead, I just take the wine bottles from him, trying not to turn my nose up at the label. It's not Nate's fault the wine is cheap and his T-shirt is old — he just doesn't seem to understand how important this is to me.

'Hiii!' Tamsin squeals as she opens the door, reaching out and pulling me into a big hug. 'I've been dying for you to get here! And Nate, it's nice to meet you.' She leans in and kisses a rigid Nate on the cheek.

'Thank you for having us, we've been looking forward to this all week, haven't we, Nate? We brought some wine.' I hold out the bottles, holding my breath for a second, but Tamsin's eyes light up.

'Yum. I love Barefoot. Come on through, guys, Seb is already cheffing it up out in the garden.' She rolls her eyes theatrically and I cast a quick glance at Nate as we follow Tamsin along the hallway, through the kitchen and out towards the garden. His eyes are wide as he catches sight of the huge American-style fridge, the gleaming range and the set of expensive Japanese knives on the counter, and he raises his eyebrows at me as I grin back.

'Guys, you made it!' Seb swipes his hands over the very manly apron he's wearing and wraps his arms around me, before turning to Nate and pumping his hand in a quick shake. 'Nate, mate. Good to see you.'

'We didn't exactly have to come far,' Nate says dryly, and my insides curl up and die but Seb lets out a hoot of laughter. Tank lies beside the BBQ and lifts his head at the noise, letting out a low growl as he fixes his eyes on Nate.

'Shush, buddy.' Seb reaches down and runs a hand over the dog's head. 'Didn't I say he was a crotchety old thing? Although we know he likes you, Hayley.'

I can't help but feel a little smug as I crouch next to Tank and he rests his head on my knee. Someone likes me better than Nate for once, even if it is only the dog.

'No designated driver tonight, right?' Seb claps a hand on Nate's back and hands him a beer. Something dark and imported from Europe, not the Bud or Corona Nate usually drinks. 'Hayley, you look lovely.'

'Doesn't she?' Tamsin comes up behind me with two glasses of wine and hands me one, before stepping back and running her eyes over my outfit. 'Gorgeous trousers, Hayls. And those wedges make your legs go on forever.'

Nate widens his eyes at me at the shortening of my name, something only he ever does, but I am deep in the warm glow of Tamsin's attention.

'I can't wait for you to take me shopping,' Tamsin says, 'I'm thinking Friday afternoon if you can swing it?'

'Won't you be at work?' Nate says, his eyes fixed on mine.

'I've got some leave.'

'But I'll be home on Friday evening.'

'I'll be back by then, we won't be gone all night.' I grin at Tamsin. 'I can't wait! I'm really looking forward to us getting to know each other better.' As I speak, Nate drops his phone on the table with a clatter, and he pulls an apologetic face.

'I bet you're glad to be back home with this one,' Tamsin says, as Nate checks his screen isn't cracked. 'It must be hard being on the road all the time. What is it you do again?'

'Pharmaceutical sales,' Nate says. 'Nothing very exciting, but it pays the bills.'

'Oh, for a regular pay cheque.' Tamsin pretends to swoon. 'Being a voice actor means everything is very ad hoc. A pain in the arse, really, but I love it. Thank God for Seb and his little production company.'

'Less of the little,' Seb swats at her with the BBQ tongs, before turning over the meat. It smells like Chinese ribs and my mouth waters. 'It keeps you in the style to which you have become accustomed. And we've also made some of your favourite shows, so hush.'

'Wow,' I exclaim, 'so you've made stuff we might have seen?'

'Well, that's debatable,' Nate says, as I glare at him. 'I just mean people watch all kinds of different stuff, don't they? Some people only watch Netflix. Some people only watch movies.'

'I know what you're getting at,' Seb says graciously, as I furiously wish the ground would swallow me up. Or better yet, swallow Nate up. 'Hopefully you've seen some of my work.' He proceeds to reel off a bunch of TV shows — mostly those three-part crime dramas on terrestrial telly — and I am gleeful to find I've watched most of them.

'Very impressive, isn't it, Nate? We've watched loads of those shows.' I dig Nate in the ribs until he grunts an assent. 'How did you get into making TV? I'd love to do something more creative than managing a bunch of babies in a stuffy old office all day.'

Seb grins as Tamsin starts to plate up the ribs, carrying them over to a table already groaning with salads, corn on the cob and fresh bread. 'Hard work and perseverance.' He winks at me, making my cheeks flush. 'I started with a media degree and went from there.'

'Nate did a media degree,' I say as we take our seats. 'Nate, tell Seb about your degree.'

'What?' Nate frowns at me as he takes a chunk of still-warm bread. 'No one wants to hear about that, Hayls. It's not like I did anything with it. Like I said, the pharma stuff pays the bills and that's the most important thing.' My cheeks burn as if I've been slapped, but Seb and Tamsin don't seem to have noticed Nate's tone.

'You have an absolute gem in this girl,' Tamsin says later, her words slurring a little as she nudges my arm. The food was a hit, every mouthful more delicious than the last, and even Nate has relaxed and started chatting more openly now he's a few beers in. 'My lovely new friend. My shopping buddy. My new partner in crime.'

I flush, enjoying the way she leans against me, as if we've known each other for years. 'I don't know about being a gem,' I say, 'but I'll take the praise if you're offering.'

Tamsin laughs and leans in to peck me on the cheek. 'I'm thrilled to find you living next door. Anyone for more drinks? We seem to have run a little dry out here.' The empty wine bottles glint in the warm glow of the solar garden lights and I am surprised to see we've emptied three bottles between us. No wonder I'm feeling a bit tipsy.

'I'll have another beer,' Nate says, pushing his chair back and following Tamsin across the patio. 'Let me give you a hand.'

I sit back, glad that he seems to have shaken off his reluctance to get to know the neighbours. Seb and Nate have spent much of the evening talking about classic cars — not something that I realised Nate was into, although he does watch an inordinate amount of *Wheeler Dealer* episodes — and it's been nice to see him relax properly. I knew once he actually met Seb and Tamsin he would love them just as much as I do.

'Enjoying yourself?' Seb asks, leaning back and putting his hands behind his head.

'It's been a lovely evening. Again.' I laugh. 'You'll have to come to us next time.' Even as I say it, I pray he says no. Our house is in dire need of redecoration, and I know I can't pull off a meal as delicious as this.

'Absolutely. I'd love to see your place.' Seb leans in close, reaching for my hair, not taking his eyes off mine. As he brushes his fingers over my temple, I shiver, something primal tightening in my stomach at the sensation of his breath on my cheek. 'Sorry, here.' He plucks a piece of blossom from my hair. 'You're shivering. Are you chilly? Let me light the pit, we can sit round there.'

As Seb fusses with the fire pit on the other side of the patio, I scrape back my chair and head inside for the loo. I'm hoping Nate isn't in there, he seems to have been gone for ages, and I just need five mins to run my wrists under a cold tap and cool myself down. Seb's closeness has left me feeling shaken.

Dusk has fallen and the kitchen is dark as I step inside, pausing on the threshold. I thought Tamsin and Nate were fetching more drinks and for a moment I'm confused, before I see the basement door is slightly open, a soft glow coming from below. Of course the Coopers would have turned their (probably not) damp old basement into a wine cellar. Nate will be all over that — while he rarely buys expensive wine for us, he's more than happy to drink other people's. Stepping onto the stairs leading into the cellar, I make my way down carefully, intent on geeing the other two up, but as I reach the bottom stair I stop. Tamsin holds a bottle of red wine in one hand, as Nate holds her other arm. They stand close together and there is an intense look on Nate's face, one I've seen before when he's deadly serious about something, as Tamsin mutters something too low to make out. My heart crashing in my chest, I clear my throat.

'Hayley!' Tamsin pastes a smile on her face, wide and beaming, as Nate drops his hand, the atmosphere shifting. 'What do you think about an Argentinian Malbec?'

'Perfect,' I say, glancing between the two of them. Tamsin is still smiling and Nate's face is impassive, slightly flushed from the alcohol. 'Is everything OK down here?'

'Peachy,' Tamsin says, stepping towards me. 'Nate was just asking me about a voiceover for an ad for some . . . what was it, Nate?'

Nate looks at her, his mouth open uselessly for just a fraction of a second before he speaks. 'A new hay fever medication — it's something only available on prescription before, but they're going over the counter with it, and they really want a big marketing push. A radio ad would be perfect so I was asking if Tamsin has any free time to come and speak to the company directly.'

'Right. OK. Always networking, eh?' I say lightly, as my pulse still skitters under my skin and Tamsin brushes past me, Nate following, leaving me to bring up the rear.

Later, the Malbec drunk and the fire pit slowly dying to embers, Nate and I head home and crawl into bed, having drunk far more than we should.

'That wasn't so bad,' Nate says as he settles onto his pillow, stifling a yawn. 'They seem all right. Not sure I want to be best pals with them though.'

'I knew you'd like them if you gave them a chance,' I say, but I don't feel smug. I can't shake the uneasy sensation I had when I stepped down into the cellar, that I had walked in on something I shouldn't have. Something private and intimate. I'm not sure if it's the booze or the memory of Nate's hand on Tamsin's arm that makes me feel slightly nauseous. 'Night.' I go to roll over, but Nate reaches out a hand and stops me, pulling me towards him.

'I was thinking,' he says, his breath minty with toothpaste, 'maybe we are ready.'

'Ready?'

Nate's fingers loop lazily over the skin on my shoulder in a way that usually makes me shiver. 'To start a family. To be parents. I think it's time.'

'Do you mean that?' Tears prickle behind my eyes and my stomach swoops like a swallow in flight, but Nate doesn't reply, just presses his mouth gently against mine. Usually I'd respond willingly, but tonight, as his mouth covers mine and his hands rise to my breasts, the only thing I can think is, *is he thinking of me? Or is he thinking about Tamsin?*

CHAPTER 7

Nate is unusually attentive over the rest of the weekend, bringing me breakfast in bed on Sunday morning (although I can't eat much of the burnt bacon sandwich he offers up — even without a hangover it would be a struggle, but it's the thought that counts). He even makes sure to lean in and kiss me on Monday morning after he's showered and dressed, and instead of feeling irritated at being woken so early, tucking my head back under the pillow, I bask in his attention and reach up to kiss him back. The uptick in attention continues right through the week, Nate calling me every evening just to ask about my day.

Maybe the change in Nate's behaviour has nothing to do with Tamsin, I think, as I absent-mindedly stir my coffee in the office kitchen on Friday morning. I've squashed down the image of Tamsin and Nate standing too close to each other for comfort, telling myself I'm seeing it differently through the lens of a memory, exaggerating the intimacy I thought I felt. *Maybe he's just seen what I saw between Seb and Tamsin and realised that we probably should work on our own relationship. Maybe he really does want us to start a family.*

A little before one o'clock Wendy appears, looking flustered. She hates any kind of change to our office routine. 'There's someone here to see you,' she says, a blonde figure hovering behind her.

'Perfect. Bang on time.' Reaching under my desk, I pull out my handbag and snatch up the denim jacket that hangs from the back of my chair.

'Oh.' Wendy looks put out, her lower lip jutting out as she watches me tuck my phone into my bag. 'Where are you going?'

I pause, feeling Tamsin's eyes on us. 'I'm not sure that's any of your business,' I say, 'but if you must know, I'm taking my friend shopping.'

'Is that . . .' Wendy's eyes go to Tamsin, raking over her clothes. 'Is that a good idea?'

'What? Is there a problem?'

'No, absolutely not.' Wendy shakes her head, avoiding my gaze by reaching out to straighten the papers in my in-tray. 'I was just worried you might not have finished the final bits Harry asked for this morning.'

Injecting a hint of ice into my tone, I say, 'Harry knows I'm taking a half day today, Wendy, and I think you know me well enough to know I wouldn't leave the office with jobs half done.'

Wendy flicks her eyes towards Tamsin and grasps my fore-arm, leaning in and lowering her voice. 'Are we not eating lunch together today? It's Friday.'

'And?' My brows knit together, and I make a conscious effort to smooth them out. Tamsin's forehead is completely wrinkle-free.

Wendy presses her lips together for a moment. 'We always eat lunch together on a Friday. The taco guy is outside, remember? You said the chicken tacos were the best you'd ever had.'

It's no good, the frown is etched into my forehead. I did get tacos with Wendy two weeks in a row, and I probably *did* say the tacos were amazing. 'Sorry, I didn't . . . I can't today. Look, Wendy, I'm sorry, but I have to go.' I raise my voice. 'There's filing in that tray — can you make sure it's done before Monday? Thanks.'

'That was very efficient,' Tamsin whispers to me with a grin as she links her arm through mine and we head to the lift. 'And aren't you impressed with me? I wasn't even five minutes late.' She casts an appreciative glance around the office as we wait for the lift, running her eyes over the cream walls, immaculate grey carpet and the glass that is everywhere, allowing a glimpse into other people's workstations. 'Maybe I should quit all this actor stuff and get myself a real office job.'

'Oh please,' I laugh, as Wendy gawps through the closest window at us. I feel weirdly like the cool kid for once. The lift doors close behind us, shutting Wendy's face out.

'She's a bit much, isn't she?' Tamsin nods in the direction of the lift doors, and I picture Wendy's face as they slid shut. 'I'm not sure how you cope with her all day.'

'She's all right, really,' I say, guilt at leaving Wendy out making me kind. Maybe I should have invited her for lunch, she was clearly assuming that we'd eat together at the taco truck . . . but then, we're not really friends, and there's a part of me who wants to keep Tamsin all to myself. 'Office life is full of Wendys, so you might want to rethink giving up the voice acting. And I'm not sure the bosses could cope with that.' I grin and gesture to her cleavage, bursting out of a neon yellow shirt.

'Well, you're going to sort me out today, aren't you?' Tamsin winks as we step out of the office and into the bright sunshine. 'I'm looking forward to having my own personal shopper for the day.'

As we walk towards the shopping mall, arms linked, our feet stepping in perfect synchrony, I don't think I've ever been happier.

* * *

Three hours later, the two of us slump into chairs in the bar-lobby at The Stratford Hotel, mere feet away from the shopping centre. Surrounded by bags, and with a credit card that is considerably lighter — something I'll worry about later, that's for sure — Tamsin calls over a server and orders us a bottle of rosé and some snacks.

'I'd call that a success,' Tamsin says when the wine comes. As she raises her glass in a toast, I catch sight of an ugly purple mark on her forearm. 'Nate is going to lose his mind when he sees that lingerie.'

'What's that?' I nod in the direction of her arm and she glances down, rubbing her fingers over the skin before she laughs.

'God, I'm such an idiot,' she rolls her eyes. 'I burnt myself on a pan last night, trying to cook for Seb. Thankfully that long-sleeved blouse I bought today will hide it when I accompany Seb to that TV awards thing next week. Although God knows what he's going to say when he sees the Visa bill.'

'I don't think I'm going to tell Nate,' I say, relishing the crisp wine on my tongue. 'I pay my own bill, so it's not like he needs to know what I've spent.'

'Oh, good for you,' Tamsin says. 'I'll have to fess up, Seb will go mental if I don't. Although we spent less than a grand so he can't complain. He's spent more than that on that God-awful wallpaper in the dining room.'

I say nothing for a moment, remembering how much I had lusted over that wallpaper when I first saw it. 'You got some nice outfits though.'

'Thanks to you! Maybe once Seb sees me in them he'll forget all about the Visa bill.' She laughs throatily. 'I never knew pencil skirts could look so good on me. I didn't think I had the figure for it. You should do this for a job, you know. You could make a fortune.'

The idea of earning money doing something I love makes my heart skip a beat, but I shake my head. 'Too many bills to pay,' I say. 'Nate would have heart failure if I jacked my job in to try and start something up on my own. And I think if I was going to, interiors are more my thing.'

'He's not very adventurous then?' Tamsin eyes me closely and I lean down to fumble with the handles of my shopping bags to buy some time as I think.

'Not really,' I say, although it's not strictly true. He's adventurous in some aspects of his life — he's more than happy to sign up for a charity skydive, but less interested in a volunteering holiday in Vietnam with me. 'Put it this way, I wanted to hike the Inca Trail for our honeymoon, but we ended up spending it in the Lake District.'

Tamsin frowns. 'What's wrong with that? The Lake District is beautiful. I used to go there on holiday as a child with my family . . . I have good memories there.'

I wince, seemingly having put my foot in my mouth. 'No, it's gorgeous. I loved it too, only . . . it wasn't the destination I really fancied for our honeymoon. I was thinking about Barbados or Thailand if not Peru and Nate would only consider the Lake District. We've never been abroad together.'

'Never?' Tamsin's mouth drops open. 'God, I think Seb would die if he didn't get at least six weeks of sunshine a year. He loves Thailand in January, Greece in August and the Caribbean in November.'

The thought of it makes my mouth water, and not just at the thought of Seb in his swimming shorts, tanned and ripped and lying on a sun lounger beside me. *Lucky Tamsin*. 'I'd love that and we probably could afford at least one trip abroad a year, but Nate hates flying.' At least, that's what he says. He used to go abroad with his family when he was younger though.

'We know what we need to do?' Tamsin daintily picks up an asparagus spear and bites the end of it. 'We need to make you fall in love with the English coastline and countryside.'

'What?' I was hoping she'd say we need to train Nate to get over his fears and jump on a flight. Maybe a private jet, courtesy of Seb's production company.

'I know a place that you will *love*,' she leans in close, her wine-scented breath hitting my cheek. 'Margate.'

Margate? Not what I was expecting. 'I know Margate already,' I say. 'Nate and I went there the other weekend to dip in the pool at Walpole.'

'So you already know about the Walpole Bay Hotel?' Tamsin raises an eyebrow.

I shake my head. 'I've driven past it but I've never been inside.'

Tamsin lets out a hoot and claps her hands together. 'Darling Hayls, we have to go. It's like no hotel you've ever visited before. There's a gorgeous terrace out the front where you can get drinks and afternoon tea, the best rooms have little balconies that look out over the sea and . . .' she pauses dramatically, 'there's a museum *inside* the hotel. It's full of old dolls, and knick-knacks, photos and letters . . . it's wonderful. Let me see when Seb is free and the four of us can spend the weekend there.' She glances down at the bags by my feet. 'Our treat.'

Honestly, the hotel sounds horrific, but the thought of spending the entire weekend with the Coopers is intoxicating. Maybe Tamsin's right — instead of moaning about Nate's faults I should try embracing the things he loves. Although, there's just one problem. I don't think Nate will ever agree to a weekend away with the Coopers.

* * *

'No, I'm not going to play golf with Seb today,' Nate says, as soon as he appears in the kitchen doorway on Saturday morning. 'I know that's what you're going to ask. And when did you give him my number?'

'He asked for it after the BBQ,' I say, leaning in for a kiss as I groan internally. Now is definitely not the time to mention the weekend away Tamsin is excited about. 'I didn't think you'd mind. You're always saying you should get back on the golf course.'

Nate tuts. 'The *driving range* so I can practise and get my handicap down. I meant get back on the course to woo the old farts that buy my meds, not to get humiliated by the next-door neighbour.'

I don't say anything for a moment, unsure of how to respond. I thought it was a nice gesture on Seb's behalf to invite Nate golfing with him and a few of his buddies. 'So . . . what are you going to do this weekend? Don't forget I have a hair appointment today.'

'Rock climbing this afternoon with a few people from work. Mike, Darren, Sarah.' Nate turns his attention to the vase sitting on the table. A large, expensive-looking one in the same shades of teal and gold as Tamsin's wallpaper. I was hoping he wouldn't notice it. 'What the fuck is this? Since when are we vase people? Shouldn't there be flowers in it?'

There probably should, but I can't bear to sully the inside with dirty water. 'I liked it, I bought it. It looks nice.' I pause. 'Sarah? Who's Sarah?'

'Some new woman in accounts. Don't you think the vase is better suited to maybe somewhere a little more . . . upmarket than our place?' Nate says, his eyes flicking towards the wall between our house and the Coopers. There is the sharp sting of tears behind my eyes, and Nate moves towards me. 'Sorry, Hayls. I didn't mean to snap. The vase just isn't the kind of thing you'd usually bring home, that's all . . . normally it's books to add to your ridiculous pile by the bed. I'm still waiting for that to topple over and kill me in the night.' He wraps his arms around me and I smile into his chest.

'Maybe it is a bit too flashy,' I mutter against the clean cotton scent of his T-shirt. 'I'll give it to your mum.' There is the rumble of laughter against my forehead and then Nate drops a kiss in my hair.

'Go and get ready or you'll be late,' he says and gently pushes me away. 'I'm going to walk up to the shop and get some more orange juice.'

Upstairs, I slick lip gloss over my mouth, watching out of the window as Nate strides up the garden path and turns left towards the corner shop. Seconds later, Tamsin hurries along her own garden path, and makes the same turn. It looks as though she calls out to Nate and I pause, waiting to see if she catches him up and whether he brushes her off if she does, but he doesn't turn around and she doesn't catch him before he turns the corner at the end of the road. I don't know why, but I feel relieved.

* * *

Nate isn't home when I get back from the hairdressers, and part of me is glad. I went all out at my appointment and now I touch a hand to my new hair. I feel completely different, I *look* completely different, as though a new butterfly-like Hayley has emerged from some ugly old chrysalis. Taking the stairs two at a time, I rummage in the back of the wardrobe for the bag I brought home from my shopping spree with Tamsin and pull out the La Perla matching lingerie set I treated myself to. Pulling out the red-and-black silk, my heart hammers in my chest. I'd picked up the cream silk set, but Tamsin had shaken her head and placed it firmly back on the rail.

'Cream is for virginal brides,' she'd whispered with a grin. 'You're a stone-cold fox who's going to give Nate the night of his life.' And she'd thrust the red-and-black silk into my hands and marched me to the till, ignoring my wince at the £650 price tag.

Now, I slip my clothes off and slide into the silk, the cold whisper of the fabric against my skin making me shiver. Standing in front of the mirror, I suck in my stomach, smooth a hand over my newly short hair and adjust my tits, just as the front door closes with a bang. *Maybe tonight is the night we make a baby.*

'Hayley? You back?' Nate's voice floats up the stairs.

'Up here,' I call back. 'Come up, I need to show you something.' Arranging myself artfully across the bed, I wait for the door to push open and relish the widening of Nate's eyes as he spots me.

'Uh . . . wow. I wasn't expecting this.' He stands in the doorway, not making any attempt to step inside. 'You look . . .'

I flutter my lashes as I look up at him, the strap of the bra digging into my shoulder in a way that I honestly don't think a £350 bra should. 'Come over here then. I bought this for you.' When he doesn't move, I run a hand over my waist, a sinking feeling dragging my stomach to my feet. 'Nate?'

He blinks, pressing his hand against the door frame as if he might fall over. 'Your hair,' he says eventually. 'Why did you get it done like that?'

Disappointment singing in my veins, I sit up. He wasn't supposed to care about the hair. He was supposed to care about the fact that his wife was offering herself up to him on a platter, in the most expensive underwear she's ever bought in her life. 'I fancied a change.'

'A change?' His voice is strangled. 'You look like . . .'

I slide off the bed and move to the mirror, raising my hand to my head again to smooth at my new haircut. At the soft, honey blonde highlights laced through the dull, mousy brown, at the gently curled waves that have replaced my limp, poker-straight locks. He doesn't say it, but I know what he's thinking.

Nate's right, I think. *I look just like Tamsin.*

CHAPTER 8

My cheeks are scalding as I pull off the underwear and reach for my shorts and T-shirt, stuffing the silk back into the bag. A total waste of £650 seeing as it's non-returnable. It's going to take me months to pay it off, but it isn't the money that makes my eyes sting and my face burn.

'Hayls, come here.' Nate reaches for me, but I shove past him, heading for the stairs. 'I didn't mean it like that . . . you look beautiful.'

'Really?' I whirl around at the top of the stairs. 'Because that isn't what your face was saying. You looked *horrified*, Nate. Like you'd seen a ghost or something. It wasn't the face of a man who wants to have a baby with his wife.' That snake of suspicion stirs in my belly again. 'I was trying to do something *nice*, something to breathe some life into . . . whatever *this*,' I wave a hand between us, 'has become.'

'Hayley, please. You're overreacting. I said you looked beautiful, it was just a shock, that's all . . . your hair . . . I wasn't expecting such a dramatic overhaul.' Nate pauses, pushing his hand through his own thick blond hair. 'Please? I'm sorry. You didn't have to do all of this.' He holds out a hand but I shake my head.

'I'm going to go for a walk,' I say, holding up a hand when he steps towards me. 'Please, Nate. It's fine, OK? You just go back to whatever important thing you've got to do and I'll be back in a little while. I need some space.'

Half of me hopes he'll follow me downstairs, push me against the wall and kiss me hard the way I imagine Seb would do to Tamsin, but there is no thud of footsteps on the stairs behind me, so I hurry outside, slamming the front door closed behind me.

I don't even know where I'm planning on going, I just walk, my skin smarting with the pain of Nate's rejection. The look on his face was priceless and not in a good way, and now it's imprinted on my brain, replaying on a loop. I'm so deep in thought I don't even realise I'm being followed until a hand lands on my shoulder and I whirl around, about to karate chop my assailant in the throat.

'Hayley! It's me!' Seb stands back, his hands held up in a gesture of surrender. 'Didn't you hear me calling you?' Tank sighs at the end of his leash as Seb peers closely at my face. 'Wow. Look at you. You look incredible.'

'Really?' My hand goes self-consciously to my new hair.

'Really.' Seb stands back as Tank tugs again at the end of the lead, keen to keep moving. 'It really suits you, you look beautiful. Although . . .' he eyes me closely and I feel my heart sink again, the glitter of the compliment melting away. 'You look like you've been crying. Is everything all right?'

'Oh. Yeah. I guess.' A long sigh escapes before I can stop it. 'Just a stupid fight with Nate.' Tears sting my eyes and the bridge of my nose fizzes at the thought of the horrified look on his face.

'Nothing serious, I hope?' Seb keeps his eyes on the pavement as we begin to walk again, Tank sniffing at the hedges as we go, and I appreciate his discretion.

'Let's just say he wasn't as taken by my new haircut as you seem to be.' I give Seb a rueful smile as he turns to look at me, a frown creasing his brow.

'Then the man is a fool,' he says after a long pause, in which I might be mistaken but it feels as if the air crackles between us.

'You look even more beautiful than before, if that's at all possible. He needs to realise how lucky he is to have you.'

That's all it takes for Seb to put a little spring in my step. He's right. Nate is lucky to have me — we're lucky to have each other, we just need to remember that. Seb and I walk in companiable silence back to the house, and he leaves me at the gate with a peck on the cheek.

'Everyone has ups and downs,' he says. 'It's important to work through things. Don't get mad about the small stuff, Hayley, but also don't stifle yourself.'

I give him a wave as he walks up his own front path. If Seb is this kind and thoughtful, no wonder the Coopers are living in a perfect marriage.

* * *

My intention is to go in the house and apologise to Nate, and explain that I understand my appearance was a shock, but he's flat on his back on top of the duvet, eyes tightly shut. I'm not sure if he's faking the heavy breathing and light snores, but I know that I am not tired yet, so I pull out a crumpled half pack of cigarettes from the kitchen drawer and make my way into the garden. Slumping into a patio chair, I light up, the rush of nicotine making me feel light-headed. I don't smoke often, usually only when I'm drinking, but tonight I need a cigarette.

I run my fingers through my hair as smoke coils lazily in the still summer evening air around my head. *It wasn't intentional*, I think. I never meant to imitate Tamsin's haircut. The hairdresser asked what I wanted, and I told her something drastic. Something to make me look like a better version of myself. And then I found myself agreeing to the blonde highlights, to the extra length being taken off, to the hot wand curling around my freshly bleached tresses to form beachy waves. I take a drag on the cigarette, the harsh smoke scorching the back of my throat. *What will Tamsin think when she sees it? Will she think like Nate, and believe I did it deliberately?* Because that's what he thinks, I'm sure of it. I exhale, my mouth dry and ashy. I think it's more likely Tamsin will be flattered, and I smile. We'll both laugh about it, I'm sure. She'll call us twins and nudge up against me in that way she has.

There is the muted sound of voices and then I hear the patio doors slide open next door. I lean over and hastily stub out my cigarette, thinking I'll bite the bullet and show her my new hair over the fence now, before I start overthinking and making it weird.

'No, Seb, I'm not saying that.' I pause, halfway to my feet when Tamsin's voice floats over the fence. 'I'm just . . . you . . . careful.'

Their voices are lowered and I struggle to catch Seb's response, but the hairs on my arms prickle to attention at the tone. 'You . . . mess . . . bad idea.' There is a hissed intake of breath, and I hurry silently across the lawn to press my face to a knothole in the fence. I can just make out the Coopers, standing on their patio. Tamsin's face is contorted with pain as Seb grips her upper arm tightly. I press my hand to my mouth, wondering if I should make my presence known. I would want someone to step in if Nate did that to me, wouldn't I? Before I can react Tamsin yanks her arm free and hisses something unintelligible in Seb's face, before spinning on her heel and marching back inside the house. Turning, I glance through my own patio doors, where I can see Nate filling the kettle at the sink, his hair rumpled as he yawns and rubs a hand over his face. He flicks it on and reaches for my favourite mug, and a fist clenches around my heart. *Nate. My perfectly, imperfect Nate.* Without looking back at the Coopers' garden, I move towards my own house, my own life.

* * *

'Good morning you two lovebirds!' Tamsin trills as she and Seb approach us the following morning. Seb's arm is draped over

Tamsin's shoulder and there is no hint of the animosity I saw between them in the garden last night, but even so I feel oddly off-kilter at the sight of them both. 'Where are you off to?'

I glance at Nate, who is shaking Seb's hand. 'Heading into town for brunch.' There's a bakery we love, and after a heartfelt apology from Nate and some rather delicious make-up sex, I'm looking forward to finally spending some quality time with Nate this morning before he's back on the road tomorrow.

'That sounds nice.' Tamsin runs her eyes over me, a whisper of a frown at her brows before she smiles. 'Hayls, you look . . . incredible! I thought you were just getting a trim?'

My hand goes to my hair. I need to stop touching it, people are going to think I've developed a tic. 'You think? It's not too . . . dramatic?'

'Fuck yeah, it's dramatic,' Tamsin laughs. 'I love it. Don't you love Hayley's hair, Seb?'

Seb looks my way, breaking off his conversation with an unusually chatty Nate, running his eyes over me as if our walk last night never happened. 'Fantastic, Hayley. It really suits you. Say, Nate was just telling me about this bakery you guys were off to and it sounds amazing. Albanian, isn't it?'

Nate nods. 'Best pastries and coffee you can get.'

'We haven't eaten yet,' Seb says, nudging Tamsin. 'Hey, why don't we join you? We haven't seen you guys all week — well, Hayley at any rate — it might be nice to catch up over a lazy Sunday brunch.'

'Great idea!' Tamsin reaches up to push her sunglasses on top of her head, the short sleeve of her blouse sliding up to her shoulder. I can't help flicking my gaze to her exposed upper arm, and the three small bruises smudging her tanned skin. Fingerprint-shaped bruises. 'I've got heaps to tell you, Hayley. Everyone keeps complimenting me on my outfits, I definitely think you have a talent.'

I don't speak for a moment, knowing that Nate will decline on my behalf. I don't think I can sit across from Seb after watching him grab Tamsin like that and not say anything.

'Sure, why not?' Nate says with a smile that doesn't quite reach his eyes, reaching down to squeeze my hand. *What the fuck?* Usually I have to persuade him to spend any time with the Coopers, so why is he so amenable now? Why today?

We make our way to the tube station, Nate and Seb deep in conversation, Tamsin chatting away beside me. I can't concentrate on a word she's saying, smiling and nodding vaguely until, when we step off the tube a few stops later, she pauses and tugs at my sleeve as the boys walk on ahead.

'Are you OK, Hayls?' Her brow is furrowed as she looks me over. 'You seem a bit . . .'

'I'm fine,' I say hastily. 'Just . . . my hair, that's all. Nate said it's really similar to yours and I was worried you thought I'd copied you.'

Tamsin lets out a hoot of laughter, causing Seb and Nate to turn and wait for us. 'You daft thing!' she says. 'It's nothing like mine. Mine is far blonder, and you haven't cut yours as short. Mine is curly, yours is straight.' She's got a point — the curls only lasted until my head hit the pillow last night.

'OK. OK, good.' I let her link her arm through mine and we follow the husbands into the bakery, Nate snagging a table in the sunshine. Through croissants and coffee for them, English Breakfast tea for me, my gaze keeps returning to Tamsin and Seb. He drops a sugar cube into her coffee and stirs it, she picks croissant crumbs off his shirt, and when I drop my napkin I see her sandalled foot is hooked around his ankle, as if they are knotted together. They don't seem like the kind of couple who hiss in each other's faces and grab at each other's arms. They seem totally, almost sickeningly in love. I'm starting to think I imagined the whole thing.

CHAPTER 9

On Friday evening Nate and I attend a charity function for his work, and while Nate glitters and shines his way around the room, fawned over by men and women alike who can't seem to sing his praises enough, I end up loitering in a dark corner alone, clutching a glass of warm white wine and alternating between feeling proud that my husband is so well-liked, to feeling like an awkward teenager at a family party. Nate drinks too much and chats incessantly all the way home to the Uber driver, not asking once if I've enjoyed myself, and when I wake up on Saturday morning there is a rancid taste in my mouth which I'm not entirely sure is down to the lukewarm Chablis.

When Tamsin appears on the front path and asks if I want to go for lunch as Nate dashes out of the house, late to play football, I jump at the chance, expecting a café in a park somewhere or maybe a walk into town and a sandwich from Pret.

'I wasn't expecting this,' I say, as she drags me into Fortnum and Mason.

'Listen, if Seb is going to fuck off for the day to some horseracing thing, the least he can do is pay for us to have a decent lunch.' Tamsin grins at me but there is a sharp edge to her voice. 'And I'm going to bet you've never been to Fortnum's wine bar before?'

'Err . . . no, I haven't. And I'm not complaining.' Linking my arm through hers we giggle our way into the restaurant and I thank my lucky stars again that Tamsin and Seb moved in next door to us.

'What's Nate doing with his day?' Tamsin asks, as the waiter pours her a glass of Bollinger, apologising profusely as the bottle drips on Tamsin's skirt and she waves him away with a smile. It's a little early in the day for me but I accept the glass she holds out.

'Football, shower, protein shake, take ages over his hair and then he's going to his mum's, I think. She lives on her own so sometimes he takes her out and stays over, just to keep her company,' I say, feeling slightly bitchy as the waiter pops caviar and tiny blinis in front of us. 'Although I don't feel I can moan about him when I'm about to drink champagne and eat caviar with you.' I watch as Tamsin uses a tiny silver spoon to scoop the caviar onto the blini and pop it into her mouth, and then I copy her.

'Is everything OK between the two of you?' Tamsin cocks her head on one side, concern crossing her features as I chew and swallow, trying my hardest not to screw my face up. I'm not sure what I thought caviar might taste like but it wasn't like this.

Forcing the fish eggs down my throat I drain my champagne glass, holding my hand over the top before Tamsin can top it up. 'It's getting there between us,' I say. 'He reacted pretty strongly to my new hair cut but he apologised.'

'He did?' Tamsin widens her eyes. 'Why? You look incredible. And you never told me how the new lingerie went down.'

I fiddle with the caviar spoon, not wanting to elaborate, hot shame still running through me every time I think about Nate's reaction to seeing me sprawled across the bed. 'It was . . . fine.'

'Just fine?' Tamsin quirks an eyebrow and as she leans over with the champagne bottle in her hand I see there are still the slight faint smudges of fingerprint-shaped bruises on her upper arm. 'Come on, aren't you going to help me with this bottle? I can't drink alone, it makes me depressed.'

'I'm trying to cut down.' The words are out before I realise I'm going to say them. 'Nate and I . . . we're going to try for a baby.'

'Oh.' Tamsin fills her own glass and then puts the bottle down. 'You don't seem . . . Hayley, are you crying? What's going on? Isn't this what you always wanted?'

Feeling pathetic I swipe at my cheeks, almost surprised when my fingers come away damp. 'It is what I've always wanted, I'm just not sure it's what Nate really wants.'

'Why?'

I press my lips together, unable to tell her the truth. That I wonder if Nate just said it because he wanted to keep me pliant and happy, leaving him free to think about other things, like his friends, and work, and all the damn hobbies he has. *Like her.* 'He just doesn't seem to really see me properly. Like, there's always something more important going on for him, even when he's not out and busy doing other things. As if there's a movie playing behind his eyes and I'll never be a part of it. I'll always be an annoyance, a fly buzzing in the background.'

'Oh no, Hayley. You don't mean that.' As Tamsin takes a sip of her champagne, I think I see her mouth curve upwards but then I blink, and all I see is concern.

'It'll be all right. We'll be fine.' I clap my hands together. 'Just a tiny blip, right? And a baby is a big deal, he's not going to say that and not mean it. Nate and I are soul mates, we can get through anything.' I sound like I'm convincing myself, not Tamsin, and I change the subject. 'What about you guys? Any trouble in paradise?'

Tamsin smirks and shakes her head. 'No more than the usual. Seb is frantically busy on some documentary, but he still never fails to notice how much I spend on the credit card.' Her smile seems forced as she pops another blini into her mouth.

'So, everything is OK?' My eyes go to Tamsin's bare arms. 'I don't want to pry but . . . I couldn't help overhearing you two in the garden—'

'Hayley? It is you! I thought surely not, but then here you are.' A familiar voice rings out and my stomach pitches as Wendy descends on our table, a beaming smile fixed to her perfectly made-up face. 'And your new friend . . . sorry, I didn't catch your name last time?'

'Wendy . . . hi,' I say, my heart sinking. 'This is Tamsin.'

'Tamsin.' Wendy barely glances at her. 'So, Hayley, what are you doing in town on a scorcher of a day like this? You always say you hate the humidity in London.'

I think I might have mentioned that once before, if that. 'Just having lunch actually, Wendy, so . . .'

Wendy doesn't get the hint, peering between me and Tamsin before her eyes rest on the plate and bottle in front of us. 'Caviar? And champagne! Are you celebrating?' She doesn't let me respond as she glances around. 'Is Nate here too?'

Tamsin presses a hand to her mouth, hiding her smile as Wendy loiters at the edge of the table. The last thing I want to do is invite her to join us, and I think I'll kill Tamsin if she does. 'No, he's at home. Did you, errr . . .' I falter as Wendy turns her smile up a notch. 'Did you want something else? It's nice to see you and everything but it's just . . . we're in the middle of lunch.'

Wendy's face changes, her smile dropping and her eyes hardening as she looks Tamsin over again. 'Of course. I'll let you get on. I just wanted to say hello and check in on you.' She gives me one last lingering look as if giving me the opportunity to change my mind and then she's gone in a cloud of overpowering perfume and a swish of her dark hair.

'Well.' Tamsin lets out the laugh she's been holding in, but I don't join in. 'That was unexpected. She really is a bit odd, isn't she?'

Unease prickles along my spine as Wendy weaves her way between the tables, pausing once to look back as she exits the restaurant. I can't read the expression on her face and I reach for the champagne, ignoring the surprise on Tamsin's face. 'That was weird,' I say. 'She said something odd about Nate the other day, too. And don't you think it's strange she turned up here of all places?' I can picture Wendy spending her Saturday's mooching around Waitrose, but she doesn't really seem like a Fortnum and Mason girl, but then neither am I really. 'I mean, she's a nice girl, but that was . . .'

'She's definitely a bit of a strange one,' Tamsin says. 'I think she probably wants to be your friend.' She lets out a laugh, loud and tinged with cruelty as if the idea is ridiculous.

I suppress a shudder, and resist the urge to look around and see if Wendy is close enough to have heard Tamsin's laughter. I wouldn't want to intentionally hurt Wendy, but she is enough to deal with at work, I don't want to hang around with her outside of work too. 'No, thanks.'

Tamsin reaches over and squeezes my hand. 'I won't lie to you, I am a bit glad. I don't think I want to share you with anyone else. In fact, if Nate's going to stay at his mum's tonight, and Seb isn't going to be back until the small hours, why don't we grab some pampering bits and I'll stay at yours tonight? We can have a sleepover, it'll be like we're teenagers again.'

The unease slips away as I grin back and raise my glass in a toast. I don't need any other friends when I have Tamsin.

CHAPTER 10

'Do we have to go?' Nate grumbles as I run the iron over a new Weekend Offender T-shirt for him.

'Yes,' I snap back, hot and flustered from the steam of the iron. The weather still hasn't broken and to be honest, I'm about ready for September to kick in. 'I thought you liked Seb and Tamsin? We've spent enough time with them.' Although if I'm brutally honest, it's usually at my instigation.

It's the tail end of August and Seb and Tamsin have returned from their holiday on one of the Greek islands in time for Tamsin's birthday. We've spent several evenings with them before their holiday — drinks at Soho House thanks to Seb's membership, a night at the theatre for some play that one of Tamsin's friends was starring in — and Tamsin and I have spent time alone together, our friendship growing stronger the more we confide in each other. I've confessed to her how lonely I find things when Nate is away, and how frustratingly boring he can be, while she has confessed that Seb too can be boring (although I'm not sure I believe her), and that she has no idea about anything financial in their relationship; Seb deals with everything. 'I could have nothing,' she shrugged one afternoon as we sat by the river with a glass of rosé. 'He could clean us out and I wouldn't even know.' The only thing that hasn't come up, the words sticking in my throat every time I try to mention it, is the aggression I witnessed and my suspicion that perhaps Seb has trouble controlling his temper sometimes.

'It's not that I don't like them.' Nate takes the freshly ironed T-shirt and pulls it over his head. 'It's the fact that there'll be loads of other people there who we don't know. Fancy wankers with loads of money and useless arty degrees. I've given up going to Luke's stag do for this.'

'You have a useless arty degree, and who even is Luke? You've never even mentioned him before,' I tut, as Nate scowls in response. 'It'll be fun. And it's at their house, it's not like we have far to go if you really hate it.'

I, for one, am looking forward to it, especially as Nate has agreed to give up his own night out to join me. Seb and Tamsin are so glittery and fabulous that I have no doubt that their friends will be the same. And if some of them are excited by my suggestions to Seb for changes to the house and garden, then maybe this is the start of me building a small network, and hopefully being able to change my career before it's too late.

We can hear the thud of the music as soon as we step out of our front door, and a shiver of excitement runs down my spine. I smile a 'hello' at the man who steps onto the Coopers' garden path ahead of me; he's dressed all in linen and sports a man bun, giving shades of early 2000s Russell Brand before he was outed as a predator. Nate's hand presses lightly against the small of my back and I'm glad he's there, nerves suddenly tickling my belly as we follow the path along the side of the house, letting ourselves in through the small side gate, as per the flyer stuck to the front door.

The garden has been transformed. The fire pit is glowing, with low chairs arranged around it in a semicircle, the sun loungers hidden out of sight. Tiny Chinese lanterns are strung between the trees, emitting a faint yellow glow, and laughter rises over the buzz of easy conversation, as people fill the lawn, effortlessly glamorous under the soft light. I smooth a hand over my dress, suddenly feeling self-conscious. A table at the opposite side of the patio is laden with finger food, but not your usual party finger food. Oysters, crab claws and tiny roast beef canapés are laid out on stoneware plates, along with buckets full of ice holding bottles of Veuve Clicquot. My mouth waters, just as Nate says with a laugh, 'That'll go straight through you.' He gestures to the seafood bar. 'Sitting out there all night in this warm weather? E coli waiting to happen.'

'For fucks sake, Nate.' Shaking my head, I move to the table and deliberately throw an oyster down my neck before pouring myself a glass of champagne.

'You found the most important part of the party then.' Seb's breath tickles the back of my neck and I turn to face him, my heart racing. 'You look . . .' he rakes his eyes over me, over the vintage Pucci mini dress I found in a charity shop in St Johns Wood. 'Magnificent.'

'Thank you.' I swallow, my mouth suddenly dry, and sip at my champagne. Nate hasn't even noticed I'm wearing a new, to me, dress. 'Where is the birthday girl? I have a gift for her.'

Seb waves a hand over the garden, over the thirty or so people dancing, talking and drinking. 'She's around somewhere. She'll be thrilled you made it.'

I remember what Seb had told me before about Tamsin, that she doesn't very often click with people. Looking around, I find it hard to believe now. The garden is full of guests and I spot Tamsin in a corner towards the back of the lawn, surrounded by a bunch of people who all look decidedly more glamorous than me. She throws her head back laughing, two of the men beside her joining in, and I press my fingers against the clasp of my clutch bag. Inside, I have a pair of earrings for Tamsin's birthday gift. They are only Kate Spade, all I could afford after my credit card blowout, but I thought of Tamsin the moment I saw them. Now though, surrounded by these bright media folk, I wonder if they just look cheap and tacky.

'Come on,' Seb takes my hand, seemingly not bothered that Nate has appeared beside me (he won't eat the seafood, but I see he's already on the champagne). 'You need to say hi to the birthday girl and there's some people you absolutely *must* meet.'

Following Seb across the lawn, my heels sinking slightly into the grass, my heart lifts as Tamsin catches sight of me, her face lighting up. She pulls me into a tight hug, pressing her cheek against mine. 'Thank God you're here,' she murmurs, 'I've been stuck with these boring production arseholes for an hour at least.'

Laughing, I pull away. 'You were very convincing,' I say. 'You looked as if you were having a lovely time. Here. I got you something.' Pressing the small package into Tamsin's hands, I wait as she feverishly tears off the paper.

'Oh.' There is a pause, and my stomach turns over. *She hates them.* 'Oh, Hayls. These are fabulous. They'll go with everything.' She holds the earrings — small flower studs, each petal a different coloured jewel — against one ear.

'Gorgeous,' Seb leans in and kisses her so fiercely I think I might blush for her, and then takes the earrings. 'Hayley, what a thoughtful gift, they're exactly Tam's style. Let me put these away before they get lost.' He's gone before the pink flush has faded from my cheeks.

'Let me introduce you.' Tamsin gestures to the small woman beside her, a thick dark fringe almost obscuring her eyes completely. 'Elena, this is Hayley. She lives next door.'

There is a pang of something I can't quite name at being described as Tamsin's neighbour rather than her friend. 'Nice to meet you. How do you know Tamsin and Seb?'

'Oh gosh.' Elena's accent is slow and drawly, the kind of accent only people with money have. 'I've known them for years and years. We were at university together. God, seems like an age ago.' Tamsin slips away to greet more guests, and Nate has also disappeared as Elena blathers on for what feels like forever, about her job and how the City isn't the same as it was before Covid and I find myself people watching, unable to get away without seeming rude. I spot Nate talking to a blonde woman, in a dress that is far too tight for her, smirking as she laughs at something he's said. 'Is that your husband?'

'I'm sorry?' I drag my gaze away from Nate, flirtatious, enchanting Nate, a Nate I never get to see any more, and back to Elena with her droning voice and thick cut fringe.

'That guy over there. The blond chap. Is that your husband?'

'Err, yes. Yes, it is.' I wish I hadn't drained my glass so quickly and cast about for an open bottle.

'Where's he from?' Elena frowns, rising up on to her tiptoes to get a better look. 'He looks familiar.'

'He grew up around here, but he's a pharma rep so he travels quite a lot,' I say. 'I thought Seb was familiar when he and Tamsin first moved in, but I guess he and Nate both just have one of those faces.'

'I guess so.' Elena gives me a quick smile, although her brow is still crinkled with a slight frown, and to my relief moves past me. 'Won't you excuse me? I need another drink.'

I barely speak to Nate for the rest of the evening, although I see him charming and flirting his way around the party. Every time I try to make my way over to him, Tamsin appears and fills my glass and introduces me to another friend or colleague, telling them how my suggestions are responsible for some of the changes Seb has made to the house and that they should probably hire me before I get too expensive. Every time I try to tell her to stop, my cheeks burning hot with embarrassment, she winks and tells me to hush, topping my glass up so that by the time the party winds down I have no idea how much champagne I've drunk but I'm delightfully tipsy.

'Having fun?' Seb's voice is low in my ear, as I whirl around to face him. With the booze making my head spin and neither Nate nor Tamsin anywhere to be seen I have retreated to the end of the garden, away from the last few party stragglers.

'Yes, it's been lovely. A real banger.' I laugh, pressing a hand to my mouth, vaguely aware that my words are slurred.

'Nate gone home?' Seb surveys the garden, somehow without seeming to take his eyes off me. *Am I imagining it, or is he looking at me differently?*

'I hope not.' A hiccup escapes, and my cheeks burn. 'Oops, sorry. Too much Veuve.' There's a sentence I never thought I would say.

'He's a fool if he has gone home without you.' Seb steps closer and I can smell his aftershave, and something else. Something uniquely him. His eyes run over my face and I swallow, my breath sticking in my throat. Butterflies are swarming in my stomach and over his shoulder I can see Tamsin throwing her arms around the Russell Brand guy at the other end of the garden. 'I mean it, Hayley. I wouldn't leave you here alone. Not when you look like that.' His hand comes up to brush my hair away where it skims the top of my bare shoulder, his palm like fire against my skin. My eyes meet his and as his mouth curves up in a gentle smile I find myself leaning in.

'Hayley?'

At the sound of Nate's voice the spell is broken and I let out a long breath, pulling back and neatly sidestepping Seb. 'Over here.' I don't know whether I am relieved or disappointed that he has appeared, drunken and dishevelled.

'Heyyy.' Nate throws his arms around me, and it's enough to sober me up. 'I think I'm done, Hayls.'

'Yeah, I think it's time we went home.' Tucking an arm around Nate, I give Seb a brisk smile. 'Thanks for a lovely party.' He nods, but there is an expression on his face that I can't read, and I hurry Nate up the path towards the side gate. *What was I thinking? What was* Seb *thinking?*

CHAPTER 11

Waking up the next morning, the sun is far higher in the sky than I expected, and I remember how dawn had almost broken by the time I eventually managed to drop off to sleep, after Nate and I had staggered our way back home.

'Nate?' When I reach for him, my head thumping a beat any rock band would be proud of, my hand only meets cold sheets. 'Nate?'

Nausea rising in my belly as I swing my legs out of bed, I stifle a burp and shrug on my robe, before making my way downstairs. I can smell coffee, and when I walk into the kitchen the patio doors are open and Nate is sitting in the sunshine, mug in hand.

'Ugh.' I shield my eyes with my hand and slump into the patio chair beside him. 'How are you even alive this morning? I feel like I woke up dead.' *Too much booze.* That's what I'm putting Seb's behaviour down to. My reaction, too.

Nate turns to me with a grin, his face a sickly shade of white. 'Berocca and strong coffee, that's how. Tamsin and Seb are offering up a full English, but I said thanks but no thanks. I thought you wouldn't fancy it.'

Sometimes I wonder if Nate knows me at all. A full English breakfast is the only way to battle a raging hangover. 'Bacon and eggs are probably the only things able to resuscitate me at this point, I think.'

The scent of sausages wafts over the fence and despite a warning roll of my belly, my mouth waters. Seconds later Tamsin's face pops over the top of the fence. She looks as though she's slept a full night's sleep and has never touched a drop of alcohol in her life.

'Mimosas are ready!' she trills, her voice like a jackhammer to my skull. 'Gosh, Hayls, you look like you need one more than the rest of us. Come on, the birthday celebrations aren't done yet. And you, Nate. I told you Hayley would be up for it.'

I half expect Nate to argue back but instead he yanks me to my feet, ignoring my groans as my head thumps and I feel slightly off-balance. I drank so much last night that I'm probably still pissed, and it's not just the thought of more alcohol that's making me sick. I have to face Seb.

'It's almost three o'clock,' Nate whispers with a sympathetic grin, as he presses a kiss into my hair. 'Eat some food and then I swear I'll let you go back to bed.'

'I'll hold you to that,' I mutter and head inside, hoping I can get dressed without throwing up.

Half an hour later I'm a mimosa in and feeling a hundred times better. There is no weirdness between me and Seb, in fact it's as if nothing has happened at all as he serves up sausages — not just any sausages, award-winning bangers from Lincolnshire apparently; Nate rolls his eyes at this — bacon, eggs, beans and hash browns.

'Oh damn, this one's empty.' Tamsin waves a bottle of champagne, a sparkly plastic tiara from the party perched in her tousled blonde hair. 'I'll grab some more.'

Shoving back my chair I follow her inside. 'Thanks for last night,' I say to the back of her head as she peers into the fridge. 'It was brilliant. Nate enjoyed himself too — it's been ages since we went to a party together.'

'It's hard not to get carried away with Seb's media lot around,' she says in a dry tone. 'Honestly, they drink the bar dry wherever they go. They're not my kind of people really, but when Seb is paying for the party Seb draws up the guest list.' Tamsin smiles but it doesn't reach her eyes. 'I'm glad you had fun though. You made some good contacts, I hope? Surely Nate can't shut you down if you have people lining up for your help?'

I press my lips together. 'I'd hope not, but . . .' Unease filters through my veins and I change the subject, not wanting to badmouth Nate when he's only feet away, especially after what I almost did last night. 'Shall I grab another bottle? Save us coming back in again?'

Tamsin gives me a thumbs up and I pull another bottle of champagne from the fridge, my eyes resting on a photograph on the fridge door as I swing it closed. I've never seen it before — or at least I've never noticed it. It's a photograph of a young woman, maybe sixteen or seventeen, her hair choppy, highlighted waves similar to Tamsin's. She sits on a concrete wall, the sea behind her, her hands tucked under her thighs as she grins wildly at the camera.

'Who's this?' A shadow blocks the light from the patio as I gesture to the photograph. I look up to see Tamsin staring at Nate as he stands in the doorway. 'I didn't see her at the party, but I think I recognise her from somewhere.'

'My little sister. She did a bit of TV work when she was younger, that's probably where you saw her,' Tamsin replies, but she's still staring at Nate, unblinking, and something prickles at the back of my neck as I glance between them. Nate stands stock still, staring back at Tamsin, his face disconcertingly blank. It's as though he's brought an arctic blast in with him and I shiver, not sure what exactly is going on.

'Nate?' I turn to him, a questioning look on my face, condensation from the champagne bottle making my fingers slick.

'Seb said where's this bloody champagne then?' Nate holds out a hand, and the spell is broken. Tamsin laughs and hands him her bottle.

'You got the bottle, you make the drinks,' she winks as she squeezes past him, and Nate turns to follow.

I stand there for a moment, not moving, before I turn back to look at the photograph again. *What was that?* I don't know why, but everything about that brief exchange has my instincts fired up. Something felt wrong, somehow, just like it did in the cellar that time, and I scrub my free hand over my other arm, feeling chilled to the bone.

CHAPTER 12

The others seem settled in for the afternoon, as Tamsin makes a fresh round of mimosas and Seb and Nate start talking cars, but I find my hangover is deepening, made worse I am sure by the unsettling feeling I had in the kitchen. I can't put my finger on it, and I reach for the glass in front of me, hoping that the booze will shake it free. I used to feel paranoid and shaky after a big night out, and maybe it's just been so long since I let loose that I have forgotten how rotten I can feel the next day.

By the time Tamsin opens the third bottle of champagne the uneasy feeling has shifted again and I have a good buzz on. Nate is a little quiet, but Seb is on top form, telling stories about his tearaway teenage years, having us all in stitches. Even though Tamsin must have heard the stories a hundred times before she laughs along with us, and the only person who seems subdued is Nate. Reaching out, I squeeze his hand and he gives a poor effort at a smile.

'. . . so many weirdos,' Seb is saying with a laugh as I tune back in.

'Speaking of which, tell them about that woman, Hayls. What's her name? The one from Fortnum's?' Tamsin nudges me.

'Wendy?' I shift in my seat, not sure why Tamsin has brought her up now. 'She's OK . . . just a bit full on, and maybe a little bit lonely? We work together but just lately it feels like she keeps popping up everywhere I go.' Unease creeps a chilly hand over my shoulders as I remember her comments about seeing Nate in Harrogate, and the way she just appeared at the table when Tamsin and I were having lunch.

'Odd woman,' Tamsin says with an exaggerated shudder.

Nate frowns, draining his beer. 'She's always been all right to me.'

Before I can ask him to elaborate — after all, he's only met her a couple of times at work events — Tamsin excuses herself to head inside for a cardigan, a chill casting over the garden now the sun has lowered in the sky, and Nate follows her inside for the bathroom. It's then that Seb turns to me.

'Feeling better?'

I nod, although the orange juice has left a sickly taste in my mouth. 'Much. I drank way too much last night. I can't remember the last time I drank like that. Goodness, I felt so foggy this morning. The night was a blur. I barely remember a thing.' *Not completely true.*

'Honestly?' Seb eyes me closely. 'Yeah, me too. Silly, eh? You'd think by now we'd learn to control ourselves. It's not like we're teenagers any more. Can't party like we used to. There are consequences.'

My mouth is dry, but my palms are not and I swipe them surreptitiously over my shorts under the table. 'Yeah.' *Where are Nate and Tamsin?* It feels as if there is a whole different conversation going on at this table, one I'm not sure I want to have.

'I admire you, you know.' Seb sits back, and I feel as though I can breathe again. 'In fact, I wish Tamsin was a little more like you.'

'What?' I shake my head. Tamsin? More like me? 'I find that very hard to believe.'

'Why?' Seb watches me curiously. 'I don't think you know how intriguing you are, Hayley. Nate Turner is a very lucky man.'

A snort of laughter escapes my nose as my cheeks burn. 'Now I know you're joking. There's nothing remotely intriguing about me.' Not compared to Tamsin with her swishy blonde hair (there really is no comparison now mine has started to grow out), her lithe body and her silver bangles.

'You're so confident, so on top of things . . . I'd love for Tamsin to be like that. She's so . . . I don't know. *Chaotic*, I guess.'

'It's my job to be on top of things,' I say briskly, although my words come out blurred with the alcohol. So much for cutting down. 'If I'm not organised at work then the whole house of cards tumbles down.'

'You're naturally brilliant,' Seb says, his dark eyes never leaving my face. I feel like a butterfly pinned to a board. 'And I think you're very much unappreciated by—'

'This conversation looks deep,' Tamsin says with a laugh as she throws herself into her chair, Nate following closely behind.

'I was just telling Hayley that our Nate here is a lucky man,' Seb says, and Nate gives him a thumbs up as he drains the last of his drink. 'But alas, I think I'm done for the night. Two nights in a row is too much for this old fella.'

Tamsin snorts, something ugly flashing across her features so quickly I'm not sure I've even seen it. 'You are joking? It's Saturday night, Seb!'

'And we spent Friday night partying until dawn,' he chides gently, linking his fingers through hers. 'Remember? Dancing and drinking until 6 a.m. this morning?'

'But that's *why* we had the party on Friday,' Tamsin snaps back. 'So we could have an intimate get together with just our good friends the following evening. Remember? God, Seb, don't be so boring.'

I glance at Nate, but he's busy popping the cap on a bottle of beer, clearly not ready to leave just yet. I thought this was an impromptu get together, but it seems Tamsin had it planned, in her own head at least. But I'm with Seb on this one — I'm exhausted and already not looking forward to the doubly ferocious hangover that I know is going to kick in by tomorrow morning.

Seb looks amused and leans back in his chair, tucking his hands behind his head. 'I'm boring, am I? OK darling, why don't you give us an idea on how to jazz things up a bit? You're always full of ideas.'

Tamsin grins, an unnerving glint in her eye. 'I know what we should do. We should swap.'

'Swap?' I glance from Tamsin to Seb, not quite sure what she's suggesting.

'Swap,' she says again and Nate finally looks up. 'Partners. Just for the night. You stay here with Seb, Hayls, and I'll go home with Nate.'

It's as though she's thrown a bucket of cold water over me and I let out a shrill laugh. 'You must be joking. You are joking . . . aren't you?'

Raising her glass to her lips as if to hide the smile lingering there, Tamsin shrugs. 'We're all adults and it's one night. Seb is boring me to tears tonight and you clearly don't want to stay out any later so let's just . . . swap.'

Seb laughs, slapping his hand on the table. 'You're a wild one, Tamsin Cooper. I'll give you that.' He leans over and kisses her neck, and I push down the nausea at the back of my throat, my hands on the table ready to push back my chair and get out of here.

'Nate?' I want him to get to his feet and grab my hand, I want us to hurry back along the path to our house where we will jump into bed together, breathless with laughter and shock at just how wild our new friends are.

'Let's do it.' Nate's tone is serious, his gaze flicking towards Tamsin. His eyes are sleepy, the way they get when he's had far too much to drink. 'One night only.'

'What?' Horror makes my voice pitchy and I stare at him. 'Nate, come on . . . this is ridiculous. It's a joke, right, Tam? Just a joke.' Where is my Nate? The man who's always on the go, always busy dashing from one place to the next but who always comes home to me? Until this moment I never realised that I love that part of him. I love him as he is, even when I wish he had more time for me. I don't know who this Nate is, sitting across the table from me.

'Come on Hayls, don't be a stick in the mud. It's just a bit of fun, that's all. We've done it loads of times before and nothing bad has ever happened. And besides,' Tamsin's tone changes, shards of shale and grit entering. 'I've seen the way you look at Seb.'

'I'm not . . . I don't—' I flounder, because it's true. I have enjoyed the way Seb speaks to me, the way his eyes linger and make me feel seen. 'Nate, I think we should go.' I get to my feet, but Seb puts out a hand and wraps his fingers tightly around my wrist, tugging me back into my chair.

'Come on, Hayls,' he mimics Tamsin. 'One night, that's all. And then we all go back to our normal boring lives.' His eyes bore into me and I look away, heat rising in my chest.

Tamsin stands and to my horror, Nate scrapes his chair back. He sways slightly as he puts an arm round Tamsin, not meeting my eyes. Tamsin, however, does, and I don't think I'm imagining the look of triumph there. 'See you in the morning, kiddos,' she says, her words falling over one another in the way they always do when she's been drinking. 'Don't do anything I wouldn't do.' She winks at Seb, and then with Nate's arm around her waist, they head inside the house.

'Nate.' His name is little more than a whisper on my lips as I hear the front door open, then close, hot tears springing to my eyes. I can't believe he would agree to this, not the Nate I know.

The Wife Swap

There is a hot breath in my ear and then Seb is gently tugging me to my feet. 'Come on little Hayley,' he says, pulling me into his arms. 'Don't be upset. It doesn't mean anything.'

I let him hold me, my eyes going to the upstairs window next door. A light goes on and then Tamsin appears, Nate close behind her, and she reaches out and closes the blinds. My heart racing in my chest, my legs like jelly, I let Seb lead me inside the house.

CHAPTER 13

Seb doesn't switch on the lights as he leads me through the kitchen, along the hall and up the stairs, his warm hand clutching my cold one tightly. I'm glad the lights stay off. I feel woozy, soggy with alcohol, my mouth dry and my mind strangely disconnected. The soft dusky darkness makes this all seem as if it's happening in a dream, as if I'll wake up in the morning with the sheets tangled around my sweaty torso. My legs still feel like jelly, my knees soft and my breath coming loud in my ears as we reach the top of the stairs and Seb pushes the door open into the master bedroom. *Tamsin's bedroom.* I pause on the threshold, Seb beside me.

'Hayley? You don't have to—'

I force myself to step into the room, the faint scent of lilacs from Tamsin's perfume still staining the air. The bedroom is immaculate, the bed neatly made. There is an open fireplace opposite the bed, a mirror to the one in my own bedroom, but where ours is soot stained with cracked hearth tiles, this is swept clean, the hearth gleaming. There are no clothes draped over a chair the way there are in mine and Nate's room, no make-up spilling out all over the dressing table. There's no sign at all that Tamsin was getting ready for a party in this room twenty-four hours ago, and somehow that makes it easier to step inside.

'It's OK,' I lie. 'I'm OK.' My toes sink into the thick, plush carpet, the exact kind I wanted for our own bedroom but Nate still hasn't got around to coming carpet shopping with me. At the thought of Nate my stomach rolls and I plop down on the edge of the bed.

Seb hovers in the doorway and I am surprised by the thought that perhaps he isn't really as into this as he makes out, but then he looks me over in a way that tells me otherwise. Greedily almost, as if I am a feast about to be devoured by a starving man.

'How about a drink?' he says, moving to a small globe on a stand in the corner of the room. He lifts the lid to reveal a tiny version of a globe drinks bar, just big enough to hold a single bottle of whisky and two tumblers. *What the fuck? Who the hell drinks whisky in bed?* This is the kind of pretentious thing Nate and I would laugh about back in the safety of our own bed.

'It's a fine single malt,' Seb says, popping the lid from the bottle and taking a deep appreciative sniff. 'No ice up here, I'm afraid, but I can do you a dash of water.'

I shake my head. If I'm going to sit here, in Tamsin's bedroom, on Tamsin's bed, with Tamsin's husband I don't want my liquor watered down. 'Neat is fine.'

Seb raises an eyebrow and pours two fingers into the tumbler. As I take the glass, I stifle a nervous smile, wondering what refreshment Nate has offered Tamsin. A bottle of the Czech lager I bought in Aldi last week? Or maybe a good old cup of PG Tips . . . Maybe he hasn't offered her anything at all and they are already tumbling around in my bed together. The thought of them together, in my house, makes something spicy and acidic burn in my veins and I sip the whisky, transferring the burn to my tongue.

Seb settles back against the pillows, glass in hand, and taps the empty space beside him. 'Come and sit with me, Hayley.' My hesitation must show as he smiles, shaking his head. 'I won't bite. We don't have to do anything, OK? Let's just talk.'

Talking I can cope with. With the whisky scorching a fiery path down into my stomach, I move up the bed, into the space where presumably Tamsin would usually lie. The pillows are plump and soft, the mattress perfectly firm, a far cry from the cheap mattress with the sagging middle that Nate and I sleep on. I take a deep breath, trying to ignore the shaking in my hands as I raise the glass to my lips again. *It's just Seb. And we're just going to talk.*

'You've done this before.' The words blurt out before I can stop them.

Seb nods. 'Only a couple of times. And only with people we really like . . . people we think are on the same wavelength as us.'

I'm not sure whether to be insulted or flattered that he thinks Nate and I might be on the same wavelength as he and Tamsin, the two most vibrant and glamorous people I know.

'Things get stale after a while, you know?' I don't look at him, but I can feel Seb's eyes running over my face as he speaks. Waiting for my reaction, perhaps? I sip the whisky again, the smoky taste on my lips making me feel even more nauseous. 'We've been together since we were twenty years old. Practically half my life. We've grown together that's for sure, but sometimes . . . sometimes you miss that spark. That somersault in your stomach when you see someone you haven't kissed before . . . someone you *want* to kiss.'

Seb's little finger touches mine now, our hands lying next to each other on the duvet cover. The pressure of his skin against mine is like an electric shock, and I can't bring myself to pull away. I know the sensation he's talking about. I haven't forgotten it. If I'm honest, it's the same feeling I've had for him before, when I've caught him looking at me in a certain way.

'I love Nate.' My voice is barely above a whisper.

'That isn't in doubt,' Seb says, his voice matching mine. 'But . . . don't you get bored, Hayley? After all this time?'

Yes, I want to shriek. *So bored! My husband promised me a baby, but he wouldn't even look at me when I was dressed in £650 worth of expensive lingerie, of course I get bored!* Instead, I push my glass in his direction, my heart in my throat. 'I'll take another drink if there's one on offer.'

When Seb slides back onto the bed, our glasses refreshed, his leg presses against mine and our shoulders touch, but I don't move away.

'Cheers.' Somewhat sloppily, I clink my glass against his. 'What was it like? When you did this before?'

Seb lets out a long breath. 'Honestly? The last time wasn't that much fun. Not for me. If I'm brutally honest, Tamsin was the one who started this game. She wanted to spice up our love life, and while it was fun the first time . . .'

I wait for a moment before I prod at him. 'The next time wasn't?'

Seb swirls the amber liquid around in his glass, a peaty scent rising to squash Tamsin's lilac perfume. 'I just didn't know we would be doing it again, that's all. It was Tamsin's idea again. Nothing bad happened — we were all consenting adults — but it wasn't what I thought it would be, that's all.' His face darkens and my heart skitters with a touch of fear, as I remember the way he grabbed Tamsin's arm, not knowing I was watching from the other side of the fence, remember the ugly, purple, fingerprint-shaped bruises etched on to her skin afterwards.

We sit in silence for a moment. The whisky has made my mouth even drier, and my head is fuzzy. I know I have drunk too much, that I'll probably have to spend the night sleeping with one foot on the floor to stop the room from spinning, but I need something to beat down the wings of anxiety in my belly. I picture the way Tamsin appeared in my bedroom window, Nate's silhouette behind her and fury replaces the anxiety, flames licking at my insides. Is he kissing her now? Pushing her gently back onto the bed? Or have they already fucked once, fast and furious, before they go again, slower this time?

'Why?' I can hear the anger in my voice now and Seb frowns in response.

'Why what?'

'Why wasn't it what you thought it would be last time? You agreed to it, didn't you?'

Seb sighs, shifting slightly beside me. I can feel the heat of his thigh through the fabric of my shorts. 'I didn't find her attractive. I told Tamsin that that would be the last time. I didn't want to do it any more.'

'So this, tonight . . .' I swallow, my tongue sticking to the roof of my mouth. 'This was all her idea?' The thought that this wasn't a tipsy, spur of the moment thing makes my limbs feel numb. How long was Tamsin thinking about sleeping with my husband? Was she pretending to be my friend this entire time? I once got thrown out of a nightclub for punching a girl who was trying to slow dance with the boy I was seeing, and I feel that familiar rage burning now.

Seb turns on his side now, his glass empty again. He reaches up and presses a hand against my cheek, forcing me to turn and face him. 'Hayley, I'd be lying if I said it was all Tamsin's idea this time . . . the truth is, I think you're beautiful. Have done since you knocked on the door to tell me to stop drilling on a Sunday morning.' He laughs, deep and rich, and a smile tugs at my own lips. 'When was the last time Nate told you that you were beautiful?'

All the time, I think, before I realise that is a lie. The last time Nate told me I looked beautiful was the day I came home with my new haircut. The hair cut that he told me made me look like Tamsin. Horror sprouts like goosebumps, prickling at my skin. Before that, I couldn't tell you the last time Nate told me I looked beautiful.

'I can't remember,' I say, my voice thick as I clear my throat, choking on disappointment and something else. Sadness, maybe.

'He told Tamsin last night at the party,' Seb says, not seeming to realise his words are a scythe, cutting me in two. 'I overheard him when I went inside to fetch more ice. They were standing together by the fire pit.'

'It was her birthday party. Obviously he told her she looked beautiful. I think I told her that too. Lots of people probably did.' Frantically, I try to embed the idea in my brain. Nate was being polite, nothing more.

'He should have been saying it to you though, Hayley.' Seb touches my shoulder, and I find I have slipped down the bed, my head resting on an almost flat pillow now. He props himself up on one elbow so that he leans over me, the scent of peat and something in his aftershave that smells like tobacco tickling my nose. My head spins, the alcohol combining with the hurt — the idea that Nate is with Tamsin now, telling her things he should been saying to me all along — to fan those flames of fury just a little bit brighter. Seb's eyes lock on to mine and I feel it — that swoop in my stomach he described. As he leans down, one hand brushing against my breast just before his lips meet mine, I let out a sigh and almost feel myself fall, the room tilting slightly. Our mouths meet, his tongue finding mine as he slides his hand under my shirt, his thumb flicking over my nipple. I run my nails down his back — how is he already shirtless? — and the groan he makes against my mouth sends a surge of heat through me. He kisses me again, harder, the way I wish Nate would, and then his hands are at my waist, fumbling with the button on my shorts. My breath sticks in my throat and I put out a hand to stop him, but then he raises his eyes to meet mine and they are full of fire, burning with want. The sensation makes me giddy, the thought that I have made him look at me that way and I nod, sharp and brief. With a wicked, knowing grin he slides my shorts off, then my underwear, and as he presses his elbows into the pillow on either side of my head, tugging at my hair in a way that sends a sharp tingle down my spine, I feel him nudge against me, and a low moan escapes as I wrap my legs around his hips to draw him in. As we begin to move together, any last shreds of guilt I feel are washed away by the feel of Seb inside me, by the gasps that I can't help uttering, by the dizzy urgency that makes me clutch at the bedsheets. As he moves faster, he leans down and catches my mouth with his, tangling one fist in my hair and gently tugging my head back. Shivers run down my spine and the thought hits me that I don't want this to end. Not yet.

Pressing my hands against his chest, I roll him beneath me, reclaiming control as I slide on top of him. Seb groans as I lower myself and our bodies fall into rhythm again, his hips rising to meet mine, as I slow things right down. My name falls from his lips, low and desperate, in a way that Nate has never once said it and I feel a surge of power run though me, as intoxicating as Seb himself. His hands grip my hips, urging me to go faster, but I keep my tantalisingly slow pace, keeping control as any last inhibitions — and any remnants of guilt — slide away completely. I reach out, placing my hand at the base of his throat and squeeze lightly, just enough to feel his pulse beneath my palm.

'Jesus, Hayley,' Seb gasps, his hands tightening on my hips as he thrusts into me, hard and relentless, until we tip over the edge together. For a moment there is only the sound of our ragged breathing. My heart is racing, my skin tingling and that's when the thought slips in — quiet, and almost easy to believe. *Maybe Seb and Tamsin are right. Maybe this is all just a bit of fun.* Nate was the one who agreed to this. We're all consenting adults. Grown-ups playing grown-up games. What could possibly go wrong?

CHAPTER 14

Ugh. The thin slant of early morning sunshine peeping through the gap in the blinds seems to fall directly across my face, as I struggle to open my eyes. My head thumps, a resounding bass line that feels as if it is reverberating through my entire body, and I am too scared to sit up for fear that I'll throw up. This is the hangover to end all hangovers.

Trying to unstick my tongue from the roof of my mouth, I force myself to open my eyes, squinting as I take in my surroundings. That's when I really do feel sick. This isn't my bedroom. This isn't my bed. And that isn't Nate, sleeping beside me. Like a freight train, the memory of last night crashes into me and I press a hand to my mouth to stifle the moan that tears at the back of my throat. *What the fuck have we done? What the fuck did I do?*

Slowly turning my head to one side, I glance across at the pillow beside mine. At the sprawl of dark hair, the bearded profile. *Seb.* I swallow, bile scorching the back of my throat as images fly through my brain, each one worse than the last. Seb, leaning down to kiss me. My nails running down his back. The sweat, sticking our bodies together. The burning hot lust that ripped through me as he pressed himself inside me, and the fury that swept my veins when I thought, ever so briefly, about Nate. *Fuck.*

We had sex. The combination of mimosas and whisky meant that I was more than tipsy — I was flat-out drunk by the time

Seb leaned over me, and now I struggle to pull back any sort of coherent, linear memory. All I have are flickering images; hot, sticky flashes of something that leaves me feeling dirty and tainted, although I have the vague sensation that at the time, I didn't feel that way. Guilt is a shard of glass in the pit of my stomach. Last night I did things with Seb that I haven't done with anyone other than Nate in the last twelve years. And from the little I do remember, I enjoyed it. I feel sick, my stomach churning and saliva filling my mouth, but I don't move. I don't want to wake Seb, sleeping beside me. I don't want to face him. This is like the worst one night stand I've ever had.

Seb lets out a soft snore beside me, and I wonder how he can sleep so soundly after what we did. And then I remember this isn't his first rodeo. This isn't the first time he and Tamsin have done this, and tears inexplicably prick my eyes.

There is the soft plink of a tap dripping in the en-suite bathroom, and something stirs in my brain. Last night, I had woken from a deep groggy sleep, something — the glow of a lamp? — pulling me out of a now-forgotten dream. I thought I'd heard someone moving around, the rustling of clothing and the soft hush of a door closing. I'd reached out, thinking it was Nate in my drunken state, but finding the bed empty, I'd rolled over and fallen back to sleep. Obviously it was Seb. Maybe he had felt guilty after all and struggled to get to sleep, although clearly it doesn't seem to be a problem for him now. The thought of Nate makes my stomach turn over again. Is he awake yet? Is he feeling molten with guilt and shame, the way I am? Or is he already planning when he and Tamsin can do it again?

It's no good. I need to throw up, wash my face and get out of here. Sliding out of the bed, I reach for my shorts and T-shirt and pull them on, tucking my phone into my back pocket and pausing as Seb murmurs and rolls over, tugging the duvet over his head. From the corner of the bedroom, Tank looks up at me with droopy, tired eyes from his dog bed. I don't remember him being in the room last night, but there were more pressing things on my mind. Now, I drift my hand over his head and then, desperate for water, I creep across the lush carpet and slip into the en suite, gently closing the door before letting out a long breath. Pouring cold water into a clean toothbrush mug, I turn the tap off tightly but still it drips, the sound scraping along my nerve edgings and when I sip the water I immediately need to lean over the toilet bowl and throw up.

What feels like hours later, but is probably only ten minutes, I sit back on my haunches and reach for the hand towel to wipe my mouth. There is still silence from the bedroom, thank God, and I wash my face, scrubbing my teeth with Tamsin's whitening toothpaste and my finger. I don't feel any better, but I know I need to go home. The thought of seeing Nate feels like a blessing and a curse — I want to see him, am desperate for him to put his arms around me and tell everything is still the same, but at the same time the thought of him and Tamsin together still burns like battery acid in my gut.

Tamsin. I wonder how she is feeling. All of this means nothing to her, I'm sure, but what if that's not really the case? What if this hasn't only fucked up things with Nate, but also my friendship with her? I'm not sure how we can ever come back from this. My skin prickles, the thought of losing both Nate and Tamsin hor-rifying, even after last night. I can smell old whisky seeping out of my pores but, glancing in the bathroom mirror, I am relieved to see I look better than I feel. OK, dark circles ring my eyes and there is a pimple loitering beneath the surface of the skin by my eyebrow, but I don't look like death. Not quite. Opening the bathroom cabinet, I snag two paracetamol and wash them down, before easing open the bathroom door and sneaking out into the hallway without waking Seb or the dog. I'm going home to reclaim my husband.

* * *

'Hello?' Slamming the front door behind me in the hopes that if Nate and Tamsin are still sleeping it will wake them, I call out but there is no response. 'Nate? I'm home.' Thick silence greets me and I pause with one foot on the bottom stair. I imagine the two of them snuggled up together in my bed, Nate's arm thrown over Tamsin's waist the way he used to do to me. Now, most evenings he rolls over onto his side of the bed, showing me his back through the thin cotton of the T-shirt he started wearing to bed a couple of years ago.

'Nate?' Fuck it. It's my house. I start to climb the stairs, trying to squash down the panic that flutters in my veins. My pulse is loud in my ears and I know I'm breathing too fast but I can't help it. *He'll be asleep. On his own*, I tell myself. Nate was really drunk last night, that's the only reason I can think of as to why he would agree to this in the first place. And when Nate gets really drunk, all he wants to do is sleep. On the landing, the bedroom door is slightly ajar and I step towards it, bile rising. I want to throw up again, a cold sweat breaking out all over my body, but I push on and shove the door gently. It swings open and the bedroom is empty.

'Tamsin? Are you still here?' Stepping inside, I run my eyes over the bed, over the crumpled duvet, still pushed back, the sheets mussed. The pillows hold the imprint of a head, and a glass of water sits on Nate's bedside table, but there is no sign of Nate or Tamsin. *Maybe they woke up early and felt embarrassed. Maybe they've gone out to get coffee. Maybe nothing happened and Nate feels bad at agreeing to the swap, knowing I didn't want to do it.* Hope surges in my chest, drowning out the fiery, sticky shame that still clings to my skin, and I hurry towards the spare bedroom. Maybe Tamsin didn't sleep in my bed at all. Relief at the idea is sharp and dizzying and my eyes go to the double bed in the spare bedroom the moment I open the door. It is made, but the cushions I stack in front of the pillows — the ones Nate hates — look disturbed, as though someone has tried to put them back in the right order but hasn't quite managed it.

Feeling better, I head downstairs. I'll put coffee on for Nate. Hopefully he'll be back soon, full of apologies and regret, carrying a bag of pastries from our bakery. We can talk about the evening, and maybe start to figure exactly where things have gone wrong between us. I think he still loves me and I certainly still love him. We've just got stuck in a rut, that's all, a hamster wheel of silence and repression. Hopefully he'll be feeling just as out of sorts as I am this morning. Maybe last night was exactly what we needed to pull ourselves out of that rut and focus on starting our family together.

Tamsin's handbag is on the kitchen counter. That's the first thing I notice when I enter the kitchen and my footsteps slow. I was hoping that Nate would come back alone, but now clearly wherever they have gone, Tamsin is going to have to come back here to pick up her bag. Pressing a hand to the coffee pot, I find it is cold, although two cups have been left on the table, one still half full of cold coffee. Nate's sliders are kicked off under the table, his sweatshirt hanging on the back of the chair. There is an unnerving feeling of abandonment about it all, a Marie Celeste vibe as though Nate and Tamsin just vanished into thin air.

My phone pings in my back pocket with a Facebook notification and I don't know why I didn't think of it before. Unlocking the screen there are no texts from Nate, no missed calls, and I dial his number, starting to pace as the call connects. I can't shake the feeling that something about the whole thing feels off. Some might argue that swapping partners with your friends for the night is off in itself, and I would be inclined to agree, but I was expecting Nate and Tamsin to be here. Or to at least have messaged, but Tamsin hasn't texted either and the way things have been left . . . nothing about it feels right at all.

The call to Nate goes to voicemail.

'Nate? Um, it's me.' My voice shakes and I clear my throat, still battling that raging hangover. 'I'm home and you're . . . not? Did you guys go for breakfast? Um, call me. Please?' I hang up and stop my pacing, unease tightening in my chest. Turning on my heel, I head back upstairs to the one place I didn't check — the bathroom. The houses on our street are old, and while many of our neighbours have updated their places to knock through the tiny box room beside the master bedroom to create an en suite, the same way Tamsin and Seb's house has, Nate and I have never had the money. Our single bathroom is at the other end of the hallway, and now I knock abruptly on the door. No answer. Trying the handle, it is unlocked and I walk in, running my eyes over the room. The towels are hung as I left them, neatly and perfectly in line on the towel rail. Nate's toothbrush sits beside mine on the sink, with no tell-tale splashes on the ceramic. Everything seems normal, except it doesn't. On the sink, beside the dry toothbrushes and Nate's favourite aftershave is his wedding ring.

CHAPTER 15

He never takes his wedding ring off. Not to shower, not to do DIY (not that he does a lot of that), *never* that I've seen in the ten years we've been married. But now he has, and it sits on the sink, glinting at me almost spitefully. Reaching out, I scoop it up and shove it in my pocket, feeling the gold burning a hole through the fabric.

Hurrying back down the stairs, I let the front door slam shut behind me as I run up the path to Seb and Tamsin's, pausing only for a second as I register that Nate's car still sits where he parked it on Friday night. The thorns from that damn rosebush tear into my bare thigh as I hurry towards the front door, and I don't knock, just let myself inside and head straight up to Seb's bedroom.

'Seb?' His head is still tucked under the duvet, the bedroom a thick fug of stale air, tainted with the faint hint of sex and farts. 'Seb! Wake up.' I lean over him and shake him by the shoulder, as Tank grumbles a low warning from his dog bed.

'Hmmm?' Seb rolls over sleepily, one arm reaching for me. Stepping back I shake my head, hissing his name again. 'Huh?' His eyes widen as he catches sight of me, before a lazy grin rolls across his face. 'Hey, Hayley. You're still here.'

'No, I'm not. Well, I am but not like that. It's Nate and Tamsin.'

'Are they back?' Seb tugs the duvet up over his naked body, clutching it to him in a way that would be comical if we weren't in this diabolical situation. 'Let me just—'

'No, they're not back. That's the problem — I don't know where they are.'

Seb is quiet, a frown crossing his features. 'Meet me downstairs. I'll just . . .' He waves a hand across his body and I nod tersely.

Moments later Seb appears in the kitchen, the dog following closely behind him. I sit at the island, a glass of water in front of me. It's all I can stomach, and I'm not even sure that will stay down. It's not the hangover making me feel ill — if anything the emotions ricocheting around my body have chased that well away.

'Coffee? I know you like an espresso.' After letting Tank into the garden, Seb moves to the machine and I shake my head. I can't believe it was only a few weeks ago that I sat here and pretended to like strong coffee, just to impress him. 'What were you saying about Nate and Tamsin?'

'They're not there.' My voice seems to be too much in this vast, expansive kitchen without Tamsin's large gestures and loud laugh to fill the gaps. 'I went home and neither of them were there. The house was empty.'

'They probably went to get breakfast,' Seb shrugs as he raises his cup to his lips and sniffs appreciatively. 'Sure you won't change your mind? It's the only thing that can chase off my hangover. No offence, Hayley, but you look like you could use a cup.'

'I don't want a fucking coffee,' I snap. 'Are you not listening to me? Nate and Tamsin aren't next door and I don't think they went to get breakfast. Tamsin's handbag is still on the kitchen counter, there are half-drunk cups of coffee left on the table. Nate's wedding ring is on the sink . . . and it just felt *off* somehow. Like they just walked out in the middle of a conversation.'

'Nate taking his ring off is hardly something to call the cops over, Hayley.' Seb smiles, a patronising, smug smile that makes me feel like a child being indulged by a parent.

'I never said anything about calling the cops.' Something about his words slick over me like grease, a thick paint that makes unease prickle over my skin. 'Has Tamsin called you, or texted you? Surely one of them would have messaged if they were heading out.'

Seb pulls out his phone and shakes his head as he scrolls. 'Nothing from Tam. Hayley, don't you think you're overreacting a bit? It's barely . . .' he checks the clock on the oven, 'barely eleven o'clock. They'll have gone to get something to eat, or for a walk or something to shake their hangovers.' He pauses, looking me over. 'Let's be honest, it was a pretty wild night.'

Bile rises, hitting the back of my throat and I force myself to swallow, not looking away from his steady gaze. 'Can you just call her, please?'

Seb sighs and dials, humouring me. Hitting the speakerphone button, Tamsin's phone starts to ring and from the sitting room Flo Rida starts to sing about AppleBottom jeans.

'That's Tamsin's phone.' Pushing myself off the stool I hurry into the sitting room before the call can go to voicemail and shove my hand down the side of the sofa, where the ringtone is coming from. Pulling out the battered iPhone, my heart sinks. 'She left her phone behind,' I say to Seb, walking back into the kitchen. 'I found it down the side of the sofa.'

'She's always doing that,' Seb says, without an ounce of worry. 'It slips out of her pocket. She wouldn't have left it on purpose, but she was quite drunk. She probably never even realised she didn't have it. Did you try Nate?'

I try Nate's number again, and it goes straight to voicemail again without even ringing. Panic flutters in my belly, when I have a brainwave. 'Find My iPhone,' I say to Seb, switching to the app.

'That'll show us where they are.' Relief floods my veins and I smile, wondering why I didn't think of it before. The relief is short-lived though, when the app tells me Nate was at our house eight hours ago. 'His phone is dead. Or off. The app can't connect.'

'Look,' Seb comes towards me and wraps his arms around me before I have the chance to step back out of his embrace. As much as I hate to admit it, the hug does feel nice and I briefly let myself relax into it before I pull away, pushing my hair out of my face to hide how flustered I am. 'They'll be back soon, I'm sure.' This time though, doubt laces his voice and I look up at him sharply.

'Really? You think that?'

There is a moment of silence before Seb sighs, running his hand over his beard. 'You know what Tamsin is like.'

'What's that supposed to mean?'

Seb reaches for my hand but I pull away, shoving my hand into my pocket where it finds the warm gold of Nate's wedding ring. 'She's spontaneous, you know that. She doesn't always think things through . . . but she does always come back, at least she has before.'

'Before? Are you saying she's done this before?' A wave of fear washes over me, leaving me cold, my skin clammy. 'What the fuck, Seb?'

'Once, before,' he says, his cheeks burning a bright pink. 'When we swapped the second time, she disappeared for a couple of days after. It's her way of processing stuff, I think. Getting the other person out of her system and making sure I miss her enough to take her back when she returns.'

'That's sick. Nate would never . . .' I trail off.

Seb laughs, a harsh scoff of laughter. 'Come on, Hayley. You must have seen the way she looked at Nate. After all, you looked at me that same way. You must have seen the attraction between them. Clearly they thought they could string the swap out a little longer.' He pauses. 'Maybe they both enjoyed it as much as you did.'

'I didn't . . . it wasn't . . . I feel disgusting, Seb. This whole thing was a mistake, and now I feel like shit. Nate wouldn't . . .' It's like he's hit me full in the face with a brick, but even so I can't wrap my head around it. Yes, I did look at Seb that way, because I was flattered by the things he was saying to me, but I never would have acted on it. It felt as though someone was seeing me properly for the first time in years, but it doesn't mean that I wanted to leave Nate, or that I loved him any less. If anything, this whole swap thing has just made me realise how much I do love Nate. And I thought — was *sure* — it would be the same for him.

'Nate loves me.' The words are little more than a whisper.

'I'm sure he does,' Seb says, his tone bland. 'But show me a man who says he could turn down a little excitement in his life and I'll show you a liar.'

I think of the receipts I found in Nate's jacket, for the expensive meal for two, and the jealousy that had coursed through my veins. It stands to reason that I had been suspicious that maybe he'd had dinner with someone he shouldn't have, what wife wouldn't be? I know Nate inside out, and I know if I'd questioned him he would have told me that dinner was for him and a colleague, that there was nothing sinister going on and I would have believed him. And as for excitement . . . I swallow, my mouth dry. Nate lives for extreme sports and taking risks.

'Nate loves me,' I say again, the words feeling too big for my mouth. 'And besides where would they even go? Nate only uses his card in his Apple wallet and if his phone is dead he won't have access to it. Tamsin doesn't have any money of her own.'

Seb lets out a snort, shaking his head. 'What the hell gives you that idea?'

'She told me. She said you have control of all her finances . . . that she only has a card in your name. That you control how much she spends.' My pulse ratchets up at the look on Seb's face, and I remember the way he grabbed Tamsin's arm in the garden. I am glad I have put the kitchen island between us.

'What?! That's total bullshit,' he snarls. 'Tamsin has more than enough money of her own — we have separate bank accounts for fuck's sakes! Jesus, Hayley, just wake up to the fact that they've gone off together for a few days. Hopefully they'll fuck it out of their systems and be home with their tails between their legs before the week is out.'

His words hit me like tiny missiles. 'You can believe that if you want, but you didn't see my house. It looked as though they just walked out in the middle of something. It felt *wrong*. And you don't know Nate, not the way I do.' My voice thickens now, my throat aching with unshed tears. 'He might be a lot of things,' — neglectful, self-absorbed and sometimes ridiculously high maintenance — 'but he's loyal to a fault. He wouldn't just leave not when . . .' I swallow down the tears, 'not when we're going to start trying for a baby. Hell, we're supposed to be visiting his mum for lunch today, he wouldn't miss that without a word. He just wouldn't.'

'OK.' Seb shrugs. 'You think what you want to think, Hayley, but don't be surprised when they both turn up later on tonight, or tomorrow, all fucked out.'

Fury sparks in my veins, and for just the briefest second I imagine grabbing Seb by the hair and cracking his face down on the kitchen island, smashing his nose against the expensive marble. 'Well, let's hope that is the case,' I say, even though the thought of it makes me feel sick. Tucking my shaking hands into my pockets I skirt past him and out towards the front door. 'For all our sakes.'

* * *

Back in my own home, I can't settle, and the fury that rushed my veins only simmers longer and hotter as I hear Seb fire up his music in the garden next door, as though nothing has happened.

I smooth down a fresh duvet cover on the bed, swiping away any evidence at all that Tamsin might have laid there, stripping the sheets and throwing them in the machine on a hot wash. The wardrobe door is slightly ajar and I step towards it, pulling Nate's work jacket off the hanger and sliding my fingers into the pockets. I'm not sure what I am expecting to find, but I come up empty, the only thing out of place is a hair on the shoulder of the jacket. It's short and stubby; some sort of animal hair by the looks of it, and I pinch it between my fingers and flick it away.

Shoving the jacket back in the wardrobe, I try Nate's phone again and again, my pulse ratcheting as it goes to voicemail over and over. After the third call I stop leaving him voicemails, and just hang up. I've run out of words to tell him I want him to come home. Instead, I have to call his mum.

'Hello?'

'Pauline, hi. It's Hayley.'

'I can see that, we do have caller ID.' Her tone is frosty, the way it always is when it's my voice she hears and not Nate's. 'I do hope you're on your way. I did tell Nathan lunch was at one thirty.'

Oh God. 'Has . . . err . . . did Nate not ring you today?'

There is a chilly pause. 'No. I haven't spoken to him since Friday afternoon when he called me on his way home.' Rainbows of smugness radiate from Pauline's voice. 'He always calls me on a Friday to let me know how his week has been and that he's on his way back.'

At any other time I would have rolled my eyes in Nate's direction and pulled a face, but I am too anxious to let her spiky barbs get under my skin. 'Right. Well, the thing is, Pauline, Nate and I aren't going to make lunch today after all. I'm really sorry.'

There is a thick silence and then she says, 'I hope you're joking. I've gone to a lot of trouble for this lunch. Is Nate there? Let me speak to him.'

Stifling the urge to scream, I draw in a breath and smile. Someone once told me if you smile when you're on the phone it sounds to the other person like you're happy. That you're OK, when nothing could be further from the truth. 'He's not feeling great, Pauline. Some stomach bug or something, we think. He's been really ill all night. He really wanted to come but . . . he just isn't well enough.'

My mother-in-law huffs her disappointment down the line at me, and I promise to have Nate call her as soon as he 'feels better'. Putting down the phone, I don't feel any sense of relief that I've dealt with Nate's mum, only anger that he's put me in this position.

By the time I go to bed, far earlier than usual, my headache has returned with a vengeance and the worry gnawing in my belly has meant that I've been unable to eat all day. I call Nate's phone one more time, and once again it goes straight to voicemail. *Is Seb right? Could I have been so wrapped up in his flattery that I failed to notice Nate's attraction to Tamsin? And what about her? I'd thought we were friends.* The sense I'd had in the cellar that something more than just idle conversation was going on, the way Tamsin had stared at Nate in the kitchen the day after the party . . . was it all leading to this? With their faces rotating on a carousel behind my eyelids, I try to sleep, seeing Nate's drunken stumble, his slurred words as he agreed to the swap. *He'll be back by morning, he has to go to work*, I think groggily, the strong sleeping pills I've resorted to taking finally kicking in. *We'll talk about it in the morning.*

Only the next morning, when I wake to a screaming alarm and sunshine streaming in where I forgot to close the blinds, the space beside me in the bed is empty. Nate never came home.

CHAPTER 16

I don't have time to decide whether I am angry, sad or worried. I am late for work, and I can't even formulate an excuse as to why I can't go in today, my brain is so foggy and thick thanks to the sleeping pills.

Instead, I call Nate's phone, listen to his generic voicemail message for what feels like the hundredth time, and drag my weary carcass into a skin-stripping hot shower. As I head out of the house twenty minutes later, I see Nate's car is still in the parking spot he snagged when he arrived home on Friday. Not sure what to think about that, I sneak a glance at next door. The bedroom curtains are still drawn and I loiter at the end of the path for just a minute, half hoping that Seb will appear and tell me that Nate and Tamsin are back, sitting in the kitchen drinking his awful coffee. He doesn't, and I hurry towards the tube station, my stomach knotted with dread.

After the Monday morning briefing, in which I zone out and don't manage to take down a single minute, I scurry back to my office, intent on texting Seb to see if he's heard from either Tamsin or Nate. As I round the corner, Wendy is leaning over my desk, her fingers deep in my top drawer.

'Can I help you?'

'Oh!' Wendy jumps and turns to face me, smoothing her hair away from cheeks that burn crimson red. 'I didn't realise your meeting was over.' She nudges my drawer with her hip, sliding it closed.

'Clearly. What were you doing rifling through my desk?'

Wendy picks up a mug from my desk, and it's not one of mine. 'I was looking to see if you had any herbal tea bags in your drawer. Someone has nabbed the last of mine from the kitchen, and I would have asked, only you were holed up in there with Harry and I didn't want to disturb you.'

'Right.' On the surface it sounds credible, but even so, there is something shifty about the way Wendy seems almost desperate to leave now. 'I don't have any.'

Wendy gives me a nod and scooping up her mug hurries out towards the kitchen, leaving me to sit at my desk and tap out a quick text message to Seb, asking if he's heard anything from either Tamsin or Nate. He doesn't reply and I squeeze my nails into my palms in frustration, tiny crescent moons etching into my skin.

'Can I get you anything?' Wendy breezes into my office with a simpering smile on her face a couple of hours later as though I never caught her rummaging through my desk at all. 'Herbal tea? I brought you a KitKat. You look a little peaky.' Her brow creases and I take the foil-wrapped biscuit from her, even though the thought of eating makes me feel nauseous.

'Thanks, Wendy.' I resist the urge to point out that she said we didn't have any herbal tea. 'In fact, can you hold any calls for me until lunchtime?' I pause. 'Unless it's Nate. Or a guy named Seb Cooper.'

Wendy nods and bobs out again, leaving me in peace and I reach for the phone and dial Nate's office. Sasha, the receptionist, answers, and for a moment my tongue sticks to the roof of my mouth. *What on earth do I say? Do you know where my husband is?*

'Hey, Sasha,' I keep my tone breezy. 'It's Hayley Turner. I just wondered if you knew Nate's agenda for the week? We have a . . .

thing . . . on Friday, and I just want to make sure he'll be back in time for it.' *A thing? Jeez, Hayley.*

'This week?' There is the clicking of a mouse and the rustle of pages. 'Errm, I don't think he's in this week, Hayley.'

'Nate's not in?'

I can almost see Sasha's confusion. 'Well, no. I don't think so. He's not booked in the diary — usually he fills it in on a Friday afternoon so we know where he is and who he's meeting for the following week, but there's nothing in there this week. Sorry.'

'Oh, my mistake.' I let out a laugh that sounds like a barrel being scraped over gravel. 'He did tell me, but I forgot. Head like a sieve, sorry.' I hang up, my fingers shaking. I don't know what to think. Did Nate just forget to fill in the diary for this week? Or was all of this planned? The thought that he and Tamsin might have cooked up this whole thing between them makes me want to collapse into a weeping puddle, and then I think about things rationally. This is *Nate*. My Nate. He can't even lie to his mum to get out of her crappy long-winded Sunday lunches, could he really lie to me over something this big? And when would he and Tamsin have had time to think this whole thing up? The only time they spend together is with me and Seb around. Tamsin and I are the ones who hang out alone together.

Clearly I'm not going to get any joy looking for Nate through his work, but what about Tamsin's? I reach for my phone, ready to call Seb, when my hand falters. There's no point in calling Seb. He hasn't replied to my text from earlier, and he clearly thinks this was all planned and the two of them will be back home before we know it. Instead, I click on my screen and pull up Google, typing in Tamsin's name, followed by *voice actor*.

The first link is a link to her website, and when I click on it her face fills the screen, familiar and somehow mocking. Her About Me page says she graduated from university after completing a drama degree and says she has worked on adverts, children's television shows and audiobooks. There is no further information though. No examples of her work, no details of an agency to go through, no contact details at all. In fact, it all looks a little thrown together and unprofessional. Undeterred, I pull up Facebook and search for her on there. I'm not active on Facebook — I have a profile, but I haven't used it for ages, being more of an Instagram woman — and it doesn't take me long to find that Tamsin must feel the same way I do. There doesn't seem to be a profile that matches her at all, although there are several Tamsin Coopers. Deleting her name, I type in Nate's name on a whim. Nate has never really used social media in the time I've known him, and my breath stops in my throat when a photo of someone who is undeniably him comes up. He is younger — much younger — but it is definitely him. When I click on the profile, most of the information is locked, the small profile picture and the fact that he only has six friends the only information available. Clicking on the friends list, I run my eyes over it. It's his four best mates from school, guys who he sees maybe once every six months or so, now they're all married with kids, a guy called Zach Smith who I've never heard of and who carries no profile picture and someone called Lolly Goode, whose profile picture is Jessica Rabbit. None of the other profiles seem to be active and Nate doesn't seem to have used his profile for years, so with a sigh, I close the screen just as a tap comes on the glass beside my desk.

'Jesus, you made me jump.' I look up as Wendy smiles cautiously at me, stepping into my booth with her arms full of a brightly coloured bouquet of flowers. 'I really didn't want to be disturbed until lunchtime.'

'It's just gone one o'clock, Hayley,' she says with a frown. 'I wanted to let you know that I followed up on that list of leads Harry sent over. I know you were going to do them, but he did want them done before tomorrow and I noticed they were still sitting in the in-tray.' She pauses, her face serious, and I want to groan aloud. *The sales leads. Probably one of the most important jobs on my desk this week.*

'And besides,' Wendy goes on, 'these just came for you. I thought you'd want me to bring them straight in, before they wilt.' She hands me the bouquet, hovering as I slide my finger under the flap of the tiny envelope attached.

'Thanks. And thanks for catching up on the leads, I appreciate it.' Wendy still doesn't move. 'You can leave me to it, it's fine. I'll put them in water myself. You go on and take your lunch break.'

Wendy leaves, pausing on her way out to lean over and gossip to one of the other admins, peeking over her shoulder back at me and my giant bouquet. Swivelling my chair round for privacy, I bite my lower lip, hiding the smile that tugs at the corners of my mouth. The flowers are from Nate, they have to be. He knows my favourite flowers are lilacs and irises, and this bouquet is full of them. At that thought, my smile drops. He knows me well enough to send me my favourite flowers, so he must know me well enough to know I am going out of my mind with worry over where he is.

'Flowers won't fix this, you shit bag,' I mutter under my breath, even though I already know I'll forgive him the moment he walks through the door. There'll be a conversation to be had for sure, but we can work through it. Yanking the tiny card out of the envelope, I run my eyes over the message, my heart somersaulting. Saliva fills my mouth and for a moment I am sure I am going to be sick, throwing up the tea I drank earlier into the wastepaper basket.

Thank you for a wonderful weekend. Love, Seb x

That bastard. Did he send me these just to mess with me? I told him how I felt, how gross the whole situation made me feel, and now he sends these, knowing that Nate hasn't come home. A cold chill runs down my spine and I suppress a shiver. There's something that feels disturbing about the whole thing . . . how did Seb even know what my favourite flowers are? I can't help but feel that perhaps the day I knocked on the Coopers' door to ask Seb to stop drilling, I made a huge mistake.

CHAPTER 17

Nate still isn't answering his phone and by the time five o'clock comes around I am nauseous with worry, exhaustion and something else I can't quite name. The bouquet of flowers sits in the wastepaper basket under my desk, and I know Wendy is dying to ask why I've dumped them. No doubt she'll pinch them out of the bin after I've left for the evening. Shutting my laptop down I hurry out of the office without making eye contact and head to the one place I really, really don't want to go.

'Hi, Pauline,' I say on the doorstep of Nate's mother's house thirty minutes later.

'Hayley.' Nate's mum stands to one side to let me in, peering over my shoulder to the street behind me. 'What are you doing here? Is Nate OK?'

I came here to see if she could answer the same question. Pauline and I have a somewhat thorny relationship, but we try to get along seeing as we both love Nate. I know Nate adores his mum, and he is really close to her after his dad died when he was a kid, so I try to keep on her good side. She, on the other hand, tolerates me because Nate is her only child and I am her best shot at getting any grandkids. It didn't stop her from wearing cream to our wedding though.

'I'm not sure if Nate's OK actually,' I say as I follow Pauline into her dated kitchen. She still has drawings Nate did in primary school on the fridge, the paper yellowed and curling.

'What on earth do you mean?' Her tone is sharp as she flicks the kettle on and dumps tea bags into mugs without asking me if I want a cup. 'You said yesterday he had a stomach bug.'

'That wasn't . . . I mean, it's not strictly true,' I say, my cheeks burning at the memory of what really happened on Saturday night. 'I was . . . away, staying with a friend over the weekend, and when I came home on Sunday morning Nate wasn't home.'

Pauline says nothing, just stares and waits for me to go on.

'He didn't come home at all yesterday, that's why we missed lunch. I didn't know what to tell you, so I just said he was ill. I thought he'd come home last night, thought maybe he'd forgotten about your lunch but he didn't and I can't get hold of him.'

Pauline has already pulled out her own mobile and is holding it to her ear. I hear the tinny tone of Nate's voicemail and Pauline leaves him a short message asking him to call her.

'Did you argue?' Pauline asks, her tone softer than the usual voice she uses when she talks to me. 'Did something happen, is that why you stayed with a friend?'

I shake my head. 'Nothing like that, not really. I just . . . Nate knew I was staying at my friend's house and I was expecting him to be home. I have no idea where he is, Pauline. I don't know what to do.'

Pauline looks away, turning her attention to the boiling kettle. 'So, everything is all right between you both?'

Something prickles at the back of my neck, the creeping realisation that she might know something I don't. 'Yes. At least, I think so. Unless there's something you think I should know.'

Nate's mum fusses with the mugs, keeping her gaze averted, but I think I see the hint of a curve to her lips. 'Look, Hayley, it's not for me to say anything.'

'Do you know where Nate is?' I shove the stool back as I stand. Clutching the kitchen counter to hide my shaking hands, I try to draw in a deep breath. 'Were you pretending just now when you called him? Has he said something to you?' My voice is pitchy, my throat closing over as I battle the emotion that threatens to spill over. 'Pauline, I'm going out of my mind with worry . . . you know Nate, this isn't like him to just not come home.'

'No, I don't know where he is, but maybe he's gone off to get some space. Clear his head.' Pauline shakes her head. 'Calm down, Hayley. Getting upset won't do you any good.' She sighs, and this time I am not imagining the smugness that flits across her features. 'I was worried this might happen.'

For a moment my heart stops in my chest and at first I think she's talking about the wife swap, when I realise that of course she doesn't mean that at all. 'What might happen?' Dread creeps over me, my hands suddenly cold.

'Hayley, I don't want to be the one to tell you this, but maybe Nate isn't brave enough.' Pauline reaches out and takes my hand, and I think how this is probably the first time she's ever voluntarily touched me. 'You thought you had him wrapped around your little finger, didn't you?' She tightens her grip on my hand, the tip of her nails pressing into my skin. 'Perhaps he's finally seen sense, finally seen you for who you really are.'

'What?' Shock makes my teeth feel numb and I yank my hand out from under hers. *She knows nothing about our marriage, nothing about us.*

'Hayley, it's obvious. Nate isn't happy. With you, or with your marriage.'

CHAPTER 18

Lies. It has to be lies. Nate would never tell his mother anything about our marriage. That's the thought I have on repeat, thumping through my brain in time with my feet as I hurry along our street, a thin drizzle soaking my hair, trying to get home so I can let the tears fall, aware that it's already too late. After Pauline dropped her bombshell, I stumbled out of her house, the scent of heavy floral air freshener and bleach in my nose, tears burning my eyes. I don't remember the tube ride home, the twenty minutes spent sitting on the Elizabeth line a terrifying gap as I find myself outside my own house. Next door, the curtains are open, and I see a silhouette pass by the sitting room window. *Seb.* My feet step towards the Coopers' garden path, my fist already raised to knock on his door when I stop. My chest is hitching, tears leaking down my cheeks and dripping off my chin, rain soaking through the shoulders of my thin shirt. If I knock and Tamsin answers the door, I will dissolve into a weeping puddle on the doorstep, if I don't fly at her with my nails first.

Letting myself into our house, I call out for Nate, even though I know he hasn't come home. There is no jacket slung over the newel post, no keys in the ugly little bowl I made at a potters in France one summer, and his shoes aren't tucked under the hallway radiator. The air does feel disturbed though, and I pause for a moment, my pulse loud in my ears.

112

'Hello?' Silence echoes back at me, but as I make my way into the kitchen there is a prickling sensation along my spine, as though someone's eyes are on me. My cup sits in the sink where I left it this morning, the cardigan I wore the previous evening still hanging on the back of the chair, but even so something feels off. Looking out of the patio doors into the garden, a bird pecking at the lawn is the only movement. 'Idiot,' I mutter under my breath, moving to the fridge to pull out a bottle of Sauvignon. Of course the house is empty. The only other person who lives here hasn't come home.

Pouring myself a huge glass of wine, I settle on the couch and turn on the TV. Some soap opera is on, the female character wailing about her husband leaving her for another woman and I switch to another channel. Has Nate used the swap with Tamsin as the perfect excuse to leave me? Even if Tamsin does come home, what if Nate doesn't? The memory of Pauline's face as she said that perhaps Nate has seen me for who I really am causes another tear to slide down my cheek. None of this adds up. Suddenly furious again, I reach for my phone and pull up the notes app, typing everything I know onto the blank yellow page. When I read it back, nothing seems to make any sense at all.

Tamsin, for one. I thought we'd become good friends, despite the short time we've known each other. We spent a lot of time together and she had confided things in me that I wouldn't have expected anyone to divulge to someone they might not trust. She'd told me that she didn't have any money of her own, but Seb says that's a lie. While she never told me that Seb was abusive, I saw the bruise on her arm, saw the way he grabbed her in the garden. Tamsin said she burned her arm cooking for Seb, but Tamsin doesn't cook, everyone knows that. The more I think about things, despite all the time we spent together, Tamsin listening to me as I spilled my guts, the less I think she actually told me about her life. I don't know where she grew up, or if her parents are still alive. I know she met Seb when they were both at university, but she never told me where that was. Was she deliberately vague so I wouldn't know where to find her when this happened, or was it just that our conversation never really got that deep?

And Nate. This is so out of character for him. But maybe he really has just upped and left, if he's even telling his mum that he wasn't happy. But if he wasn't happy, why say he was ready to start a family, when he knows that's all I've ever wanted? Something about the idea that he would promise me something so huge, while the next minute agreeing to swap partners with Seb and Tamsin seems terribly cruel. And I never thought Nate was cruel.

And then there's Seb. Beautiful, glamorous Seb. There's something about him I can't put my finger on, and it's not just the way he seems so casual about the fact that Nate and Tamsin appear to have run off together. Why isn't he worried? Does he know more than he's letting on? My head spinning from confusion, lack of sleep and way too much wine I try Nate's phone one more time before I head upstairs to bed. There is no answer.

* * *

I see it the moment I step inside my bedroom, my hand fluttering to my throat. *I knew it.* I knew something felt off as soon as I stepped inside the house this evening. It might seem like nothing to anyone else, but I know I didn't leave the opened parcel of books on the end of my bed. My heart in my throat, I tiptoe across the bedroom, reaching out for the parcel with shaking hands. Three books sit inside — *What to Expect When You're Expecting, The Day-by-Day Pregnancy Book* and *The Modern Midwife's Guide to Pregnancy, Birth and Beyond* — the books I had ordered on Friday morning at work, following mine and Nate's decision to start trying for a baby, before any of this wife swap stuff happened.

They were due to be delivered today, but with everything that happened the books were the furthest thing from my mind. But the fact that they are here, opened and on my bed means . . .

'Someone's been in here.' My voice is a whisper but it seems to fill the empty room as I pluck one of the books from the box. There is a prickle between my shoulder blades and I whirl around, my pulse crashing in my ears but there is no one there. The book in my hand slides to the floor, and I swipe my palm over my trousers, dread and unease building in a tidal wave. *Was it Nate?* If it was, if he'd come home, why put the opened parcel on the bed and leave? Why not return my calls? Shaking my head, I try to dislodge some sort of sensible logic from it all, but I can't. Someone left this opened parcel on my bed and it wasn't me.

Stooping to pick up the book, I pause as something glints in the light where the bed frame meets the carpet. *An earring.* Pinching it between finger and thumb I hold it up to the light. It's a familiar flower-shaped stud earring, each petal a different colour and my mouth goes dry. It's one of the Kate Spade earrings I bought Tamsin for her birthday. *Was she wearing them the night of the swap?* I swallow down the bile that rises in my throat. *Or is it her who has been in my house today, leaving the parcel of pregnancy books on the bed?*

When my phone rings in my pocket, I jump, a shriek escaping my lips. It's a withheld number and I almost drop the call my hands are trembling so much.

'Hello? Nate, is that you?' There is the rush of static on the line, and the faint blare of something that sounds like a car alarm. 'Nate? Where are you?'

Movement outside catches my eye, and keeping the phone pressed to my ear, I move to the bedroom window. Yellow light spills in a faint puddle across next door's lawn from their kitchen patio doors, and as the clouds move on the night breeze, the moon makes an appearance. Silver moonlight hits the trees at the end of our garden and the shadows move again, triggering the security light over our kitchen window. Adrenaline spikes in my veins and I draw in a shuddering breath. *There's someone out there, in the garden. Watching me.*

'Hayley?' The voice on the other end of the phone is barely more than a whisper. I can't tell if it's Nate or Tamsin or someone else entirely over the sound of the car alarm in the background. On legs that feel like overcooked ramen I move to the door and snap off the bedroom light. Swallowing hard, I peer out of the window again. The figure is still there, casting an elongated shadow across the lawn from the edge of the trees. I can't breathe, fear closing my throat.

'Hayley?' The voice whispers in my ear again and I close my eyes, sure I am about to have a heart attack.

'Nate? Is that you? Tamsin?' My voice is thin and reedy, panic clutching me in a vice-like grip. 'Where are you?'

The call drops as the figure at the end of the garden suddenly darts into the trees, disappearing out of sight. I let out a long breath, only to realise something truly disturbing. I can still hear the car alarm going off, even though the person on the other end of the line has hung up. Whoever called me is outside my house.

CHAPTER 19

'Are you sure you weren't imagining things?' Seb's brow is creased as he pushes a mug of tea towards me. 'You seem a bit . . .'

It's almost midnight, and after seeing the dark figure at the end of the garden and realising whoever called was outside my house I had raced next door, hammering on Seb's door until he yanked it open and I tumbled into the hallway, my hands shaking and my breath sticking in my throat. I can smell the wine from earlier on my breath and I shake my head.

'I wasn't imagining it, Seb. I could still hear the car alarm after whoever it was had hung up. There was someone in the garden and they were watching me.' Shuddering, I scrub my hands over my arms. I can still feel the prickle of their eyes on me.

Seb sighs and stifles a yawn, but I don't feel guilty for waking him up. 'Maybe it was just kids playing a prank? It's Halloween soon.'

'Fuck's sake, Seb, really?' I snap, my nerves so taut they're fraying. 'It's not Halloween until the end of next month, and besides, it's midnight! Who lets their kids parade around the streets scaring people at midnight?' Seb's face darkens, and I swallow a dart of fear. 'Sorry, I didn't mean to snap at you. I just meant . . . it's late, and . . .' Horror washes over me. 'They said my name, whoever it was on the other end of the phone, before they hung up. What if it was Nate or Tamsin? What if they're in trouble?'

Seb moves around the kitchen island and slides onto the stool beside me. I can smell the pomade he uses in his hair, and the faint whiff of stale beer on his breath. Clearly I wasn't the only one to have had a drink this evening. 'Do you think we should call the police?'

Part of me thinks that is the perfect solution, call the cops and let them figure things out, but the other part of me knows it's pointless. 'And say what? We swapped partners,' God, saying the words out loud make me feel grubby and tainted, like I need a shower, 'and now our respective other halves have disappeared together? To be honest Seb, I don't think they'd take us that seriously.'

Seb passes a hand over his chin. 'I guess you're right, it is a crap idea, I don't know why I suggested it. If they were in trouble, they'd call 999 before they called either of us, wouldn't they? And why would Tamsin say your name and then hang up? I suppose when you think about it logically . . . You're tired, you've had a drink . . .' His hand slides over mine and gives it a reassuring squeeze.

At his words, I nod, exhaustion washing over me. Seb's right. If it was Nate or Tamsin and they were in a mess, they'd call the police, not me. Maybe it was kids messing around in the garden.

'Yeah,' I say. 'Maybe you're right. The fence panel behind the trees at the back of the garden has been broken for ages, I keep asking Nate to replace it but he never seems to have time.' Swallowing down a pang at the feel of his name on my lips, I force a smile. 'I'm sorry if you think I've overreacted and I'm sorry I got you out of bed.'

Seb's eyes rest on my face and I shift on the stool, warmth rising on my cheeks at the thought of Seb in bed. The memory of the other night is still bright in my mind, at least the parts the booze didn't tamp down. 'I wasn't sleeping.'

'Well, even so,' I laugh, a brittle noise that pierces the thick tension that has filled the air. 'I should go. I was just being silly, I'm sorry.'

Seb's hand shoots out and wraps around my wrist, and I notice a scrape along his knuckles. 'Stay.'

'What?'

'Stay. Sleep here tonight.' Seb's tone is serious, but as he catches sight of the look on my face a bubble of laughter escapes him. 'Not like that, silly. Sleep in our spare bedroom. You're clearly jittery after that phone call, and I doubt you'll sleep in that empty house all alone. I won't sleep either, if I think you're up all night worrying, and I've got a really long day tomorrow crammed full of meetings, so I could do with some shut-eye.' Seb smiles, but I don't respond, not all sure if I'll sleep any better under the same roof as him.

'You know it makes sense, Hayley. Stay here — at least you know I'm just down the hall if something happens.' My eyes widen and he laughs. 'Not that it will. You're just . . . welcome here, that's all. If it'll make you feel safer.'

Maybe it *would* make me feel safer, I think, the thought of going back to my dark, empty house making my stomach drop, although I still don't want to picture Seb lying in his bed just down the hall.

'I'll be . . . well, you know where my room is,' Seb says, a few minutes later as we stand on the threshold of the spare bedroom. 'Just shout if you need me, but honestly, Hayley, it'll be fine. Get some sleep, you look exhausted.'

Wishing Seb a good night, I close the door to the spare room and survey my surroundings. The windows look out on to the street outside and I close the curtains, immediately feeling safer. The bed is a lavish four-poster, almost too big for the room and I gingerly lower myself onto the mattress, perching on the edge of the bed. Although Seb had referred to this room as the 'spare' room, I could be forgiven for thinking the room belongs to Tamsin. While it doesn't seem to have been decorated recently — the wallpaper is old-fashioned and flowery, tendrils of green inching between once-bright peonies, and the paintwork on the skirting boards and windowsill is chipped and yellowing — Tamsin's things are everywhere. An antique dressing table sits in the corner and is covered with make-up tubes and bottles, the small three-way mirror splattered with tiny drops of foundation. On the free-standing full length mirror beside the dressing table hang the beaded necklaces I've seen her wear before, tangled together in a jumble. Unable to sit still, I move to the wardrobe, opening the doors to see a row of brightly coloured outfits — including some that look more like costumes than actual everyday clothes — hanging inside. Some sit on hangers, others slip precariously, silk and chiffon dangling towards the pile of shoes and boots shoved in the bottom of the wardrobe in a disorganised heap. On top of a chest of drawers sit mannequin heads, each one topped with a different coloured wig, some long, some short, curly and straight, and I reach out and stroke one. It has never crossed my mind that perhaps Tamsin's hairstyle isn't her actual hair. This room is completely at odds with the other parts of the house that I've seen — totally different to the brand-new, super modern kitchen and the sterile bedroom that Seb took me to — but it is one hundred percent Tamsin, and I feel a tug of something that makes me feel queasy at the thought of sleeping in here.

Fighting my nausea, I slip into the bathroom next door and wash my face and brush my teeth, using a brand-new sealed toothbrush I find in the medicine cabinet. As I scrub my molars something tugs at the back of my mind, a thought I can't grasp properly, and I let it swirl down the drain when I spit, hurrying back to the bedroom.

The bed is comfy, the room is dark and the only sound is the rustle of the trees outside the bedroom window. By rights I should be out like a light, but I can't sleep. I'm not sure if it's worry about Nate, fear of the mysterious figure watching me from the end of the garden, or the close proximity of the man who started all of this but my eyelids ping open, over and over, as I see two o'clock, two thirty and then three o'clock on my phone screen.

At three fifteen, I shove back the covers and slide out of bed. Maybe a glass of water or a cup of chamomile tea will help. Pulling my clothes back on, I tiptoe down the stairs, my bare feet cold on the oak flooring of the hallway. Just before I enter the kitchen, I have to pass Seb's study, the door left slightly ajar. Curiosity draws me in and I take a step closer. When Tamsin gave me a tour of the house when we first met, she'd skipped past this closed door, telling me it was Seb's study and that no one was ever allowed in there.

'Not even you?' I'd asked, dumbfounded by the idea that there was a room in her own house that she couldn't use.

Tamsin had shaken her head and laughed. 'I wouldn't want to,' she'd said, 'it's a tip. He's so private about his work, it wouldn't be worth the aggro if I did go in there.'

I hadn't thought any more about it since, skipping past the closed door and not even noticing it on my subsequent visits to the house, but now the door stands ajar and the curiosity becomes a bright, burning flame. Without thinking, I push the door and step inside. Tamsin wasn't wrong when she said it was a tip. A laptop sits on the battered desk, stacks of paper piled up around it, and the wastepaper basket is overflowing with food wrappers and chunks of paper. Leaning over, I spot a Post-it note with a scrawled telephone number and 'irises' written on it. Remembering the bouquet I received at the office, a sour taste fills my mouth and I turn my gaze to the paper stacks. Most of them look like scripts, some with red pen scrawled across the front in indecipherable handwriting, others with a black cross marked over them, presumably destined to join the other scripts that fill the bin. A plastic in-tray holds mail, and my nosiness takes over. I don't understand why Seb wouldn't allow Tamsin to come into his study — I get that he probably is a little precious about his work, aren't most creative people? — but there don't seem to be any filthy secrets locked away in here. Shuffling through the envelopes I see a royalty statement for Tamsin — not enough money to change the world, that's for sure — a postcard from someone named Wills, a credit card bill and a water bill. It's the bills that give me pause. Both have been opened, the envelope carefully slit open presumably with the letter opener that lies on the desk next to a dirty coffee mug, but the name on the front isn't Seb's or Tamsin's.

Frowning, I tug the credit card bill gently out of the envelope. It's definitely been sent to this address, but the name on the bill is Alex Small. Racking my brains, I try to remember the name of the last people who lived here, and then I remember they were the Lleshis, a fiery couple originally from Montenegro. I don't remember anyone named Alex Small living here. Maybe the bill was sent here in error and Seb or Tamsin opened it by mistake? Feeling off-kilter, I tuck the mail back into the in-tray, and squeeze past the office chair, my foot slipping and tilting my balance. My hip knocks against the paper stack on the edge of the desk and for one heart-stopping moment I think the whole thing is going to tumble down with a crash. Putting out a hand, I let out a long slow breath, manoeuvring the scripts back into place before leaning down to pick up whatever I slipped on. It's a photograph, matte with age and over-exposed. It shows a girl sitting on the grass in the late evening summer sun, a man in the background shading his eyes as he looks in her direction. A cigarette dangles in one hand, the smoke curling lazily around her head as she holds up two fingers on the other hand in a victory sign, a smile splitting her face. I can see shades of Tamsin in her, and I realise it's the same girl from the photograph on the fridge, although maybe a few years older. Tamsin's sister. Goosebumps rise on my arms as I remember the way things had felt off when I asked Tamsin about her, Nate appearing in the doorway, and I scrub the photo over my jeans, wiping off my fingerprints before laying it on the desk beside a stack of scripts. As I turn, my shin catches the sharp edge of the bottom drawer of the desk, where it isn't quite closed. Pausing for a moment, I strain to listen for movement overhead and when there is only silence, I slide the drawer open.

I only want to see if there are any other photos of the girl, but when I slip my fingers inside the drawer and see what's inside my heart goes cold.

CHAPTER 20

It's me. The thought hits me full in the face as I pull out the small stack of photographs. They aren't of the girl, of Tamsin's mysterious sister, they are of *me.* Bile rises, hitting the back of my throat as I flick through them, not caring about the smudges my fingers leave on the glossy finish. There is me, hand in hand with Nate as we walk towards the tube station. Me, in the garden, smiling at Nate as he lounges, unfocused and blurry, in the background. Me and Nate at our favourite restaurant, the light catching my hair as I sit with my back to the window. Me, in a faux leather jacket that I bought from a vintage stall at some market, a bag of groceries in one hand as Nate strides ahead of me. It's the final photo that makes my blood really run cold. It's me, alone. The lighting is dim and my eyes are closed, my hands tucked under my chin in the way that Nate tells me makes me look like an angel, before he laughs uproariously, because he knows that's the one thing I'm not. *I am asleep, in my own bed in the house next door.* A low groan escapes, and I press my hand over my mouth. Every photo is unposed, taken without my knowledge, but this — this is horrifying. For a dizzying moment I am sure that I am about to vomit all over the floor. *When were these taken? And who took these photos?* My mind is racing and I feel hot and clammy, my forehead damp when I press my fingers against it. None of the occasions captured in the photos are particularly memorable and I feel exposed, as if I've been caught outside with no underwear on.

Returning my attention to the drawer, I dig inside, wondering what else Seb is hiding. A sheaf of papers, neatly stapled together, lies under the empty photo packets and a page torn from an old newspaper and I scan it quickly, pausing to go back and double check what I'm reading. It's a life insurance policy, for two million pounds. For Tamsin. My stomach lurches at the idea of what this could mean, but before I can think about it any further there is a creaking of floorboards overhead, and then the flushing of the toilet.

Shit. Tossing the photographs back into the drawer, I make my way carefully past the script stacks and out of the study, easing the door gently closed just as I hear Seb's footsteps on the stairs. By the time he reaches the kitchen, I am standing at the sink, a glass of water in my shaking hand.

'You're up early.' Seb opens the fridge and swigs directly from the milk carton, a habit I've nagged Nate about more than once.

'Couldn't sleep.' I try on a wobbly smile, my fingers clutching the glass so tightly that I'm surprised it doesn't shatter. 'I'm not sure if it's being in a different bed, or I'm still anxious about someone being outside the house, but I think I'm going to head home now. Thank you for letting me stay.'

There is a heavy pause as Seb says nothing for a moment, just stares at me, his eyes seeming to bore into my soul. 'Any time.' His eyes don't leave my face, and panic swarms like angry bees in my veins. *He knows. He knows I was snooping in his study.* It takes everything I have not to peer past him at the study door, making sure I really did close it. 'Mi casa es su casa.'

'Thanks.' I smile tightly and, keeping my eyes averted I go to move past him, but his arm shoots out and blocks my path.

'Your phone.' He nods at the kitchen counter, where my phone sits beside a small puddle of spilled water. 'You don't want to forget that now. What if Nate calls you?'

Nodding a thanks, I snatch up my phone and hurry out along the hallway, not breathing until my own front door slams closed behind me. My pulse roars in my ears as I lean against the front door, my breath panicked and gasping. I don't want to think about how Seb might have reacted if he'd caught me snooping in his study, but I'm pretty certain he wouldn't have been happy. I think of the photos, of how unguarded and vulnerable I look in them, and of the life insurance policy. *Has Seb done something unspeakable? Did Tamsin and Nate walk out of the house on Sunday, or did something unimaginable happen?*

CHAPTER 21

'There's clearly something wrong.' Harry, my boss, says in a sharp tone. He's called me into his office, slamming the door closed on Wendy's prying eyes. 'You've been off your game all week, Hayley. I haven't had a single one of the cost reports I've asked you for, and the follow up on the sales leads came from Wendy's email account. She also tells me you're not taking any calls?'

Fucking Wendy. My skin prickles every time I think about Wendy at the moment. I've never really given her much thought before, even though I get the feeling she would like us to be friends, but after finding her snooping in my desk, and now her going to Harry about me, it feels as if something has shifted. *Is she after my job?* Something tightens in my chest at the memory of her asking about Nate and the Michelin-starred restaurant in Harrogate, and I wonder if it's something more precious to me than my job that she's after. Before he met me, she would have been just Nate's type, pretty with glossy hair and a cracking figure.

'I've got some personal stuff going on,' I say, as Harry clears his throat, my eyes filling with tears as if I've cued them up. 'I'm sorry, Harry. I haven't been sleeping well.' That, at least, isn't a lie. I didn't sleep this morning when I slipped back to my own house in the early dawn hours. Instead, I took a long hot bath and tried to figure out exactly how I'm going to get back into Seb's study and snoop some more, because why does Seb have photographs of me in his desk? And why were there two bills in the name of Alex Small? Who is Alex Small? And do they know where Tamsin might be?

'Is it Nate?'

My head snaps up at Harry's words. Nate and Harry have met a few times, even played a charity golf match together. 'Have you spoken to him?'

Harry frowns, confusion crosses his features. 'No. Why would I? I just assumed that since you said personal issues, and Wendy . . . well, Wendy said she thought you two might be having some problems, that's all. Look, Hayley, I don't mean anything by this but perhaps you need to take some leave? You've got holiday accrued, so maybe take a few days off to get your head together, just until you're over whatever it is that's going on.'

My instinct is to refuse, to tell Harry that I am perfectly capable of doing my job, and then to ask Wendy what the hell she thinks she's doing, speculating to my own boss about my personal life, when I realise that this could be exactly what I need. 'OK, thanks Harry. I promise I'll be back soon, I just need to . . .' I flap a hand, suddenly emotional.

Harry glances at the clock on the wall behind me. 'It's three o'clock, Hayley. You may as well leave now, and I'll start your leave from tomorrow. Take a week, and then see how you are.'

Thanking Harry, I hurry out of his office, pausing only as I see Wendy hovering by my desk.

'Are you all right?' She screws up her nose in concern. 'I hope you didn't mind me talking to Harry, but I've been worried about you all week.'

'I'm fine, honestly.' I reach for my phone, my lanyard and my keys. 'I'm going to take a few days off, if you'll be OK holding the fort while I'm gone?' Not that there's much of a fort to hold down, but I'm not keen on letting Wendy know that.

'No problem,' she beams. 'I do hope you and Nate get all of this sorted. I thought I saw him the other day, you know.'

'Me and Nate . . . ? Wait . . . you saw him?' My heart seems to stutter in my chest and I grip my keys tightly, hiding the trembling in my fingers. 'Where?'

'Oh, out Stratford way. I was going to the shopping centre and I could have sworn it was him, walking on the other side of the road. It wasn't, though. At least, he never turned around when I called out to him.' Wendy cocks her head on one side. 'You two are OK, aren't you? Only you don't seem yourself, and . . .'

'We're fine,' I say with a forced smile. 'Everything is fine. I'll be back before you know it.' I'm sure Wendy didn't see Nate — of course she didn't, but she loves to stir up a bit of drama — all I want to do now is get out of here and sneak my way into the Coopers' house before Seb gets home from work.

* * *

I never would have said that I had childbearing hips (much to Pauline's disgust) but I'm tempted to reevaluate things as I struggle to fit through the tiny open kitchen window at the Coopers' house. There was no key left handily under a rock, although Seb has graciously left the key in the lock of the rear patio doors. The only problem is that to be able to get to those keys, I am going to have to squeeze through the small kitchen window, the one that doesn't latch properly. I thank God as I finally pop through the gap, gasping as I land awkwardly on the kitchen counter, before sliding to the floor, my heart racing.

Please God, don't let them have an alarm. Suddenly the terrifying possibility smacks me in the face and I freeze, cursing myself for not thinking things through properly. Instead, I had hurried home from the office, my mind alive with the thought of getting back into Seb's study to figure out why there are photographs of me in his desk, and who Alex Small might be. I had stopped only to tap on the front door before heading round the back to peer through the patio doors into the kitchen, double checking that Seb really was still out, before I'd clambered up on to a patio chair and shoved my body through the window. Now, I sit against the kitchen cabinets, waiting for the shrill beep of an alarm I never knew they had to split the air. It doesn't come. The house remains silent and after a few minutes I let out a long breath and get to my feet, my knees wobbly with adrenaline.

I forgot about the dog. My heart leaps into my throat as a low growl comes from the other side of the kitchen door. Slowly, I crack the door ajar and peer into the hallway to see Tank standing guard, his hackles up.

'Shh, Tank, it's just me.' I open the door and hold out a hand for him to sniff. 'Hey boy, come here. Come on. You know me.' Tank visibly relaxes as he ambles towards me and I let out a long, shaky breath as I pet him on the head, thanking my lucky stars that the old dog likes me. He leans against me for a moment and then shuffles back to his dog bed.

The door to the study is tightly closed and I offer up a prayer to a God I am not sure I believe in as I try the door handle. Clearly, He is on my side as the handle moves under my palm and I once again find myself inside Seb's inner sanctum. The same mess spills over the desk, the same piles of scripts and paperwork, and I'm not surprised seeing as it was only a little over twelve hours ago that I was in here. Seb's laptop is missing, which is also not surprising if he's gone to work, but the charger still snakes out of the wall. Taking care not to knock over the teetering piles of paperwork, I pluck the bills from the in-tray and smooth them out. Both are in the name of Alex Small, and I cast the water bill aside in favour of the credit card bill. Running my eyes down the list of purchases made, there isn't a lot of information. This person has bought sushi, trainers from a Nike store, chocolate from Hotel Chocolat. Whoever they are, they can afford to splurge on luxuries. An item further down catches my eye, sending a tingle down my spine. A mobile phone store, one of those little stands you see in the shopping centre. I only recognise it because I'd taken my phone there a few months ago to get the screen fixed. Was Alex Small helping Tamsin? Is that why Tamsin left her phone behind, because someone had already got her a new one?

Galvanised by the thought that this Alex Small must be someone Tamsin knows, I start to search in earnest, trying hard not to think about the pile of photos of me in the drawer. The photo that I slipped on earlier, of the young woman who bears a resemblance to Tamsin pops into my mind and I pause, my fingers brushing over the edge of the desk. I had left the photo beside a stack of scripts, I was sure of it, when I reached out to stop them from toppling over. But it's not here now.

Could the woman in the photograph be Alex Small? It makes sense, at least on the surface. Who would know better where Tamsin might be than her sister? I feel that tug of recognition again when I remember the photo, the way the girl was smiling with a cigarette in her hand. I have seen her before, I am sure of it. Maybe Tamsin is right and I saw her in something on TV, but even so, something about her nags at me.

Sliding open the bottom drawer, I rifle through the photographs of myself, my mouth twisting with distaste, but the photo of the girl is gone. My fingers brush over the old sheet of newspaper underneath the photos and I carefully pull it out, intrigued to know what Seb has kept tucked away from prying eyes. My mouth goes dry as I run my eyes over the page. It's an obituary page — nothing exciting or unusual there — only, the page contains a name I know. *My grandmother's name. Nita Thompson, survived by her daughter, Annabel, and granddaughter, Hayley.* Why would Seb have this? Ink smudges my fingers and I shove the page back into the drawer as if it might burn me. *Coincidence*, I tell myself. My grandmother's wasn't the only obituary on that page. But even so, I know everything about this feels wrong.

Turning my attention to the bookcase, I run my eyes over the titles on the shelves, looking for anything that looks out of the ordinary. A book that doesn't sit right, false spines that could lead to a hidden pocket. Maybe I've watched too many movies, but I can't shake the feeling that Seb is hiding something bigger than creepy photos of his next-door neighbour . . . maybe it is just that this Alex Small knows where Tamsin is, but maybe it's something more. At the very least, I'm going to search as thoroughly as I can to see if I can turn up any information on where I might be able to find Alex. Because if Alex *is* Tamsin's sister and she knows where she is, then maybe I'll find Nate.

The bookshelves are neatly stacked, and at first glance nothing seems out of the ordinary. I think I can pluck out the books Seb chooses to read — there is a copy of Walden's *Civil Disobedience*, the entire set of Mick Herron's *Slow Horses* novels, travel books by Paul Theroux and a copy of *The Journals of Sylvia Plath* which in all honesty could belong to either Tamsin or Seb. It's only when I crouch down to the bottom shelf, to the battered, double-stacked copies of psychological thrillers by Gillian Flynn, Ruth Ware and Alice Feeney, that something seems odd. The bottom of the bookcase seems to be a solid panel, but as I crouch down my foot catches the front of it, causing the panel to swing in on itself. Lying flat, I reach a hand into the cavern inside the bookcase, expecting only to find dust bunnies and hoping not to find a dead mouse or worse. My fingers grope about, and I am just about to give it up as a lost cause, when my thumb brushes something solid. Adjusting my angle I reach in again, my fingers sticky with cobwebs, and I grip whatever it is between my finger and thumb, inching it slowly towards me.

'Come on,' I hiss under my breath as the item slides out and I sit back on my haunches, sweat prickling under my arms. It's an envelope, thick and bulky, the flap unsealed. It's not without some trepidation that I slide my finger under the flap and pull out the contents, partly terrified at the thought of there being more pictures of me hidden away in Seb's study. There are a whole wedge of credit card bills, all in the name of Alex Small, dated back six months at least. The address on them isn't much help — they are mostly addressed to this house, seeing as it's been a little over six months since the Coopers moved in, with one at the back of the pile holding an address in Notting Hill. Frowning, I move onto the next item. It's a driving licence, but again it's no use. It's dated 2009, and it's the paper counterpart only, again in the name of Alex Small. The final item in the envelope is smaller, thicker, and when I tilt the envelope to tip it out, my pulse starts to thud in my ears, and my tongue snakes out to lick at my dry lips. It's a passport. Old, for sure. It has the burgundy cover of the old European Union passport on it, and I'm not sure why anyone would keep that, until I open the cover to find it is still in date, the expiry not until 2027. It's not that though that makes my breath catch in my throat, and the polished oak floorboards seem to tilt beneath my feet. The name in the passport is Alex Small, and I feel a small sense of triumph at finding I have their name, date of birth and place of birth at my fingertips. Everything I need to track down who I think might be Tamsin's sister on the internet. That is, until I look at the passport photo. It's not the young woman's face staring back at me. It's *Seb's*.

And then I hear the front door slam closed.

CHAPTER 22

It's Seb's face in the passport. Seb is Alex Small. And now Seb has just walked back into his house — the house I have broken into. *Fuck.*

Lifting my eyes to the study door, relief washes over me in a cold, sweet wave at the sight of it pulled tightly closed. Sliding the passport into my back pocket, and then shoving the paperwork back inside the cavity inside the bookcase, I scrunch myself into a tiny ball, my calves knotting as I wait, straining to hear where Seb is. My heart stops dead in my chest as footsteps tap along the hall, pausing outside the study door. *Please*, I think, *please don't come in here*. Seconds pass, moments that feels like hours before the footsteps move on, the stair risers over my head creaking, and then minutes later the sound of the shower running comes from above and I slowly unfold myself and get to my feet.

I have to get out of here before Seb finds me. To go out of the front door means passing the staircase and that's too risky — if Seb takes that moment to cross the landing for whatever reason he'll spot me straight away. It's safer for me to sneak back along the hallway and out through the kitchen patio doors and then out through the side gate. Hopefully Seb will just think he's forgotten to lock the patio doors.

The key to the back door is cold between my fingers, but as I reach to twist it in the lock I turn to ice.

'What are you doing here?'

Closing my eyes for a brief second I draw in a breath and push a smile onto my face. *Act normal, Hayley.* 'Seb! I knocked but you didn't answer . . . I tried the back door and it was open, so . . .'

'So you thought you'd just walk in?'

I turn now, my smile wobbling across my face. Seb stands in the kitchen door wrapped only in a towel. 'I wanted to surprise you actually.'

He steps towards me, his smile mocking as my pulse skitters under my skin and I grope for the door handle behind me. 'Well, you certainly did that.' His smile drops. 'But I'll ask you again — what are you doing in my house, Hayley?'

I glance towards the fridge, my mind working overtime as the passport burns a hole in my back pocket. 'I was going to cook you dinner, as a surprise for when you got home. You said you were going to have a long day, and I wanted to thank you for last night . . . for letting me stay and everything.' I swallow, my tongue sticking to the roof of my mouth.

'You're going to cook for me?' He looks puzzled, his hands gripping the edge of his towel at his waist, and I wonder if I imagined the look on his face as he stepped towards me. 'Wow. No one ever cooks for me. What are you making?'

Fuck. I had forgotten that Seb fancies himself as a bit of a chef. And I have no ingredients with me and no idea what he has in the fridge. I know my own fridge is bare, the loss of Nate taking up my every waking thought, leaving no room for whether there's milk or bread. 'Well,' I fumble, 'it wouldn't be a surprise now, would it, if I told you? Maybe you should . . .' I gesture to the towel, the shower still running overhead, 'get showered and stuff and I'll, um . . . get cracking.'

Seb gives me a long look and for a drawn-out, heart-stopping moment I think he's going to refuse, before he nods briskly and turns on his heel, heading back upstairs. Sinking against the kitchen counter I rub my hands over my face. What the hell was I thinking? Fighting the urge to flee, I move towards the fridge and open the door. I guess I'd better try and figure out dinner.

* * *

'It really is like we've swapped,' Seb says, appearing in the doorway with his hair still damp, the fresh scent of lemon and sandalwood filling in the air. 'Something smells delicious. I don't think Tamsin has ever cooked for me.'

Sweating, I push my hair off my forehead with the back of my hand as my gut clenches. Does Seb wish he had swapped for real? The idea that the swap might have been all his idea, not Tamsin's, after I found those photographs of me makes me want to run as fast as I can and never look back.

While Seb showered I found steaks in the fridge, salad, baby potatoes and garlic, items even I can throw a dinner together from. A bottle of Malbec is breathing on the table and I am praying that I can pull this off without Seb realising I have broken into his house to spy on him.

'It's just steaks and a salad,' I say, tossing the dressing over the salad. The steaks are oiled and resting on the side waiting to go in the pan and Seb leans over and prods at one of them. He stands a little too close for comfort, his shoulder nudging mine.

'Want me to cook these?'

'Sure,' I shrug, ducking out from under his arm and carrying the salad to the table. Being in close proximity to him makes my skin prickle, and even an inch of distance is better than nothing. Seb throws the steaks into a sizzling hot pan and I take a seat at the table, relieved to let him take over.

'I take it you haven't heard from Tamsin?' I say, pouring the wine.

Seb shakes his head. 'Nothing yet. And I'm guessing you didn't hear from Nate either. What about your place? You haven't seen anyone lurking about since last night?'

'No. Nothing.' I sip the wine, hoping it might dissolve the knot in my chest. 'Maybe you were right, it was just kids.' My gut tells me otherwise, but I also know that Seb is hiding something too. *Did he break into my house and watch me sleeping before he took that photograph?* I sip the wine again, but it burns like acid as it travels down my throat.

'Well, let's enjoy our evening. Here,' Seb carries two plates over to the table and loads salad and potatoes next to the steaks before raising his glass. 'To us. Who knows, maybe the two of us will end up making the best out of this situation.'

Horror inches its way through my veins, sharp and spiky, and I reach for my wine glass again. 'I thought you said Tamsin would come back soon — that she'd done this before?' *He can't actually think it's funny to make jokes about us swapping for real?*

'She will.'

He sounds so confident. So sure. Does he know something I don't? All I've felt since I got home to an empty house on Sunday is worry and fear, but Seb doesn't seem to be the slightest bit worried, even though it's been two days now with no word from either Nate or Tamsin.

Slicing into the steak, I swallow down the spurt of saliva that fills my mouth at the bloody juices that run from the meat. Seb has served the steak rare, without asking my preference. 'Tell me some more about you,' I say, forcing the meat to my lips. 'I feel like even after everything that's happened I barely know you.' *Tell me why there is a passport in a different name in your study.*

'There's not a lot to tell,' Seb says, shrugging casually yet eyeing me closely. 'I've told you all the important things. I went to uni, graduated, met and married Tamsin, set up my production company. I'm not sure what else you want to know. Unless . . .' his gaze flicks down to my chest and then back to my mouth, and he raises an eyebrow.

Heat rises, flooding my neck and cheeks a dark crimson. 'I was just taking an interest, that's all.' Part of me feels the more I dig into Seb the closer I'll come to figuring out exactly why Nate and Tamsin have disappeared. 'I guess I'm just trying to figure out why Nate would do this to me. I thought I knew him so well, but maybe I didn't after all.'

Seb frowns, but it looks insincere as if he's trying out a look of concern, but it falls flat. 'I mean, Hayley . . . maybe it's time you just—'

Something hits the sitting room window, a loud crack against the glass that makes me shriek and drop my fork.

'What the hell—?' Seb is on his feet, heading into the sitting room as I scrape back my chair. My heart is pounding so hard I feel as if I can barely breathe, panic clawing at my insides.

'What is it?' I gasp, pressing my hands to my chest as Seb peers out of the window, into the street. Dusk is falling, the sky a deep shade of lilac, and there is the faint hint of jasmine on the still-warm air. 'Seb, someone was out there.' This is like last night all over again and I feel that familiar sensation of someone watching me. I tug my cardigan closer around my body, wrapping my arms around myself.

Seb shoves past me, the front door flying open as he hurries out on to the garden path. I linger in the hallway, my nerves endings singing as I wait for Seb to come back inside. Is it the same person who was watching me last night? The thought makes me nauseous and for a moment I am glad to be here, in Seb's company, before I remember the passport in my back pocket.

Moments later Seb reappears, shaking his head.

'Who was it? Do you think we should call the police after all?' Even though the thought of it fills me with dread, the very idea of what Seb, Nate, Tamsin and I agreed to do being made public is so shameful and embarrassing I want to die, the thought of someone watching us — watching *me* — is just as bad.

'No,' Seb laughs, although he looks a little pale. 'Why are you shaking? It was a bird, that's all. It flew into the window. Broke its neck.' He laughs again and something cold inches along my spine.

'A bird?'

'That's all it was. Still want to call the police?'

'No, I—' My cheeks flame and I turn away, embarrassed. He must think I'm a maniac, seeing things in every dark corner, but then . . . he's the one with the secret. He's the one with the passport in a different name. 'Let's go and sit back down. I could do with some more wine.'

Now I know there isn't someone peeping in the window at us, I grit my teeth, swig my wine and prepare to do what I came here for. Figure out who Alex Small is and why Seb has a passport in his name. Why there are photographs of me and a copy of my grandmother's obituary in his desk. I turn the conversation back to Tamsin.

'I know you're not concerned, Seb.' In fact, he seems more concerned with keeping my glass topped up and giving me lingering glances than anything else, and I think of the life insurance policy hidden away in the bottom drawer. 'But don't you think the two of us are owed an explanation, at least? Is there . . . somewhere you think Tamsin might go? A family member maybe?' My stomach flips. Now I know Alex Small isn't Tamsin's sister, I wonder who Tamsin's sister *actually* is, and how on earth I am going to find out why Seb has a passport in that name.

'No, I don't think so.'

'Nowhere? I've tried Nate's mum but she hasn't seen him, he's not at work . . . none of his friends have seen him . . . I thought maybe Tamsin might have somewhere the two of them might have gone. Her sister's house, perhaps?' With a dry throat and butter-flies swarming in my stomach, I throw out a name, just to gauge his reaction. 'Was her name Alex, or did I dream that?'

Seb's head snaps up and his gaze is dark as he stares at me. 'Alex? Where did you get that name?'

Fear makes my tongue too big for my mouth, and I stumble over the words. 'I . . . don't know? I thought Tamsin said her sister was named Alex.'

Seb frowns, shoving his chair back and reaching for my still-full plate. 'Tamsin doesn't have a sister.'

'She does.' I stand too, my eyes going to the fridge, running over the magnetic calendar with Tamsin and Seb's schedules on, searching for the photo I saw stuck there at the party. 'She told me she has a younger sister who used to do TV work.'

Seb's eyes are hard as he steps between me and the fridge, blocking my view. But not before something catches my eye. 'She doesn't have a sister, Hayley. I think it's time you left. Breaking into my house was enough, don't you think?'

Seb grips me by the upper arm and marches me towards the front door, my feet barely touching the ground as he deposits me on the path outside, the door slamming closed in my face. If I didn't think Seb had something to hide before, I certainly do now.

CHAPTER 23

I don't sleep. At least, I don't think I do. I toss and turn all night, my mind racing, and every time I close my eyes I see Seb looming over me, his grip tight on my arm. At this rate I'm going to die of exhaustion before I figure out what has happened to Nate and Tamsin. I must snooze eventually because the ping of my phone wakes me, dragging me out of a nightmare in which I am locked in a dark room, unable to find my way out, calling for Nate as my fingernails scratch at concrete walls. Jolting awake, I reach for my phone, squinting at the screen. There's a text message from an unknown number and I scramble to sit upright, dropping my phone in my haste to swipe the screen open.

Let it be Nate. The thought pulses through my mind, bright with hope as I open the message, disappointment swiftly chasing it away to be replaced by confusion.

DON'T TRUST HIM

Who sent this? Was it Tamsin — is she trying to warn me against Seb? Or Nate? With fumbling fingers I tap on the screen to call the number but it goes straight to a generic voicemail.

My stomach sinks and I feel that now familiar sensation of the room seeming to spin. Right now, I don't feel as if I can trust anybody . . . and that includes whoever sent this text message. Pushing back the duvet I head for the shower, standing under the hot water for far longer than necessary as I try and process everything. Should I go and visit Nate's mum again today? Maybe she knows more than she's letting on. But what did she mean by suggesting that Nate has seen me for who I really am? I know she's never liked me, but I'm not sure how far she would go to try and get rid of me, to get Nate to agree to divorce me and move on with someone she deems more appropriate. Tamsin is exactly the kind of woman she pictured for Nate. She wouldn't speak to Tamsin the way she does to me.

Obviously, I don't feel I can trust Nate right now after the way he just upped and left — does the text message refer to him? But what could he have done that's so bad that means he's left without a word, vanished without a trace? Could something have happened at work, some drug trial gone wrong? But Nate would tell me about that, we would have talked about it and found a solution. And that still doesn't explain where Tamsin comes into things. After all, she suggested the swap and Nate — uncharacteristically — was only too keen to agree to it.

And as for Seb . . . I don't trust him an inch. The passport in a different name is a clear sign that he's lying about his name, if nothing else. What is he hiding? The photos of me — *in bed, Hayley, he was watching you sleep* — the way he seems so placid and friendly on the surface, but once you dig deeper there's a darker side to him. And then there's the life insurance policy in Tamsin's name . . . none of it feels right. I shut off the water but the shiver that runs down my spine has nothing to do with the cool breeze wafting over my damp body.

Something felt off the other night, the night I saw someone in the back garden and now it comes to me. Seb had said he was in bed, although not sleeping, and when I'd gone to brush my teeth something had tugged at my brain. He'd smelled of beer and day-old aftershave, not toothpaste. Granted, I may have hammered on his door before he'd had a chance to brush his teeth, but I'd also noticed a scrape on his knuckles as he'd reached out. A fresh scrape, the wound barely dry, as if he'd just caught himself on something. Something rough. Like a broken fence panel. *Was Seb the one watching me?* The idea of it makes my stomach roll, and I press a hand to my forehead. Everything about all of it — Seb's attention towards me from the day he and Tamsin first moved in, the way Nate was so hostile towards them but then merrily agreed to go home with Tamsin that night, the idea of the wife swap itself — all of it seems blurry and confusing, as though I am missing pieces or watching through a warped lens . . .

A hammering on the door jolts me from my thoughts, my pulse racing. I pull on a sundress, glancing at my phone as I tug it over my head. There are no further text messages, and it is far later in the day than I thought it was, the bedroom stuffy and stifling in the thick afternoon heat. Sprinting down the stairs, I yank the door open and skid to a halt, the last person I wanted to see standing on the doorstep.

'Seb.' Stepping out on to the garden path, I pull the door to behind me rather than inviting him in. 'What are you doing here?'

He gives me a sheepish smile. 'I wanted to apologise. I was going to bring you flowers but the last bouquet didn't seem to go down too well.'

I frown, my stomach pitching. *How does he know that?*

'You didn't bring them home,' he says, with a small shrug, as if reading my mind. 'I guessed at what you'd like but I suppose . . . perhaps it was inappropriate of me. Anyway, I just wanted to say I'm sorry for how I behaved last night. I think I might have overreacted.'

'Don't worry about it. It's all forgotten.' I cross my fingers behind my back hoping God doesn't strike me down for lying.

'Could I come in? Apologise properly. Explain myself, if you'll let me.'

The thought of Seb being in my house makes my insides shrivel. I don't really want to be alone with him, not after the way he was last night. It was as if a mask fell away to reveal who he really is, and the memory of it makes me go cold all over.

'I was actually just on my way out.'

Seb looks a little taken aback. 'Oh, well . . . maybe I can walk with you? Take you out for a late lunch maybe? Please, Hayley. I'd really like to make it up to you.'

If I say no, will he just hassle me until I agree? Seb's mask might have fallen away, but the blinkers I was wearing have too, and I don't buy his charming, apologetic act. The last thing I feel like doing is spending time with Seb after the way he behaved last night, but I'm also not stupid enough to throw away the opportunity to try and dig for more information. Maybe if I let him tag along, he'll let something slip.

'Sure. OK. I was only going for a walk anyway.'

We don't speak, not about anything of importance, until we reach the pub that sits on the canal. By some miracle, despite the warmth of the afternoon there are tables available in the sunshine and I snag one while Seb goes inside to order us sandwiches and cold cider. I slide my phone from my pocket, but there are still no other messages.

'Fruity cider OK?' Seb hands me a pint glass, condensation running over my fingers as he slides into the seat opposite me, clinking his glass against mine. 'Listen, I really am sorry about last night, it just threw me for a loop, you know? I wasn't expecting you to be in the house first of all, and I guess I just . . .' he trails off.

'I'm sorry if I took you by surprise.' I sip the cider and wait for him to continue.

'I guess it just hit me yesterday, you know? The fact that Tamsin might not be coming back.' He fiddles with the napkin-wrapped cutlery he brought back to the table with him. 'Before, I'd always heard from her by now, but I guess this time it's the real thing for her. She really has left me.'

His words are like a thousand tiny teeth, nibbling away at my insides. Because if he thinks Tamsin has left him for Nate, that means Nate has left me for Tamsin.

'. . . never realised.' Seb is still talking.

'Sorry, what?'

'I said, I guess she was miserable with me and I never realised. I suppose I was like you with Nate — I thought we were happy, that our marriage was a stable one. It just goes to show you never really know who your partner is.'

Fury flares in my veins and I grit my teeth. We are nothing like Seb and Tamsin, Nate and I. Nate isn't a bully, doesn't hurt me, and neither of us fantasise about sleeping with other people. At least, I never have. Not seriously.

'You really have no idea where she could have gone? She really doesn't have any family?' The photo of the young woman, Tamsin's sister, is bright in my mind. She definitely said it was her sister. Why is Seb lying about that too?

'None,' Seb says, staring down at the beer mat he's picking to shreds. 'I feel like such an idiot. I gave her everything and she's just tossed me aside like I'm rubbish by the side of the road.'

To be fair to him, I do understand that feeling. That's exactly how I feel Nate has treated me, if he really has left of his own accord. But still, things don't seem to be adding up.

'She has an audition tomorrow,' I say quietly, not sure if I should be reminding Seb of this. 'I saw it on the calendar stuck to your fridge last night. At the Brompton Studios, out past Heathrow.'

'And?' Seb's brows knit together and he leans in closer, his dark eyes never leaving my face.

'I'm going to go there. Confront her. Nate hasn't signed into the diary at work, so even if he is working no one at his office knows where he is. But Tamsin will still show up for an audition, right? She can't afford not to. It's not like she's employed, if she misses an audition surely that's a black mark against her name for any future work.'

Seb lets out a long sigh as the server approaches our table with our sandwiches. He waits until she leaves before he speaks. 'You really think she'll show up?'

I shrug. 'I don't know. I'm going anyway — I can't just leave things like this, Seb. If Nate has left me for Tamsin I deserve an explanation at the very least, and if I can't speak to him then I'm going to demand answers from Tamsin.'

'I don't think this is a good idea.' Seb's voice is low, and he seems reluctant to meet my eyes.

'Why? What's the worst that could happen?' In my eyes, the worst has already happened. I've lost my husband and someone I thought was my friend, and I'm not just going to lie down and accept it.

'You don't know her the way you think you do,' Seb says. 'She's . . . Tamsin can be reactionary. She can lash out if she's cornered. I don't want anything to happen to you.'

'Reactionary how?'

Seb pauses, his brows knitting together. 'She flies off the handle if you cross her. I've seen her yell at store assistants, at wait staff . . . she even—' he breaks off abruptly.

That doesn't sound like the Tamsin I know. I think about the champagne bottle dripping on her expensive skirt in Fortnum's, the way she waved the waiter away with a smile. Surely she would have reacted differently if she really is the way Seb says she is. If anything, from what I've witnessed, Seb is the one who can't control his temper. But then, did I ever really know Tamsin that well at all?

'I'm going,' I say. 'You said you would usually have heard from her by now, so clearly something isn't right. I need answers, Seb.' I leave my untouched sandwich and half-drunk pint of cider and get to my feet, suddenly keen to be away from him. 'And there's nothing you can do to stop me.'

CHAPTER 24

My mind is still turning over Seb's words the next morning as I sip on a cup of tea, killing time until I need to leave for Tamsin's audition. *You don't know her the way you think you do. She can lash out if she's cornered.* I never got that impression from Tamsin, but then despite our closeness over the few months, my belief that we were friends, I didn't really know her that well. *Maybe she really did burn herself cooking. Maybe I misread the altercation in the garden that time.* But then I remember the way Seb's face changed when I mentioned Alex's name, the way he flipped on me and marched me out of the house. Now I regret telling him about my plan to confront Tamsin at her audition, but I had thrown the words out in anger, furious at the idea that Seb thought he could tell me what to do. Regardless of whether Tamsin lashes out or not, there were still photographs of me, taken without my knowledge hidden in Seb's desk. Seb is lying about something.

Throwing the dregs of my tea into the sink, I grab Nate's car keys and reach into the understairs cupboard for a jacket, pausing at the sight of Tamsin's handbag thrown into the far corner. I had tossed it there in fury when I came back from Seb's on Sunday evening, after I realised she and Nate had disappeared together, forgetting all about it until now. Resisting the urge to rifle through it, I tug it to the front of the cupboard. I don't have time to look through her things now, I have to get to the audition before she does and find somewhere to lurk where she won't spot me.

Flying out of the front door, aware that the morning seems to be trickling away from me, I pause as I step out into the street where Nate's car is parked. At first glance nothing seems out of the ordinary, but as I look closer the car seems to be leaning at an odd angle.

'What the . . .' Moving around to the passenger side of the car I can see the front tyre is flat. Completely and utterly flat. 'Fuck.'

It wouldn't be the first time Nate has had a slow puncture on the car. He does so many miles that we're lucky the car is still standing. He's had punctures, wing mirrors clipped off, huge scratches in the bodywork from overgrown bushes as he rockets down country lanes, and I've thanked God more than once that it's a company car. I pull out my phone, intending to call the mobile mechanic about a new tyre, when I stop, my phone half-way to my ear. It isn't just the front tyre. The back tyre is flat too.

Crouching down, I prod at the front tyre with one finger. This is no simple puncture. There is an inch-long gash in the side of the tyre wall, a neat plunge with something sharp. As I move to the other tyre, I find the same thing. A perfect, neat inch-long slash in the rubber. Someone has done this deliberately. My knees give way and I crash down onto the tarmac, grit and stones digging into my skin.

'Are you OK, miss?' A teenage boy stands over me, frowning, his acne-scarred cheeks pinkening.

'Fine, thank you.' I push myself up to standing. 'Just a little accident.'

He nods and goes on his way, and I lean against Nate's car and stare at the Coopers' house. The car is parked directly outside our front gate — a small miracle for our street — and just feet from the Coopers' front garden. *Should I knock and ask if Seb saw anything strange last night?* Shaking the thought away, I head back towards my own house. I didn't exactly leave things in a good way yesterday afternoon with Seb when I stormed out of the pub. *And what if it was Seb? What if he was the one who slashed the tyres, furious after the way I spoke to him?* As I reach my own front door, the Ring doorbell stares back at me and I wonder why I didn't think about it before.

* * *

It takes me a moment to update the Ring app on my phone. I hadn't wanted it, hating the chime and the thought that Nate could see me going in and out all day long, not that I ever had anything to hide. It was more the fact the camera was at such an unflattering angle, making me appear dumpy and twice the size I really am.

The icon refreshes on my phone and I log in, praying it's the same login details Nate uses for everything. It is, and seconds later I'm looking at the street view from the camera affixed to my front door. The car is in the perfect position and my pulse spikes, anticipation making my fingers swipe too far as I run the timeline across the bottom of the screen. Suddenly I am looking at Nate and Tamsin on Saturday night, Nate turning to look over his shoulder at her as she almost tumbles into the rose bush, alcohol making her unsteady on her feet. There is no audio, but I catch the glimpse of a smile on his face as he turns and offers her a hand. She takes it, looking up at him from beneath lowered lashes like some sort of cut-price Princess Diana, and a spurt of white-hot rage laces my veins. Nate, however, simply hauls her into a steady upright position, and places his key in the lock. There is no smile on his face now, and something about his expression makes me jab at the screen and pause the recording. He looks . . . angry, almost. But I don't understand why. Clearly he's not cross with Tamsin, he smiled as he helped her regain her balance. Is it me? Is that who he was angry with? Did he not really want to do the swap after all? The thought that Nate only agreed to the swap because he thought it might be what I wanted makes my heart contract. As they step inside the house, the door swinging closed behind them, the video runs on, activated by a moth who hovers close enough for the security light to switch on.

It's as if a lightbulb goes off over my head and I groan aloud at my own stupidity. If the Ring camera caught the two of them coming into the house on Saturday night, then surely it would have picked them up leaving? I can watch the footage and see what time they left . . . and *how* they left, because half-empty coffee mugs and Tamsin's handbag left on the table doesn't scream leisurely Sunday stroll to me. Sliding the time bar along the bottom of the screen, I search for the next recorded movement. At 2.45 a.m. a figure appears at the end of the path and I pause it, my pulse skipping. I can't zoom in close enough to make out the person's features, but they seem to be male. Running the footage on, I don't know if I am relieved or disappointed when the figure passes the house, out of sight. The footage scrolls on, picking up a fox sprinting across the road, another fat moth hovering in the porch, and then the sun is rising and I appear on the screen, pale and dishevelled, unaware that my life is about to unravel. Frowning, I stop the video and rewind it, going back to the time frame where Nate and Tamsin appeared. This time I let it run without skipping, but nothing new comes up. The same dark figure appears, the same fox runs across the street, the same moth hovers in the porch. But there is no sign of Nate or Tamsin leaving. I don't understand why the cameras wouldn't have picked that up. I run it for a third time, this time keeping my eyes on the timestamp at the bottom of the frame. The video doesn't skip. They simply don't appear on the camera at all.

I don't know what to think. What I hoped would steer me towards some answers just seems to have raised more questions. Glancing back down at the screen, I see the footage has continued rolling and I see myself leaving for work, my face drawn as I turn back to lock the door. The postman leaves the package of books in the porch, his hair dampened by rain. Seb appears on the doorstep, the two of us leave, and then I see myself returning from the pub yesterday afternoon, fury and despair written all over my face. There is no sign of anyone collecting the books from the porch, and a shiver runs down my spine. Was it Nate? Tamsin? How did whoever it was get into the house without being picked up on the camera? I scrub my hands over my arms, a sudden chill seeping into my bones. Will Nate be watching this? Will he use it to check to see if I'm coping? Is he even able to see it? Or is it simply a case of out of sight out of mind?

Movement on the video drags my attention back and I press a hand to my mouth. In my excitement at realising I might be able to see when Nate and Tamsin had left, I almost forgot about the slashing of my tyres. Now, at 11.27 p.m. according to the time stamp, someone approaches the car. My heart is in my throat as I slow the footage, but whoever it is walks on, a woman following behind moments later. Hoping this isn't going to be a waste of time as well, I continue watching as the fox reappears, and then at 1.54 a.m. as the moon disappears behind a cloud, a figure appears. Leaning forward, my palms are sweaty as I pause the video. The figure approaches from the left-hand side of the camera, stopping as they reach Nate's car. They look around, over their shoulder, and I think I see them glance fleetingly up at my bedroom window, before they slink around the boot of the car to the road. To the passenger side. Holding my breath I roll the footage, watching in horror as they duck down, disappearing out of sight for a few seconds before they pop up again and move towards the front of the car, disappearing again seconds later.

'You bastard,' I hiss, rewinding the video. The figure is wearing a sweatshirt with the hood pulled up over his face. He is of slim build, but that's pretty much all I can make out. His features are darkened by the hood, but even so there is something familiar about him. As he pops up into the frame again, I slow the video down, watching as he glances over his shoulder once more, tucking something — presumably whatever he used to slash the tyres — into the front pocket of the sweatshirt. He comes back around the front of the car and breaks into a light jog, coming back the way he first appeared.

Sitting back against the sofa I press a hand to my mouth. The figure is familiar — he's a similar height and build as Seb. Nausea washes over me, my stomach cramping as shock renders me speechless. Seb? Could Seb be the one who slashed my tyres? My lips feel numb, and I run my tongue over my teeth. I roll the footage back and watch it again, my eyes aching with the concentration. Seb slashed my tyres just hours after I told him I was going to drive out to Tamsin's audition and confront her. Clearly he doesn't want me speaking to her. Getting to my feet, I begin to pace, my mind working overtime. No matter how I look at things, no matter how much Seb tries to tell me that Tamsin isn't the person I think she is, everything always keeps coming back to him. I know he's behind all of this somehow, and I need to get inside his house — properly this time, planned and with no chance of getting caught — and find out exactly what the hell he is hiding.

CHAPTER 25

Even if I hadn't spent all this time searching through the Ring camera footage, I still wouldn't have made it to Tamsin's audition on time using public transport, so that's that plan out of the window. Instead, I turn my attention to the handbag tossed into the cupboard under my stairs. Pulling it out, I run my fingers over the soft leather. It's some Italian designer that I've never heard of before, but judging by the way the leather feels butter soft beneath my fingertips, I am sure it costs far more than I could ever afford. I don't care about that though — for once I am not coveting Tamsin's accessories. I am coveting what might be inside the bag . . . like her house keys.

I need to get into Seb's house, and I can't keep breaking in. It's bad enough that he's caught me once already, and I am aware that the old lady who lives across the street from us never leaves her sitting room window. If I let myself in with a key, it stands to reason that I have permission to be there.

Upending the bag on to the kitchen table, I rake through the items one by one. There is a Charlotte Tilbury lipstick in *Pillow Talk*, and I remember asking Tamsin what shade she was wearing one evening after work, when we went for drinks. I'd gone out the next day and bought the same colour, believing Tamsin when she told me it was a shade that suited everyone. Everyone except me, it seems. I had worn it once, tossing it into the bottom of my make-up bag when Nate had commented on it with a wrinkle of his nose. It was too nude, too meh, too *bland* for me, making me look even more washed out and pale, and I had been annoyed at wasting £29 on it, not realising it came in different shades. Tamsin's is worn down to a tiny stump, the outer casing scratched and battered.

There is a packet of tissues, a biro without a lid, hair grips and a book with a title that makes me snort aloud. *The Zen Monkey and the Lotus Flower: 52 stories to relieve stress, find happiness and live your best life.* Is this a joke? Tamsin has been reading how to live her best life, all while turning mine upside down, tugging at a loose thread until the entire thing unravels. With a primal yell, I pick up the book and tear off the front cover before hurling it across the kitchen. It crashes against the patio doors with a thump before hitting the floor, and hot tears scorch my eyes, my chest hitching. *Keep it together, Hayley.* I breathe in deeply through my nose, trying to get my emotions under control. There'll be time later, when I find Nate and get to the bottom of exactly what the fuck is going on here, to rage and shout and toss things across the room.

Something falls to the floor with a clatter and I stoop to pick it up. *Tamsin's house keys.* The bunch is small — just the front door key, what I assume to be a back door key and a simple keychain in the shape of a daisy. Nothing like my unwieldy bunch, which includes keys that Nate and I have long forgotten what they were for, and a bunch of keyrings I've picked up over the years. I tuck them into the pocket of my jeans, a wave of relief washing over me at the thought of not having to squeeze my hips through the tiny kitchen window again. Retrieving the torn book from the floor, I scoop everything on the table into a pile, ready to return it to Tamsin's bag, but when I lift the leather strap, the bag still feels oddly weighty, as if something is left inside. Opening the zipper fully, I peer in, swishing my hand around. There is nothing in it, and yet, it still feels too heavy to be completely empty. Impatient now, I tug the bag closer, yanking the zippered edge far apart and sliding my hand inside, running my fingers along the silky interior. My fingers rub against a line of stitching in the inside fabric and I pause, my spine tingling. Twisting the leather so that the interior lining is exposed, I can see a small line of stitching where an invisible zip hides a secret pocket. My hands shaking, I tug on the tiny zip tag and inch it open, sliding my hand inside.

I knew it. There's something in here. My fingers close around a small solid object and I tug it free, my heart in my throat. It's a phone. A tiny old-fashioned Nokia, with no camera, and a screen so small you'd struggle to read a text on it. Turning it over in my hands, I let out a long breath. Clearly Tamsin was hiding this from Seb . . . why else would it be tucked inside her bag, in a secret pocket? Pressing down on the power button I wait a moment, but nothing happens. The screen stays blank. The phone is dead. It's an old model — the kind I had way back in the early 2000s — and when I reach into the small pocket again I come up empty. There is no charger, and I'm not even sure where I would get one for a model this old. I'm pulling my own phone out of my pocket to google the best place to buy an old phone charger when the chime of the Ring doorbell ricochets through the house.

'Shit.' My phone drops to the floor as I scramble to shove Tamsin's belongings back inside her bag, with the exception of the tiny, dead phone which I stuff into my pocket. 'Just a minute,' I call out, knowing, just *knowing*, it will be Seb. Shoving Tamsin's handbag behind a cushion as I hurry past the sofa, I pause at the front door and take a deep breath, smoothing my hair down. *Be cool, Hayley.*

'Oh.' The person on the front doorstep is the last person I expected to see, and I peer past her, as if reassuring myself Seb isn't following behind.

'I'm sure you weren't expecting me, but I thought I'd just pop by,' Wendy says with a bright smile. 'Gosh, I didn't realise you lived on such a lovely street.'

'Um . . . thanks?' *Why is she here?* I draw in another deep breath, adrenaline still flying around my body at the thought of having to confront Seb over my flat tyres.

'Really lovely and quiet, you lucky thing.' She glances over the wild rosebush in the direction of the Coopers. 'And what about the neighbours? Do you get on well with them?'

'Fairly,' I manage, my mind racing. *Is Wendy just being friendly, or is there an undercurrent to her tone?* I'm not sure if I'm reading into something that isn't really there.

'Always good when you get along well, isn't it? Look, I know I should be at the office, but don't panic, everything is all in hand.' Wendy peeps over my shoulder into the hallway and I turn, half expecting to see someone standing behind me. 'Can I come in?'

Part of me wants to shriek no in her face and slam the door, but that's not going to help. Instead, I stand to one side with a wan smile and she steps into the hallway.

'Oh, gorgeous wallpaper,' she says, sliding her cardigan off and hanging it over the newel post, where Nate usually leaves his jacket.

'It's old,' I say. We haven't redecorated anything in the house apart from the sitting room since I inherited it from my grandmother.

'Vintage, you mean,' Wendy says with a wink, following me as I lead her through into the kitchen. 'Oh gosh. It really is vintage in here.'

'We keep meaning to update things, but you know how it is . . .' Lord knows why I am explaining myself to Wendy, of all people. 'I'm sorry, Wendy, but . . . why are you here? Has something happened? Do I need to come back to work?'

Wendy hikes her huge handbag up over her shoulder and tilts her head, her forehead crinkling in concern. 'Honestly, Hayley, I came by to see how you are. I've been worried about you.'

'You have?'

'Yes. I mean, I know you said you're taking time out for personal reasons, but we're friends, aren't we? We've worked together for a long time. Obviously I'm going to worry about you.'

Friends? I wouldn't exactly call myself and Wendy friends, but I guess we have worked together the longest out of everyone else in that office. I was only going to work there for a year or two, just until Nate and I got ourselves on our feet after I inherited the house, but now it's eight years later and I'm still there.

'Right.' I force a smile, but all I can think about is Tamsin's house keys and the tiny mobile phone stuffed into the pocket of my jeans, and figuring out when Seb is going to be out of the house for a while.

'Anyway, I was wondering if you wanted to come for dinner with me and Matt one evening? Nate is invited, too. That is . . . if he's around?' She widens her eyes and I realise this is a snooping mission. Wendy is the brave soldier doing a recce for information for the rest of the office gossips.

'He works away, Wendy. You know that,' I say tightly. 'I'm still sorting a few bits out here so I'll take a rain check for now. Maybe once I'm back in the office.' Immediately I could kick myself for saying that. I gently grip Wendy's elbow and turn her around, pointing her back towards the front door. 'I appreciate the visit though.'

'Oh yes, the office.' Wendy pauses and I grit my teeth. 'When do you think you might be back? Only, there's a woman who keeps calling for you.'

'A woman? Who?'

Wendy shrugs. 'She won't leave her name. She's called twice, but every time I say you're out of the office she just hangs up.' She peers at me closely, as if trying to read answers from my face, and I battle to keep my face blank.

Could it be Tamsin? But why wouldn't she call my mobile? And then I remember, her phone was left down the side of her sofa, and obviously she doesn't have the little burner phone I just discovered hidden in her bag. It would be easy for her to get my office number. But why would she be calling me if she's run off with my husband?

'Well, gosh, I have no idea who that might be,' I manage to press out from between dry lips. 'I guess it must be a client. Give her my email address if she calls again . . .' I trail off, my mind working overtime. 'Tell her . . . tell her I'm on leave, but I am responding to emails. If it's important I'll get straight back to her immediately.'

'OK.' Wendy gives me a quizzical look. 'Well, I'm glad you seem to be . . . *fine*.' She gives me a sharp-toothed smile, quick and pointy, as I guide her over the threshold and back out on to the garden path.

'Thanks for stopping by.' I grip the door, ready to close it in her face if I have to. Behind me, I hear the slam of a door closing somewhere next door. The walls are so thin between the houses, and I realise to my disappointment that Seb must still be home.

Wendy smiles that pointy smile again and begins to walk away, but she turns before I can exhale in relief. 'Oh! Just one more thing,' she says, delving into her suitcase sized handbag. 'The real reason I came.' She digs around and pulls out a jiffy bag, the envelope still sealed.

'What's this?' My name is written in block letters in thick black Sharpie on the front.

Wendy shrugs. 'It came to the office for you, special delivery. I would have opened it like the rest of the post in your absence, but it's quite clearly marked private and confidential.' She runs her eyes greedily over the package, her curiosity a bright, burning flame.

'Great, thanks. I appreciate it,' I say, waving the package at her and closing the door in her face before she can speak again. Leaning against the front door, I finally let out the long, stifled breath I've been holding, closing my eyes for the briefest of seconds before I rip open the jiffy bag.

A slim journal falls into my hands, the maroon cover stamped with *2017* in gold leaf. It feels expensive, the leather cover soft and buttery, like Tamsin's bag, and I open it to the first page. *It's a diary.* A diary, filled with page after page of neatly sloping handwriting. Handwriting I recognise. This is Tamsin's diary.

CHAPTER 26

Feeling slightly grubby, the good girl in me not comfortable with the idea of reading the innermost thoughts of someone I believed to be a friend even if she has betrayed me, I open the diary cover and smooth the first page over with one finger.

It seems fairly innocuous. Tamsin writes about having coffee with a friend, someone named Florence who she hasn't seen for years. There is a tiny part of me that smarts with jealousy at the thought of Tamsin having someone else, a friend she's confided in other than me despite what's happened. There is no date at the top of the page, and I have no way of knowing how recently this occurred.

There's a reason this has been sent to me. I don't know who sent it — I can only assume it was Tamsin — but if she sent it to me at work, then it means there's something in here that she wants me to know. My head spins, confusion crinkling my brow. Nothing, and I mean *nothing* seems to have made sense since the moment Nate agreed to the wife swap.

My hand goes to my pocket. I need to see what's on the burner phone, read the diary and get into the house next door so I can snoop properly on Seb and find out what he knows. Because there's something odd about the way he seems so nonchalant about Tamsin and Nate disappearing together. It's almost as if he was half expecting it to happen, which maybe he was, given the fact he's said that Tamsin has done this before. But surely, even if she has done this kind of thing before, shouldn't he also be getting worried by now?

As if I have conjured him up out of thin air, there is the sound of footsteps on the path outside and I move to the window to see Seb striding down his front path towards the road. I'm not sure if I imagine the way his gaze flicks towards my lop-sided car and my hand goes to my pocket again, to the tiny daisy keychain on Tamsin's house keys. I could go in now, I think, my pulse starting to race. I could let myself inside and root through his things in the hope that some light will be shed on this whole horrible mess. I am halfway down my own front path when common sense comes knocking. It's the middle of the afternoon. Seb clearly hasn't been at work today, and I have no idea when he's due to return to the house. For all I know, he's popped out for a pint of milk. It makes more sense to find out when he's going to be gone for a good chunk of time and then let myself in.

Ducking back inside, I call a mobile mechanic to come out and change the damaged tyres on the car, and then head straight for the kitchen and pour myself a large glass of wine. I don't care that it's barely three o'clock — it's five o'clock somewhere — and after dealing with Wendy and having Tamsin's diary literally fall into my lap, I think I'm going to need a drink. Curling up on the sofa, I take a large gulp of wine and open the cover of the diary, Tamsin's familiar writing sprawling across the crisp, white pages. *Come on, Tamsin*, I think, the wine already buzzing through my veins, *show me your secrets*.

* * *

Hours later, with the wine long gone and a thumping headache pounding at my temples, I am halfway through the diary and my stomach is growling. Placing the journal face down on the coffee table I head for the kitchen to pour a glass of water and pull a microwave lasagne out of the freezer. Nate would be horrified to see the crap I eat when he's not here — after being on the road all week he likes a home-cooked meal when he comes back, and sometimes that's the only time I eat properly. The thought that Nate might not come back at all makes my breath catch in my throat and I stab at the film on the ready meal a little too harshly, blinking back tears.

As I wait for the food to ping, I think over the diary entries so far. Towards the beginning it was bland, dry drivel about her day. The coffee with an old friend, the audition where she swears she bumped into Jude Law (although he never responded when she called his name), the sushi she ate on the tube, even though she knew everyone on that train hated her for it. I wanted to skip past these parts, but I am forcing myself to read slowly, to absorb every word just in case there's something in there that I'm missing. Some code or something that Tamsin thinks only I will understand. I'm glad I have taken my time, because the last couple of entries have been different. Her mood, and writing, has shifted. Rather than writing about mundane, everyday things she's started talking about her feelings. The microwave pings and I scoop out the hot plastic tray with a tea towel, juggling it in one hand as I return to the sofa, and the diary to reread the last entries.

Sometimes I wonder what I'm even doing this for. The years I've put in hardly seem worth it for the reward.

I frown at this. Does she mean her job? I understand that it might be hard to not have a steady income, but Seb earns enough for both of them to live on comfortably. Unless she doesn't mean work at all.

*I'm all about a can-do attitude, but lately I just feel as if
I can't do it any more. It's a relentless merry-go-round that
never seems to slow. I thought there would be cycles . . . a
calm to follow the storm, but just lately it all feels like storm.*

My skin prickles at this, my nerve endings singing as the hairs
rise on my forearms. Could she be talking about Seb? I think of
the way he grabbed her by the arm, the way her face screwed up
in pain. I wish there was a date on the page, so I could figure out
when exactly she's talking about.

*Sometimes I look at him and it's as if the years have
melted away. He still looks like the same boy I saw standing
on the fringes of the party, that first time I laid eyes on him.
I remember him standing in the kitchen, a beer in his hand,
and thinking, 'Oh, that's you, is it?' Now though, he might
look the same but he's not, not on the inside. He's harder,
angrier, more brittle.*

I think of Nate at these words, wondering how I failed to see
how similar he and Seb can be at times. Nate was soft, vulnerable,
when I first met him. I remember thinking as I passed him his
change over the bar how calm he was. Placid, kind, not leering at
my tits or clicking his fingers when there was a queue for drinks.
He was always surrounded by people, but never seemed to realise
how well-liked he was, how the girls followed him with their eyes
and how the boys laughed loudly at his jokes. Now, sometimes,
when he's tired after a long week on the road he can snap, his
tone sharp and his eyes cold, and it catches me by surprise. I do
it, too. I know I do, sometimes I even enjoy the way my words
hook under Nate's skin like little barbs, if it means we can make
up again later. Maybe we all grow harder and more brittle with

age and experience, but something about the way Tamsin writes makes my stomach sink, a dragging sensation that I fear will pull me under completely.

Lies. So many lies. All the time, about everything. This life he has constructed, it's all a house of cards and I will be the only one not surprised when it crashes down around him. For now, I'll just nod and smile, agree with everything, sit with the others as they all say how well he's doing and I'll pretend like everything is OK. I'll pretend I don't know what he did. I'll choke down the fear that grips me by the throat every time he catches my eye, giving me that look. The look that tells me that if I cross him he'll shut me down. He'll silence me for good.

The slam of a car door makes me jump and I drop the diary as I get to my feet, moving to the front window. Dusk has fallen and I peer out into the darkness, the outline of my tilted car just outside the gate a reminder that someone wants to shut me down too. *Seb?* The thought that Tamsin might have been living with an abuser feels even more real now I've read her diary entries. I had hoped I was mistaken that time in the garden, hoped I might have seen something that didn't really happen, but Tamsin's words . . . she sounds desperately miserable and, more importantly, afraid. Afraid of what Seb might do if she steps out of line. The idea that Seb is more than just a man who controls his wife with his fists crawls up my throat and threatens to choke me.

A shape moves at the periphery of my vision and I instinctively draw back from the window, adrenaline spurting through my veins. I watch as someone creeps along my front garden path, coming from around the side of my house and crossing the street. They are wearing a hoody, the hood drawn up, and I think of the footage on the Ring camera, of the person who slashed my tyres. Was it Seb? Or someone else? The figure turns back as they reach the pavement on the other side of the road, glancing back over their shoulder and I shiver, tucking myself out of sight, not sure if someone really is watching me or if I am just being paranoid. I was stalked back in high school, by a boy who followed me to school, who watched me through my bedroom window and lurked around every corner I turned. He denied it when I confronted him, told me I was mad, but I remember how it felt and this is the feeling I have now. Of eyes on me, all the time. Fumbling for my phone, I tap the screen for Nate's number with a shaking hand and wait for it to connect. Unsurprisingly it goes straight to voicemail and I leave a message, my voice trembling.

'Nate, wherever you are, please come home. Whatever has happened we can fix this, nothing is unforgivable. Please? I'm scared.'

Moving away from the window, I stoop to pick up the diary from the floor, pausing as a slip of paper falls out from between the back pages. It looks like a newspaper article, clipped neatly so that only the headline and a photograph remain. It's old, the paper soft and worn and I catch my breath as I read the headline.

MISSING GIRL FOUND DEAD AFTER FOUR DAYS

My ribs feel compressed, caught in a vice and I struggle to draw in a breath as I stare down at the photograph. My hand covers my mouth and for a moment I think I might be sick, because I know her. I recognise this girl, this missing girl who was found after four long days. She's the girl from the photograph on Tamsin's fridge. She's the sister Seb swears Tamsin doesn't have.

CHAPTER 27

Is that what he meant when he said she didn't have a sister? Shock makes my knees wobbly, and I crave the nicotine rush of a cigarette. Still clutching the clipping I rummage in the kitchen drawer for the battered pack of emergency Benson and Hedges and a lighter, and stumble out into the garden, pausing as I step outside to scan for movement at the end of the garden. Satisfied there is only the swaying of tree branches, and no sinister figure loitering in the shadows, I light the cigarette and draw in a long breath, the crackle of embers and the taste of smoke in my lungs immediately slowing my pulse. Blowing out a long stream of smoke, I inhale again immediately, drawing so hard this time that my head spins from the rush of nicotine.

'Fuck,' I breathe out, pressing my other hand to my forehead, before I run my eyes over the newspaper photo again. It's her. At least, I think it's her. There's only one way to be sure. My eyes flick over the fence towards the Coopers patio doors. I need to check the photo on the fridge and see if it really is the girl in the article. Stubbing out my cigarette I light another, the craving still not satisfied even though I feel sick, as I ponder Seb's words. *She doesn't have a sister*. I thought he'd meant that Tamsin had never had a sister, something that I knew he was lying about because Tamsin had told me herself she had a sister. Did he just mean that Tamsin didn't have a sister *any more*? *So many lies*. Tamsin wasn't wrong when she wrote that in her diary. Fear swirls in my stomach, icy ripples branching out into my bloodstream.

'That's not what I said.' The words float over the fence and I pause, cigarette halfway to my mouth as confusion ripples through me. For a moment I think I must have spoken aloud, before I realise Seb is pacing the patio next door, his phone clamped to his ear. 'That's not . . .' he sighs with frustration and I carefully stub out my fag and lift my chair, moving silently closer to the fence.

There is a scuffing noise, and I peep through the tiny knothole to see Seb toeing the edge of the patio slabs, his white trainers scraping at the green tinge that grows around the solar lights, as Tank sniffs at a bush before letting out a long stream of piss against it. Seb's brows are drawn together as he turns and paces across the patio, his shoulders hunched.

'Are you kidding me?' he hisses, and I press my face right against the fence as my breathing threatens to drown out his voice. 'No. No. We stick to what we agreed—'

I watch as he balls the fist of his free hand and kicks out at the fire pit, narrowly missing the glass edging.

'I am fucking calm,' he says in a low voice, heading back in my direction. I pull back away from the fence, the lighter balanced on the arm of my chair hitting the patio with a tinny clash as the security light goes on overhead, illuminating my garden. Tank lets out a sharp bark and Seb's head snaps up, turning to look in my direction. 'I have to— I've got to go.'

Shit. Pushing my chair away, I am leaning over on the pretence of picking up the lighter when Seb's face appears over the top of the fence.

'Hayley. I didn't realise you were out here.'

I straighten up, plastering on a wimpy smile and hold up the lighter. 'Just having a cheeky cigarette. Nate doesn't like it when I smoke.'

'Is Nate back?' Seb's face darkens and my mouth goes dry, but it's not from the nicotine.

I shake my head and force myself to push another cigarette from the pack, even though the thought of smoking another one makes me feel nauseous. 'No, he's not. I would have told you if he'd come back. Tamsin would be back too, wouldn't she?' *Who was he on the phone to?* 'Have you heard from her?' The air seems to thicken and every muscle in my body tenses.

'No.' Seb's tone is short, and I hear Tank snuffle against the fence line. 'And I don't know that I'd want to speak to her right now. I've got shit going on at work, idiots who aren't listening to what I'm saying, and I haven't told anyone there that she's gone off. If I talked to her right now, I think I'd explode.' He pushes a hand through his hair and seems to visibly sag before me. 'Sorry. It's been a bit much today. Do you mind?' He gestures towards the lit cigarette in my hand and I pass it over the fence willingly.

'I know how you feel,' I say. 'I've had a bit of a day too. The car has two flat tyres. I didn't realise until I went to leave the house this morning.'

'*Two* flat tyres?' He raises an eyebrow. I could well believe he had nothing to do with it if I hadn't seen the figure on the Ring camera footage. The figure who I could have sworn was him, but now looking at the confusion on his face, I feel less certain. 'Want me to take a look?'

Seb looks innocent, his face pleasantly blank, but there is still a ripple of unease travelling along my spine. 'I've called a mechanic.'

'How long are they going to be? I don't mind taking a look for you. It's the neighbourly thing to do, right?' He smiles at me, but I don't feel reassured.

'Uh, sure. OK. I'll meet you out the front.'

Hurrying back inside, I tuck the newspaper article back into the diary and stash it under the sofa cushions before hurrying out to the front of the house. Seb is already on the pavement, stroking his chin as he eyes up the car.

'Weird,' he says, crouching down beside the rear tyre, He pokes at it, pressing down hard on the rubber. 'Hayley . . . this is deliberate.'

'Really?' I widen my eyes. Does he think I'm stupid? Or is he trying to convince me that he has nothing to do with this?

Seb gets to his feet, his expression quizzical. 'Did you not look at the tyres? Did you not see the holes in the sides? Someone has stuck something in the wall of both tyres — a knife, I'd say, if I had to guess.'

I'm not sure he does have to guess. 'Did you see anything?'

'Me?' Seb cocks his head on one side. 'Why would I have seen anything?'

I shrug. 'I don't know. The car is parked next to your garden path, and it must have happened sometime between me coming home from the pub yesterday and earlier today when I left the house. I don't know. Maybe you might have seen something . . . you don't go to bed early.'

Seb shakes his head and I can't tell if the regret on his face is real or manufactured. 'I did last night. I was asleep by eleven.'

I don't believe him. 'I can check the Ring camera,' I say, testing him. 'It will pick up whoever did this, the car is parked close enough to the camera.'

'Oh.' Seb looks shocked for the briefest of seconds before he composes himself. 'Well, that's great. I never even realised you had one of those.' A light goes on behind his eyes. 'Does that mean . . . ?'

'No,' I say, immediately knowing what he's thinking. 'I already checked. There's nothing on there to show Tamsin and Nate leaving on Sunday morning. Weird, eh?'

'Yeah. That is really strange.' Seb seems to deflate and his gaze flicks over my shoulder, to my front door and the camera winking there. 'I don't know about you, but I could use a drink. Do you want to come over to mine? It must be a terrible shock, finding out that someone did this to your car deliberately.'

I give a thin smile, doing my damnedest to make it seem genuine. Honestly, I would rather head back to my own house, lock the doors and get into bed with his wife's diary, but I realise that this is the perfect opportunity for me to get inside the house legitimately. There will be nothing to stop me from checking the fridge for the photo of Tamsin's sister, and if I'm lucky I might even be able to slide it into my pocket while he isn't looking. 'Sure,' I say, rearranging my face to look suitably anxious, which isn't hard given the way my pulse skyrockets when I'm around Seb, and not in a good way. Not any more.

I am on my guard as I follow Seb into his house, hoping that the Ring camera will have picked us up standing on the pavement together. The things written in Tamsin's diary, the underlying note of fear that laces her words seems to have seeped through my pores and into my bones. I'm on edge, my insides frantic with the beat of a thousand butterfly wings.

Seb leads me directly into the kitchen, exactly where I need to be.

'Wine? Or something stronger?' Seb seems more relaxed now we are inside, away from the car, and he smiles as he holds up a bottle of Au vodka.

'Just tea for me, thanks.' The wine buzz from earlier has faded to leave me feeling dehydrated and headachy, and besides, the thought of being even slightly tipsy and off my game around Seb makes me uncomfortable.

'It must have been a bad day,' Seb teases, seeming more like his old self. 'Are you sure I can't tempt you? I won't lie, I'm going to have a shot of this.' He twists the cap on the vodka, before leaning into the freezer and pulling out a shot glass.

'No, just tea is fine. I can make it.' Filling the kettle, I glance towards the fridge, but can't see the photo of Tamsin's sister from this angle. Seb sits at the table, shooting his first shot and then pouring another that he sips slowly.

'So,' he says as I take a seat opposite him with my cup of tea. From here I can see the fridge from the front and side, and I discreetly run my eyes over it. For a couple who seem so minimalist — at least downstairs anyway — it strikes a jarring note that the fridge is covered with postcards, reminders and memos. 'You didn't go to the audition after all?'

'Nope,' I shake my head. 'I would never have made it on public transport, not in time to get there before Tamsin and surprise her. And obviously I couldn't take the car . . .' I pause for a moment, taking care not to stumble over my words. 'I thought you said it wasn't a good idea for me to go anyway.'

Seb stares at me for a moment, his gaze boring into me until I feel the prickle of sweat under my arms and along my collar. 'I just didn't want something to happen to you, that's all. I told you, Tamsin can be unpredictable, especially if she feels trapped, or tricked into something. There's no telling how she will react.'

Something about his tone raises the hairs on the back of my neck. 'Well, I didn't have to worry about it in the end, thanks to whoever decided to slash my tyres.' Seb says nothing, just takes another drink. 'This tea needs milk.'

Shoving back my chair I head to the fridge, pausing at the door. The takeaway menus and old postcards still litter the front, but the calendar — the one that showed Tamsin's audition — is gone. Pulling out the milk, I top up my cup, ruining the tea and shove it back in the door of the fridge. I can't see the photo of Tamsin's sister. Lifting the edge of a takeaway menu with one finger I check behind it, but the photo isn't there.

'Looking for something?' Seb's breath is hot in my ear as he leans in close, and reaches for the vodka bottle.

'No,' I manage, my tongue sticking to my teeth. 'Just looking at this menu . . . I don't think I've eaten a proper meal since Nate left.'

'Me neither. Apart from your delicious steaks, anyway.' Seb sinks another shot, as my heart sinks alongside. The drunker he gets, the meaner he's going to get, according to Tamsin's diary. 'Anyway, you didn't need to worry about seeing Tamsin at the audition. She didn't show.'

'She . . . didn't show?' Something about the way he says it makes my knees feel wobbly and my eyes shoot to the fridge door again, still searching out the photo that I know now is missing.

'Nope. I know this, because I did.' He gives me a self-satisfied look.

'You . . . did?' I don't sit back down at the table. Instead I pick up my cup and toss the tea into the sink, ignoring Seb's raised eyebrows. The sooner I get out of here the better. 'Wow. I didn't think you were going to . . . I mean, weren't you worried she would react badly if she saw you? Feel trapped?' I think for a moment my heart is going to burst out of my chest as Seb turns his dark eyes on me, his fingers gripping the shot glass so hard I think it might shatter.

'I knew she wouldn't show,' he says, the faintest tinge of a slur to his words. 'But I wanted to make sure.'

How did he know she wouldn't show? The memory of waking up the night of the swap to find the bed empty, sure the closing of a door had jolted me from sleep hits me like a sledgehammer. 'Didn't there . . .' I swallow, my throat thick. 'Didn't there used to be a photo on the fridge? Of a girl? Tamsin's sister.'

Seb frowns, shoving back his chair so hard it makes me jump. 'I already told you, Tamsin doesn't have a sister.'

'My mistake.' On legs that don't seem to want to work properly I skirt past him. 'I should go. Thanks for the tea.'

It's only once I am safely back in my own house, the curtains drawn, the doors locked and the diary on the bed beside me that I let myself breathe. *Why did Seb leave the bedroom the night of the swap?* I had been so drunk, only half-conscious when I woke, that he could easily have left the house and I wouldn't have known. Maybe he wasn't so keen on the idea of the swap as Tamsin was . . . and he seemed shaken by the fact that we have a Ring camera on the front door. I scrub my hands over my face. Seb didn't want me to go to the audition, claiming that he was worried she would be volatile if she saw me, yet in the next breath he was telling me he was sure Tamsin wouldn't show . . . but he went along himself to check.

The thought hits me, straight in the solar plexus and I sit up with a gasp. I definitely heard a door slam at Seb's house when Wendy was standing in my house handing over the diary at a time when I should have been chasing down Tamsin. If Seb had gone to the audition that day . . . who was in their house?

CHAPTER 28

Was it Tamsin? Nate? Did Seb lie to me and not go to the audition at all, because he already knew there was no way Tamsin could have been there? Part of me wants to laugh in my own face. Tell myself I've watched far too many Netflix documentaries and the idea that my next-door neighbour might have found a way to get rid of his wife and my husband while I was sleeping beside him in their bed is utterly ridiculous. That it's simply a case of my husband finding Seb's wife more attractive than me and they split together. But then, I look down at the diary, the corner of the article about the missing girl peeping out from between the pages, and I know there's more to it than that.

I open the diary to the last page I read, but I don't see the words. I only see the photograph of the laughing girl, pinned with a magnet to Tamsin's fridge, my stomach lurching at the memory. I hear her tell me that's her sister, telling me she did TV work when she was younger, that's how I vaguely knew her face. I know I didn't imagine all that, so why is Seb lying to me? The photo was on the fridge when Tamsin hosted her party, and she and Nate vanished the following night. Seb is the only one who could have removed the photo since then, but it doesn't make sense why. *What does he know?* If Tamsin really is the one who sent me her diary with the clipping inside, it tells me that she wants me to dig around. She wants me to find out the truth.

Turning my attention back to the diary I pick up where I left off. Tamsin has mentioned the fact they are moving, and I find myself wanting to skip ahead to see if she mentions me. She talks about that first day, the day I saw them together on the path, laughing and kissing.

> *It feels as though we have done the right thing, although I am not sure how long this feeling will last. I could feel eyes on us as we unpacked the van, but he told me I was being ridiculous. Paranoid. That no one else knows why we are here.*

My skin prickles at that. She makes it sound as if there were another agenda for them moving here, instead of what she told me. That they wanted a bigger place to start a family and could finally afford it. A dart of betrayal pierces my heart. I had imagined us raising our kids alongside each other, the children being friends just like us, and now it sounds as though this wasn't the only reason they moved here. Suddenly hot under the duvet, I shift my legs into the cool spot. It sounds as though they were here for another reason entirely.

> *He hasn't changed, and I am not sure why I thought he might have done. This evening I went down to the basement, planning on picking out wine for drinks with the new neighbours (once again, I am reduced to being a 'neighbour') and he followed me, pressing himself so close to me that I thought he was going to kiss me. Instead he asked me if I was happy. I told him I was, but I lied and he knows it. I'll only be happy when I know the truth about what happened to Lola.*

Lola. The name sends a shiver down my spine and I unfold the article, running my eyes over her face. Goosebumps rise on my arms and the sense of dread that creeps over me forms ice crystals in my veins. At the bottom of the clipping, underneath the picture are the words:

Lola Goode, 21, missing since Friday evening

I hadn't noticed them before, and I swallow hard. *Goode by name, good by nature.* The words swim into my mind unbidden, and I run my eyes over her face. She does look good by nature. Her smile is sunny and the light catches her blonde hair, giving her a soft, golden halo. An angel, with no idea of what's coming to her.

The final diary entry is short, less than a page. The first line reads, *Things are coming to a head*, the rest of the entry scored out with thick, black marker pen. As I raise the book towards my bedside lamp a piercing scream comes from the garden, the frantic, terrified cry of a hysterical woman. Leaping from the bed, I drop the diary to the floor as I run to the window, my chest tightening and my breath coming in loud pants. There is nothing to be seen save for a patch of white moonlight puddling across the lawn. Then the scream comes again, making me shriek aloud in return.

Turning back to the bed I rummage through the bed clothes for my phone, jabbing at the nine on the screen before turning back to the window. If I call the police, what do I say? Will they come out if I tell them I saw nothing but heard screaming? The scream comes again, but from further away this time and then a fox appears at the edge of the garden, carrying something small in its mouth. Relief washes over me and I clear my phone screen. *A fox, that's all.* Probably glad of something organic to eat instead of rubbish out of the bin. The fox trots across the lawn, jumping the fence out into the street and I let out a breath, but it catches in my throat as I stare at the trees by the broken fence panel. I could have sworn I saw movement out there, a larger shadow moving stealthily away from the house. Too big to be a fox. More . . . human sized. My fingers itch for my phone, to press nine three times, but I don't. Part of me knows I won't be a priority, and another part of me — a dark, twisted part that I thought I'd long put to bed — wants whoever it is, whether it's Seb, or Tamsin, or even Nate, to challenge me. To show themselves.

Shivering, I close the curtains tightly and climb back into bed, trying to calm my racing heart enough to finish the last diary page. Still, only the first sentence is visible and I hold the book towards the lamp again, trying to read the words through the thick marker pen. Parts of the page have melted away under the ink, leaving a soft-edged gap in the paper, but towards the bottom I think I can make out a couple of words. Party. Lola. *Rev* — Revenge? Revelation? . . . *hurt me*. And then, in the final sentence I think I can make out the words, 'help' and 'Nate'.

I sit up. Why is Tamsin writing about Nate in her diary? This doesn't feel . . . illicit, as such, but it still feels off. She hasn't mentioned me by name at all in the diary, but here is Nate's name, barely visible beneath the vicious strokes of marker pen. The more I discover about Tamsin, the more I realise that perhaps we weren't really friends the way I thought we were. I had thought that she might have mentioned my name, might have talked about meeting me, our connection, the fun times we spent together shopping and talking about our marriages, but there is nothing. Just Nate's name scored out in black pen.

Did she use Nate? The notion strikes me, as hard and fast as a cobra bite. She used the wife swap to get Nate alone. Seb was abusing her, hurting her, and she needed to get away without raising his suspicions. The calendar on the fridge wasn't just a gentle reminder to the two of them of the appointments and meetings they had booked in — it was a way for Seb to log where she was all the time, leaving her no room to escape. Tamsin has used Nate to get away from her horrendous marriage, and it's worked. Maybe she didn't think I was strong enough to help her but Nate . . . Nate is. Did Nate know that this was her plan? I would be inclined to say he didn't. Usually, Nate can't keep a secret to save his life, to the point that he has to buy my Christmas present on Christmas Eve so he doesn't spoil the surprise. But if Tamsin used Nate to escape from Seb . . . why hasn't Nate come back?

CHAPTER 29

Panic makes my fingers and toes go numb, and I grip the edge of the bed as vertigo makes the room spin. What if Nate hasn't come back because he *can't*? The panic drains away to be replaced by a sharp, clinical anger. Tamsin, always smug and smiling, hiding the true nature of her relationship with Seb. By involving Nate, pulling him in to help extract her from her toxic, violent marriage, she's put him in danger. I think again of the cold, empty space beside me in the bed that night of the swap. I have no idea where Seb went or how long he was gone for. It could have been five minutes or five hours. Did he know what Tamsin was planning? And could he realistically have done something to the pair of them while I was sleeping? I think back over our interactions at the party, and the days leading up to it. Seb was overly attentive to me at the party, I remember that. I had got the distinct impression, after months of light flirting and dancing around each other, that that night, if I had given him the nod, he would have taken me indoors and encouraged me to break my vows to Nate. Was he attracted to me, and completely oblivious to the way Tamsin was feeling? Or was it just a ruse to make her jealous, to make her realise that their marriage might not be perfect, but it would hurt a hell of a lot more if someone else had him?

Nausea rises and I swallow hard, still gripping the edge of the bed. This is all my fault — if I'd known who these people really were, I never would have allowed myself and Nate and to get so tangled up with them. I can't help but wonder if Nate was aware of how Tamsin felt about Seb. Something inside me shrivels a little, like a plant without enough water, at the idea that perhaps Nate and Tamsin were closer than I realised — closer than even Tamsin and me. I think of the way they stood together in the cellar, her hand on his arm, and the sensation I'd felt that there was more to it than simply choosing a bottle of wine. If Tamsin had confided in Nate and he had agreed to help her then maybe there is something here that could point me in the direction of where they are. Nate is organised, neat, methodical. If Tamsin came to him with the seed of an idea I know that Nate would act on it. He's not always the most thoughtful guy, but he does like to be seen as the guy to go to when the chips are down and I know that the idea of Tamsin being in danger would appeal to his heroic side. He'd go all out to find a way to help her get free of someone who might be abusing her, but I thought he might have confided in me too.

Maybe he was afraid of putting you in danger. The thought is sweet and welcome, like a cold drink on a hot day, and I feel a surge of love for my husband. Of course, that could be the only reason why Nate wouldn't have told me about Tamsin. He would have been worried that I might act on it — he knows how impulsive I can be, and how obsessive I can get about things if I have too much time to think on it. One thing I do know, is that if Nate knew about Tamsin's plan to disappear then there will be something here, somewhere. He would never have left me to deal with the fall out alone, not without leaving me some sort of clue.

Not caring about the late hour, and the fact that my exhaustion is bone deep, I scramble off the bed and head for the wardrobe. If he planned this, he would have packed a bag. Throwing open the doors I scan over his rail of clothes, the neatly pressed shirts that he sends to a dry cleaner because I never get the collars right, the suit jackets and polo shirts. Sliding my hands into trouser and jacket pockets, I come up empty, save for a single unused tissue. Checking the drawers, all I can see missing is a pair of grey sweatpants and a black T-shirt, which I guess he must have been wearing when he left, the clothes he wore to the party tossed hurriedly into the laundry hamper.

I leave the bedroom and head downstairs to the dining room. Nate always leaves his laptop bag behind the door in there, tucked out of sight. When I flick on the light, I can see it's still in the same place he left it last Friday night, I don't know whether to be relieved or worried. Relieved, because access to his laptop means access to his mind, and worried because if Nate did know Tamsin's plans and knew he might not be back, there's no way he would have left his laptop behind.

Tamping down the anxiety that claws its way from the pit of my stomach to my shaking fingers, I take a deep breath and open the lid of the laptop, confidently typing in Nate's password. HAYLEYMAY2805. The screen judders, a warning box flashing up, and I frown, deleting the characters and retyping, more carefully this time. The screen judders again and something molten pours over my skin. Tugging my shirt away from my chest, I flap my hands to cool my cheeks. The password can't be wrong. It's been HAYLEYMAY2805 since the day we got home from our honeymoon. I'd even laughed at him, telling him anyone could crack the code and get into his laptop, urging him to change it to something more sophisticated. Clearly, years later, he's decided it was time to change it.

'Fuck's sake, Nate,' I mutter under my breath as I sit back, shoving my hands through my hair. 'Why now?' Drumming my fingers on the table, I rake through my mind, trying to figure out what he might have changed it to. I try the name of his first pet, a scruffy dog he absolutely adored, but that too causes the screen to judder. Aware that I probably only have a couple of attempts left to get it right, I flex my fingers over the keyboard. The only other thing that means anything of significance to Nate, and it's something that could be a safe password, is when Chelsea won the Champions League in 2021. Pulling out my phone, I google the match, knowing that Nate will use a name and a date, it's just a question of figuring out which. Reading over the match stats until I feel confident, I type into the password box. KANTE290521. I can't help but punch the air when the screen unlocks — Kai Havertz might have scored the winning goal in that match but I know the way Nate's mind works. I knew he would have used the man of the match over the most obvious name. Now, the screen shows his homepage, and my feelings are a little less stung over being replaced as Nate's password.

Praying that his emails aren't also password-protected — I don't think I can go through the pressure of figuring out another one — I click on the icon, sighing with relief when they open. There are hundreds of unopened messages and I scroll back to the end of last week. Most of them are from his other team members, some pharma companies and lots of spam for things he's bought online and inadvertently signed up for mailing lists for. Moving to his deleted folder, I scroll through there too but it's much of the same. Junk mail, sales offers and a bunch of emails from porn sites, that I don't know if Nate has watched things there, or if it's just spam. Either way, I scroll past without stopping, my heart in my mouth. His folders are full — for someone so organised, he doesn't seem to delete anything properly — and I realise there is an easier way for me to search what I'm looking for.

Typing 'Cooper' into the search bar brings no results. I don't know what Tamsin's email is, never having had cause to send her one, so I try 'Tamsin' too, but there is nothing. They've never communicated this way, at least, it seems unlikely. Blowing out a long breath I scroll through the deleted folder, just in case she's using some odd combination as her email address, and it's a while later when, my eyes aching and a yawn tearing at the back of my throat, I finally spot something that halts my scrolling. It's a receipt from Argos, telling Nate his order is ready for collection. *We haven't ordered anything from Argos.* That store is for cheap furniture, paddling pools that you throw away at the end of the summer and crappy electronic devices like karaoke machines and . . . throwaway mobile phones. The receipt is for two Nokia mobile phones, the same phone as the one Tamsin had in her bag. The room spins for a moment, black spots dancing at the edges of my vision. Suddenly, it doesn't feel as if Tamsin has used Nate to escape from her abusive marriage, knowing he's such a good egg he wouldn't be able to refuse. Suddenly it once again feels as though Nate and Tamsin are having an affair, Nate buying burner phones so the two of them can talk undiscovered.

There is a pounding in my ears and I have to resist the urge to sweep Nate's laptop off the table and send it crashing to the floor. Instead, I shove my chair back and march to the kitchen, pulling Tamsin's phone from her handbag before yanking open the junk drawer. I checked it before for a charger cable, but now I check thoroughly, dumping the contents all over the kitchen floor. Raking through the same pile of old keys and crap there is still no charger. I check the other drawers, the top of the fridge, the drawers of my granny's old Welsh dresser in the dining room. It's only as the first fingers of dawn are creeping over the horizon and the entire contents of Nate's bedside table are scattered all over our bedroom floor that I finally hit the jackpot. Coiled into a neat pile, in typical Nate fashion, is a black cord with a charge end that can only fit the burner phone I hold in my hand. As it slots in easily, I breathe out, my hands shaking as I wait for the phone to charge enough for me to turn it on.

After what feels like hours but is merely minutes, there is finally enough juice to power up the phone. My chest tightens as I press the button for Tamsin's call log, feeling an odd sense of nostalgia as the green screen lights up. The call log shows only one number, and it hasn't been saved as a contact. Without stopping to think I jab at the call button. The ringing is in stereo, and it's only when I pull the phone away from my ear that I realise I can still hear it — the phone is here, ringing, in my house. Scrambling to my feet, I follow the sound of the ringtone past the spare bedroom (the room that I wanted to turn into a nursery) and into the main bathroom at the end of the hall. The ringing is louder now, but still muffled and in my exhaustion it takes me a few moments to realise that it's coming from behind the bath panel.

'Nate, you fucker.' I hang up and get on my hands and knees to pop the bath panel off. Reaching into the gap, I feel around until my hand closes around the boxy, plastic frame of a second burner phone, my fingers sticky with cobwebs. This phone still has two bars of charge, and shows one missed call from an unsaved number — clearly the call I just made from Tamsin's phone. Popping the bath panel back on I sit with my back against it as I pull up the text messages on Tamsin's phone. There are dozens of messages, all from the same unknown number.

This is the safest way for us to talk.

My heart sinks at the first message, sent from Nate's phone to Tamsin, even as I try and pep talk myself. It could just be he's helping her. It doesn't have to be an affair.

Does she know?

Tamsin's text to Nate makes my stomach roll and for a desperate minute I think I will throw up the few sips of tea I drank next door.

*Don't mention her. If we're going to do this she can't know
anything.*

I don't know how to feel about Nate's response, still uncertain
if they are in the midst of a torrid affair, or if it is simply that Nate
is trying to help Tamsin escape Seb's clutches.

The meal was delicious — parfait to die for!

From Tamsin to Nate. Now, I do feel sick. The memory of the
receipt I found in Nate's trousers looms bright in my mind. *Steak,
cheesecake and that fucking parfait.* I believed him when he told me
he was working late, meeting a colleague.

Wait. I found the receipt in his jacket pocket weeks before
Tamsin and Seb moved in. It's like I've been slapped, my cheeks
burning, and I press my hand to my mouth, sure now that I'm
going to vomit. Dropping the phone, I head back into the bedroom and rummage in the wardrobe, pulling out the jacket Nate
wore that night. The receipt is still scrunched into the inside
pocket, forgotten about by Nate, but not by me. Smoothing it
out, my eyes travel to the bottom of the receipt, to the date and
time stamp. Part of me — the part that idolises Nate and doesn't
want to contemplate a future without him, the part that would
have done anything to be with him — tries to rationalise it, telling myself they could have gone out for dinner any time, but the
date on the receipt is 7 June. A full two weeks before Seb and
Tamsin moved in. Did Nate and Tamsin know each other before
the Coopers moved in next door? Part of me hopes the parfait was
from an entirely different meal . . . but I know that's grasping at
straws.

I crumple forward, my forehead hitting my knees as sobs
threaten to strangle me. How could they do this? Was Nate the

reason for Tamsin moving in next door? Was that why she, so glamorous, so *exciting*, wanted to befriend mousy old me? Rage coils in my chest and I think if she was standing in front of me now I wouldn't be able to stop myself from striking her, hard enough that she understood how badly she's hurt me. Angrily jabbing at the phone screen, I move through the rest of the text messages, intent on putting together a parcel of evidence to show Seb. Fuck Tamsin, fuck Nate. I don't even care if Seb wants to kill her for having an affair, because I feel the same way. And then I stop, rereading the final text on the screen, from Tamsin's phone to Nate's.

> *Don't say anything to Alex, Nate. You must want to know the truth about Lola as much as I do. After all, you were there that night.*

CHAPTER 30

Everything tilts. Lola — that's Tamsin's missing sister. And Alex
... The passport I found in Seb's house with his photo ... it was in
the name of Alex Small. Before I get the chance to process things
any further, the doorbell rings.

'Shit.' Getting to my feet, I glance in the mirror, pausing to
smooth my hair down. I've not slept a wink, my face pale, dark
circles ringing my eyes. I look as if I have the flu, and I frantically
tap at my cheeks trying to draw some colour into them. The wrin-
kles in my clothes are a dead giveaway that I've been wearing them
for far too long, but there's nothing I can do about it now as the
chime pierces the air again.

'Coming!' I hurry along the hallway and yank the door open,
surprised to find it is completely light outside. 'Oh.'

Wendy stands on the doorstep, wearing a dark grey hoody over
running leggings and carrying a greasy paper bag in her hands. She
makes no attempt to hide the shock on her face as she looks at me.
'Hayley. Are you . . . all right?'

'Fine. Just busy. What are you doing here? Shouldn't you be
at work?'

'I'm going in later, I've got a dentist appointment this morning. It's eight thirty in the morning, Hayley. You're off work.' She
peers behind me and I tug the door closed, hiding the explosion

of chaos in the kitchen at the end of the hall. 'What's got you so busy?'

Something about her tone makes me falter, her words carrying an edge of concern, but needles of suspicion still dig under my skin. Wendy is wearing a hoody — Wendy never wears hoodies. Not once in all the years I've known her. The image of the hooded figure leaning down behind Nate's car pops into my mind and I frown. 'What do you want, Wendy? I told you, I'm in the middle of something.'

She raises her eyebrows, and then pulls that face she does at work when I pull her up on stuff she hasn't done. Crocodile tears brimming at the corners of her eyes. 'I came to see how you are.' She holds up the paper bag, the grease spots and waft of meat making my stomach growl. 'I brought you breakfast, from that bakery you like. I wanted to see how you are, that's all . . . we're friends, aren't we? That's what friends do.'

Friends? Maybe in Wendy's eyes. From where I'm standing it feels more like keeping tabs. Maybe she's hoping I won't ever return to the office. 'Thanks.' I take the paper bag, the scent of sausage rolls making my mouth water. 'But you didn't have to come over. I'm fine. You could have sent a text.' I know I sound ungrateful, but all I want to do is get rid of her and her big nose, poking into my business. I need to get back to figuring out what the hell is going on with Nate and the Coopers.

'I did.' Wendy's eyes are full of worry as she watches me intently. Aware of the chaos I've created in the house overnight, I step out on to the garden path, pulling the door closed completely behind me as Wendy takes a step back. 'I sent you a few WhatsApp messages, I tried to call a couple of times but . . .' she shrugs. 'I didn't know if you had anyone checking in on you. I know you lost your parents and now Nate isn't around . . .'

'Wendy, when you said you saw him, first in Harrogate and then again later, in Stratford . . . was he . . . with anyone?'

'With anyone?' Wendy bites her lower lip. 'I mean . . . I thought he was with you in Harrogate, remember?' A flush washes over her cheeks, making her look younger and when she speaks again her voice is soft. 'Hayley, has Nate left you? Is that what's going on?'

'He hasn't—'

'Wendy!' A familiar voice comes from the other side of the rose bush and I freeze, my eyes going to Wendy's face. Her frown drops and she beams as she turns to face Seb.

'You know each other?' I ask, as Seb joins us on the garden path, Tank on a lead clipped to his waist. *What the actual fuck is going on?* I'm starting to think this is all a horrible nightmare and I pray that I'll wake up at any moment.

'Well—'

'Not really—'

They both speak at the same time, laughing over each other as I stand there, stony-faced, my heart clattering in my chest. The way Wendy smiles up at Seb, who is looking particularly fine this morning in a running singlet and shorts, Apple watch strapped to his wrist, is sickening. Does she know what he's really like? Is she part of all this?

'I saw Wendy the other day,' Seb says, turning his laughing eyes on me now. 'She was looking for you, but you were out somewhere. I'm so sorry, Wendy, I completely forgot to let Hayley know.'

'When was this?' I don't believe him. I've barely left the house the last few days — I hate getting the tube and I haven't been able to go far with two flat tyres, although that will change after today, once the mechanic has been. Besides, when I did leave the house it was with him. 'Wendy, why do you keep coming round? I told you I'm fine. You don't need to be here.'

'And I told you I was worried.' Wendy flicks a concerned glance in Seb's direction. 'You're going through something . . . emotional.

You don't have a lot of support, and with Nate gone and that fence panel broken at the back of the house . . .'

Fear whips through me, liquefying my limbs. 'How do you know about that?'

'You . . . told me?' Wendy frowns, stepping forward with one palm raised as if taming a wild animal. 'Hayley, you really don't seem fine to me. You told me about the fence panel months ago, remember? You asked why I didn't just text you, but I did. You never replied.'

Pulling my phone from my pocket, I check WhatsApp. There are six or seven messages from Wendy, all unread. 'I just didn't see them, that's all. It's no big deal.'

'Wendy, I'm sure Hayley appreciates your concern,' Seb puts an arm around her shoulder and gently guides her back towards the pavement. 'But you can see, she's fine. And I'm right next door.' He adopts a sober tone. 'Obviously we're going through this together, and Hayley knows she has my full support.'

'Together?' Wendy turns back to look over her shoulder at me and I nod, although I don't want to elaborate. 'Well . . . if you're sure you're OK, Hayley?'

'I'm fine,' I manage, forcing a smile. 'Thanks for checking in though. And for the food.' I hold the bag up like a trophy, finally sighing with relief when she turns onto the road and makes her way towards the tube station. The relief is short-lived when I realise that Seb is coming back up the path towards me.

'Hayley.' Seb adopts a concerned frown that lacks sincerity. 'Wendy seems nice . . . if a little intense. Are you sure you're OK? You look a bit . . .' he trails off. 'Did something happen? Did you find something out?'

'What? No.' My voice is a little pitchy and I clear my throat to cover it. 'Everything's fine.'

'Shall I come in for a coffee?'

Absolutely fucking not. Even if I hadn't trashed the house over-night there is no way I feel comfortable being alone with Seb after reading Tamsin's diary, and finding the text messages between her and Nate. I feel as much in the dark as I did that first morning when I came home to find Nate and Tamsin gone. The difference is, I no longer think that Seb has no idea what happened between Nate and Tamsin leaving the garden next door and now.

'I've got somewhere I need to be.' As the words leave my mouth, I realise they are true. I need to dig into Lola's disappear-ance, and I'll feel safer doing that well away from home.

'Really?' Seb runs his eyes over me and I feel every moment I've been awake claw at the back of my eyes.

'Really.' I swallow, not liking the way he stands so close that I can smell the faint whiff of yesterday's aftershave. 'So, I'd better get going.'

'OK. I'll catch up with you later.' Seb gives me a long look, before turning and jogging back down the path, turning right towards the park, the dog bouncing along beside him. It's only once he's out of sight that I remember to breathe again.

* * *

Twenty minutes later, after the quickest shower known to man and a cup of very strong tea — never have I wished harder that I liked coffee — I have the two phones, the diary and the article tucked into my bag and I am headed for a coffee shop I like in Mile End. Call me paranoid, but I can't help checking over my shoulder as I hurry towards the tube station, sure I will see Seb or Wendy on my tail. I make it to the coffee shop without incident, feeling a pang of something I can't name as I enter. Nate and I used to come here a lot when we first moved to the house, before he started working as a pharma rep. We'd come on a Saturday morning, get coffee for him and peppermint tea for me, before heading over to Hackney for a wander around the market. I blink back tears as I place my order and find a table at the back, in a small booth that will give me some level of privacy.

Logging on to my laptop, I pull up Safari and type in Lola's name, my heart crashing in my chest as her face appears on the screen. The first photo that comes up is the one from the newspaper clipping, the same headline blaring across the screen. I run my eyes over the article. I remember seeing this on the news, although not every detail. Lola Goode had gone to a party in Brighton, where she was studying a BA in Fine Arts. Glancing at her photo again I can see her as an art student, wafting around in floaty dresses, paint stains on her hands. There had been a lot of people at the party, some who weren't invited according to the article, and it had been held in the grounds of an old manor house, the gardens overrun with students who had had far too much to drink. Lola hadn't returned to her digs after the party, and it wasn't until two days later that her flatmates had called her family to ask if she'd returned home as she still hadn't turned up.

I take a break, sipping at my peppermint tea as I think about how Tamsin must have felt, receiving that call, a prickle of guilt running down my spine. I never went to university, but I did grow up in Falmer, which is only a short drive from Brighton. I'd worked in a pub in the town centre and spent most of my time feeling irritated by the brash, braying university students, claiming to be skint but splashing their parents' cash on pints of lager and shots of jaeger bomb. Nate had been the exception.

Scrolling down the Google page, I click on article after article, slowly piecing together the story being told by the media. Lola had been at the party, she'd drunk too much, her clothes were revealing. She'd left the party at some point without saying goodbye to her friends, although someone reported that they saw her leaving with a man. It all sounds so familiar — a story that has been told by the press a hundred times before. After her flat-mates called her family, they drove down to Brighton and started searching. There's a photo of Tamsin on one news site, looking unrecognisable. Her face is drawn, she's too skinny, and her hair is pulled tightly back into a ponytail. She wears a Juicy Couture tracksuit, her eyes focused on the ground as she leaves a property that is presumably Lola's flat.

Another article tells how Lola was found four days after the party, in the woods that backed on to the manor house, by a dog walker, naturally. It's always a dog walker or a jogger. She was found under a tree, lifeless and pale, her skirt rucked up above her knees, although they said there was no sign of sexual assault. There had been no attempt to hide her body, and at first there was speculation that it was simply a tragic accident.

It's the last article on the page that makes my hand tremble so hard that peppermint tea slops over my legs, the scent of mint clinging to my trousers. Dated a few weeks later, I read how Lola was found to have a wound to the back of her head, consistent with blunt force trauma, throwing off the theory that this might have all been just a tragic accident.

Two men are said to have been aiding police in their enquiries, however both men have been released and no charges are being brought.

It's not the wording that makes me sick to my stomach. It's the photograph of two men leaving the police station, their names in tiny font under the photo. *Alex Small and Nathaniel Turner.* Seb and Nate's faces stare back at me, their expressions grim. Seb and Nate. Both suspects in Lola's disappearance.

CHAPTER 31

I always knew Nate was keeping a secret from me. I never challenged him on it. There were plenty of times when I wanted to, but I knew deep down from the moment we started seeing each other that there was a small part of himself that he had closed off from me. There was something about the way he never wanted to talk about university, even though we started seeing each other just weeks after he graduated. The way he leapt at the chance to move into my dead grandmother's house with me on the outskirts of London, even though we'd only been dating for a little over six months. Not that I had been sad about it — I couldn't afford to live in Brighton for much longer, not on a bartender's salary and Nana's house came mortgage-free — and I'd known even as I told Nate about the house that I wanted him to come with me. I'd tried to prompt him a few times, to reassure him that he could tell me anything and it would never change the way I feel about him, but he never opened up. Not once.

Now, I stare at the grainy newspaper photo. Nate's eyes are cast down as he leaves the police station, his hair sticking up at the back in that tufty way it has when he's been running his hands through it. In contrast, Seb appears more confident, glaring at the cameras as he strides away, no Tamsin in sight. *Both of them were suspects in Lola's disappearance and subsequent death.* Is that why

Seb changed his name? I wonder how Nate felt when he came home and I raved about our new neighbours — no wonder he had been so hostile to them both, when this was the dark cloud hanging over them. He must have been terrified that Tamsin or Seb would spill the beans to me . . .

I run a hand over my face, suddenly overwhelmed. *What does this mean for us?* If I pull at these strands, does it mean that everything is going to come crashing down around us? There is a part of me that wants to jump in Nate's freshly repaired car and drive until I reach the end of the world, but then there is the other part of me. The part of me that would do anything for Nate. Anything to get him back, anything to keep him. When I started digging into Lola's disappearance I didn't know what I expected to find, but whatever it was it wasn't this. And now . . . it seems as though all of this is related to Nate and Tamsin's disappearance. I think of her diary entries, the undertone of fear lacing her words as she spoke about Seb — Alex, whatever he wants to call himself — and my stomach lurches.

'Excuse me.' My mouth is dry, butterflies swarming around my insides as I suddenly feel light-headed, sure I am about to throw up. I tap on the edge of the table next to mine, disturbing a woman with a baby. 'Would you mind watching my things for just a moment? I need to use the bathroom.' I don't have time to pack up my laptop, my stomach somersaulting as if I am on a rollercoaster. The woman nods but I am already squeezing past her, intent on getting to the bathroom as soon as I can.

Moments later, I lean over the toilet in the café, swiping my hand across my mouth, the sour taste of vomit on my tongue. Weak and shaking, I stumble out of the stall towards the sink, grateful that the bathroom is empty. I slurp icy water from the tap and rinse my mouth out, the edges of my hair dipping into the cold stream, before raising my eyes to my reflection. I look horrendous. My eyes are bloodshot, my skin grey and my hair sits in lank handfuls around my face. I no longer have to worry about resembling Tamsin, with her glowing complexion and her bouncy, golden curls. I look like a monster, something dragged from the depths of the ocean.

They've all been lying to me, all this time. Nate must have recognised Seb the moment he met him — did he recognise Tamsin too? The idea that the three of them have been carrying this huge secret around behind my back cuts deeper than any knife could have. It is as if I am the old Hayley again, the Hayley I was before Nate came into my life. The Hayley who was invisible to everyone else, a ghost lurking on the fringes. I rush back into the stall to throw up for a second time.

* * *

Exiting the bathroom, I feel less shaky. I've splashed my face with cold water, tied my hair back and pep talked myself. This doesn't mean that Nate doesn't love me. This doesn't mean that he and Tamsin are having an affair. But it could potentially mean something much, much worse. My steps falter as I approach my table. The woman sitting on the table next to mine is gone and for a moment I feel a flash of panic, sure that baby or no baby the woman is an opportunist thief and I have just handed her my laptop. The panic subsides as I see it peeping out of the top of my bag, and I pull it out, checking my purse and phone are still there. They are, as are the two burner phones still tucked into the side pocket. Feeling guilty for assuming the woman would rob me, I open the lid of the laptop to close it down properly.

Fuck. I freeze, my fingers still gripping the lid. A Post-it note is stuck to the screen, the edge curling slightly. In block capitals it reads, HE'S NOT WHO YOU THINK HE IS. The room spins and I blink, trying to right myself before I slam the lid and shove the computer into my bag.

Pushing past the small queue of customers snaking towards the café doors, I shove my way out onto the street, my chest hitching as panic sits in a ball somewhere right above my heart. I scan the street, looking for the woman with the baby, searching for her dark hair and red top among the sea of people filling the pavement but there's no sign of her. I pause for a moment, trying to weigh up which direction she might have gone in, when a flash of blonde hair catches my eye on the other side of the street.

Is that . . . ? A bus pulls up right across the street, blocking my view, and I step off the pavement, intent on crossing before I lose sight of Tamsin. Because I am sure it was her standing on the other side of the road. A horn blares and I leap back onto the pavement with a yelp, holding one hand up in apology to the irate driver of a black cab, the other pressed to my racing heart. The bus pulls away and I sprint across the road, searching for the bob of a blonde head. I see her, maybe fifty feet ahead of me, her blond curls catching the sun as she weaves her way through the crowd towards the tube station.

'Tamsin! Hey, Tamsin, wait!' I call out, but she either doesn't hear me, or is choosing to ignore me. I press on, closing the gap between us, stumbling over an elderly man pulling a shopping cart. 'Sorry! I'm so sorry,' I pant as he shouts after me. My bag is heavy on my shoulder, sweat starts to prickle on my spine, but I keep my eyes on Tamsin. After days of trying to figure out where she is, where *Nate* is, I can't afford to let her go now. I want answers, and I'm going to force her to give them to me.

As we reach the tube station I close the gap, my feet aching in my thin sandals as I reach out and yank on the strap on Tamsin's bag, pulling her to a stop.

'Hey!' Tamsin turns and I feel the triumphant smile die on my face. It's not her. It's not Tamsin, it's some other woman with bouncy, golden curls and a taste for brightly coloured harem trousers.

The woman looks terrified and cries out, 'She's trying to steal my bag!'

'No, no, I'm not, honestly.' I raise both hands in a gesture of surrender, shaking my head. 'I'm really sorry, I thought . . .' the words catch in my throat as my cheeks burn a hot, vivid pink. 'I thought you were someone else. I thought you were . . . my friend.' Hot tears sting my eyes as the woman gives me a look that could kill.

'Fucking maniac,' she hisses, glaring at me as she walks backwards towards the tube, only turning her back when she's certain I am not going to follow her.

'Sorry,' I whisper again, ignoring the stare of a small child being whisked past me by her mother. As the blonde woman descends into the depths of the tube station, I lean against the cold tiled wall, sinking down until I hit the dirty floor. I was sure, *so sure*, that it was Tamsin ahead of me. Slinking my fingers into my bag, I pull out the Post-it note. HE'S NOT WHO YOU THINK HE IS. It could only have been Tamsin who left that note. Does that mean she's the one who's been watching me? She must have waited until I left for the bathroom. I imagine her telling the woman with the baby that she could go, it's fine, she's a friend of mine. A fat tear runs down my face.

'Here you go, love.' A man in a suit chucks a pound coin down in front of me, and I don't know whether to laugh or cry even harder.

HE'S NOT WHO YOU THINK HE IS. At the moment, no one seems to be who I think they are, and I think again of the article about Lola, how she didn't go home after the party, and my stomach lurches. I know Seb isn't who he claims to be — I know he's really Alex Small, the man accused of being involved in Lola's disappearance and subsequent death. But what about Nate? Is Tamsin trying to warn me about him too?

CHAPTER 32

'No, I'm sorry, that's not possible. You aren't a police officer.' The café owner stares at me, arms folded across her body as she shakes her head. She couldn't be more hostile if she tried, and I know I've drunk my last latte in here.

'You don't understand,' I say. 'She was in here earlier, a blonde woman with curly hair, probably wearing lots of bangles. She . . .' I break off, knowing when I'm being stonewalled.

'I don't care.' The café owner raises an eyebrow. 'She didn't steal anything from you, and I'm pretty sure it's some sort of GDPR infringement if I just hand out CCTV footage willy-nilly.'

Leaving the café, I could cry. I was sure that if I could just take a peek at the CCTV footage I would see Tamsin entering the café and leaving the note. It never even occurred to me that the owner wouldn't let me see it.

Back at the house, relieved to see that the mechanic has been and changed the tyres, I take a nap. When I wake nearly four hours later, I am stiff from lying in one position, my eyes blurry and I sit up with a gasp, remembering the events of the morning. I need a shower, a long one with water so hot it stings, to wash my hair and put on clean clothes. I need to feel human again before I can even think about Tamsin, Nate and Seb/Alex and everything that happened with Lola. I run my tongue over my teeth, wincing at the fur coating them, as tears sting my eyes again. I can feel myself sliding back, the dull pull of depression yanking at my shoulder the way I yanked at that woman's bag earlier today outside the tube station. I won't let myself slide back into that dark place I was in before Nate and I got together, that Hayley is long gone. I have to make sure I figure out exactly what Seb knows about what happened to Lola Goode. And I need to get Nate back.

I feel a hundred times better after I shower and dress, and I am aware that I haven't eaten properly for days. Pulling overly ripe tomatoes, cheese and garlic from the fridge, and a bag of pasta from the cupboard I set a large pan of salted water to boil and flick open the diary, rereading it as I begin to chop tomatoes.

I need vegetables — I can't remember the last time I ate a proper meal and I'm starting to feel as if I might get scurvy. The giant pimple hovering under the skin by my hairline is a sure sign that I'm not taking care of myself. In an attempt to make myself feel safer, I also order a security camera complete with alarm, to put up at the back of the house, covering the tree line by the broken fence panel. I'm hoping that that, combined with a decent meal means I'll sleep a little better tonight.

My eyes scan over the diary pages, searching for any sign that Tamsin thought Seb could be dangerous, mentally logging each phrase. Did Tamsin think Seb could be the one who hurt Lola? The idea of it makes my brain hurt. I can't see Tamsin being the kind of person who could live with someone knowing they might have harmed someone she loved, but then before all of this I could never have seen Tamsin as the kind of woman who would let a man hurt her, physically and emotionally. Maybe she's afraid he was responsible for what happened to Lola, and she's been too scared of repercussions to leave. Until Nate came along.

I wonder if all of this is some kind of punishment for Seb, and I have been caught in the crossfire. I still don't want to think about Nate, about his involvement with Lola, my fragile brain not ready to face up to something that might hurt so deeply that I may never recover.

I am lost in thought, mindlessly chopping the tomatoes, so when the sound of someone clearing their throat comes from behind me I almost slice the top of my finger off. Whirling around with a stifled shriek, I hold the knife aloft as I come face to face with Seb.

'Seb? What the actual fuck?' He is standing behind me in the kitchen, the patio door behind him slightly ajar. Blood rushes in my ears and I battle to hold the knife steady, my fingers trembling.

'Woah, calm down. No need for all that.' Seb holds his hands up in a gesture of surrender, the smile on his face faint and unsure.

'What are you doing here? How did you get in?' Keeping the knife on him I glance behind his head to the patio doors and the tree line beyond. 'Have you been watching me?'

'What? Watching you? No, I haven't.' Seb shakes his head but keeps his hands raised. 'Hayley, any chance you can put the knife down?'

Shifting slightly so that I block his view of the diary on the counter behind me, I shake my own head. 'You just broke into my house, Seb.'

Seb laughs, lowering his hands. 'Oh God, Hayley? Really? It's not like you haven't done it to me, let's be honest.' A fiery blush creeps its way up my cheeks. I don't have any comeback to that. 'I tried the front door and there was no answer. I don't know if your doorbell is out of battery, so I tried knocking too but there was still no answer. I was worried about you, Hayley. You didn't seem yourself this morning, when Wendy showed up. You seemed . . . I don't know. Erratic? Off-key? Tamsin mentioned before that you'd struggled with depression so I was concerned for you, especially with Nate not being here. I thought I'd check round the back and there you were, in the kitchen.'

Unease makes my palms sweaty and I almost drop the knife. I don't remember telling Tamsin about the time before I met Nate, about the depression that sat on my shoulders, an unbearably heavy weight.

'Look.' Seb comes towards me, reaching out and gently taking the knife, laying it down on the table behind him. 'I was concerned, that's all. All that talk about someone watching you from the tree line . . . I wanted to make sure you were OK.'

I push him away with one hand, turning my back on him. The diary is there in plain sight and I shift to block his view. Under the pretence of scooping up tomatoes, I shove the diary in between two of the cookbooks that rest against the tiled wall between two bookends, before throwing the garlic and tomatoes into a pan.

'I'm fine, Alex.'

Seb stills as the full force of the name hits him. 'What did you—?'

'Alex,' I say, lifting my chin. I can barely breathe my heart is racing so hard, and I wish I still had the knife, but Seb stands between me and the table. 'I called you Alex.'

'My name is Seb, Hayls. You know that. I knew I was right to come over. Did you bump your head?'

'No, I didn't. And I know your name isn't Seb. I know you're a liar.'

Something seems to break inside Seb as he lowers his head, his shoulders rounding. 'Hayley, you don't know what you're—'

Tamsin's words, scrawled across the pages of her diary, float through my mind. *Things are coming to a head.* It certainly feels that way. 'I know your real name is Alex Small. I know about Lola.' I fix my gaze on him, wishing more than anything that I could have just kept hold of the knife. 'I know all of it.'

CHAPTER 33

I don't know what I expected. For Seb to rush at me, to wrap his hands around my throat? For me to lunge for the knife, the two of us grappling in a bitter battle to the end? None of that happens. Instead, Seb stares at me as if I am speaking a foreign language.

'How?' is all he says.

'I'm not an idiot,' I say. 'I knew something was off the moment I saw Lola's photograph on the fridge. I thought I recognised her and Tamsin said she'd been on TV as a kid, but that wasn't it. That wasn't where I knew her from. Then you told me Tamsin didn't have a sister.'

'I didn't lie about that,' Seb says wearily, pushing a hand through his hair. 'Tamsin doesn't have a sister any more. Lola is dead. You said you knew everything so you must know that.'

'I know that you were a suspect in her disappearance.'

'Do you have anything to drink? And something's burning, by the way.' Seb slumps into Nate's usual seat at the table.

I switch off the gas burners; the tomatoes are a sticky, charred mess. Then I pour us both a shot of Nate's good whisky and sit at the table opposite Seb, pushing the thick tumbler towards him. He takes a sip.

'Blue Label? Nice.'

I say nothing and leave my glass untouched, waiting for him to speak. He takes another mouthful of whisky, rolling it around his mouth before he finally swallows.

'Lola was Tamsin's sister. But she died. You already know that.' His words are stilted, as if it pains him to speak her name aloud. 'I didn't have anything to do with it.'

'That's not what the police thought.'

'I know. I was there.' Seb gives me a hard stare, his face like granite, and my limbs seem to turn to water, fear spiking in my veins. I haven't forgotten the way he grabbed Tamsin in the garden. 'That's the only reason they pulled me in, Hayley. Because I was at the same party.'

If that's the case, why didn't they pull in every male at the party? Every girl too? Why just Seb and Nate? I shift in my seat and hold my tongue, waiting.

'Look, I'm here now, aren't I? I'm not in prison, I was never charged. I never did anything to Lola.' Seb's nostrils flare, his frustration evident.

'They must have thought you had reason to want to harm Lola, surely? If they called you in for questioning. Seb, there must have been a reason.' *Be honest,* I want to beg, *tell me everything you remember about that night. What did you see? What do you know?* 'The police don't bring you in for questioning just because you went to the same party.'

Seb stays silent for a moment, and I almost pity him as I watch the internal struggle go on behind his eyes. He's unsure how much I really know — despite my warning — and he's uncertain how upfront and honest he can afford to be with me.

'We argued that night. Me and Lola,' he admits, the words pulling out of him like taffy, his reluctance written all over his face. 'Tamsin and I . . . we were already casually dating by then. Just seeing each other, nothing serious, but Tamsin wasn't there that night. She'd gone back home to see her mum. I think she was pissed off to be honest, that Lola was going to be at the party and she wasn't. It was a third-year bash and Lola was only a first year — she shouldn't have been there at all.'

'But she was.' I can picture her now, in the white top and lilac skirt she was found in, her blonde hair plaited into a crown around her head. Bright, vivacious, thrilled to be included in something she knew she wasn't supposed to be a part of.

Seb nods, his expression sombre. 'She was. Lola saw me talking to another girl — it was all completely innocent — but Lola was off her face. She went mental at me, started screaming in my face that I was cheating on Tam . . . I only realised Lola was her sister after she'd been yelling at me for about ten minutes. I hadn't met her before.'

I wonder if Tamsin knows that one of the last things Lola did was defend her sister. The idea brings a lump to my throat and I swallow hard. 'Then what happened?'

'I shouted back at her. I was furious, she was yelling all sorts of accusations and I really liked Tamsin . . . I was worried what people might tell her. I could feel myself losing my temper so I . . . I left.' Seb shrugs. 'By myself. Only someone said they saw Lola leave with a man . . . and that it was me.' He raises his eyes to mine. 'It wasn't me. I swear on Tam's life. Whoever Lola left the party with . . . whoever took her out to the woods . . . it wasn't me.'

CHAPTER 34

I feel sick at his words, but things still don't add up. Seb must know that Nate was also brought in for questioning by the police — is he pushing me to see if I know that? I can't bring myself to bring up Nate first, wanting to see exactly how much Seb is going to reveal of his own accord.

'If you were so innocent, why did you change your name, *Alex?*' I can't help the sneer that tinges my words. 'I saw the passport in your house, amongst other things.' *The photos of me, taken without my knowledge, the life insurance policy taken out on Tamsin.*

Seb looks at me, his brow furrowed. He looks dreadful now, the cocky, confident smirk that usually sits on his face well and truly wiped off. I hate to admit it but he looks weak, a shadow of his former self, and if this was the Seb who had greeted me at the door the day I knocked and asked him to keep the noise down, I doubt there would have been any spark of attraction at all.

'Have you ever been arrested, Hayley?'

I shake my head. I haven't, although there was an occasion once where I thought I might be. Every teenager fucks up occasionally, don't they? People at school were always gloating about being brought home in a police car after fighting, or shoplifting. 'No, of course I haven't.'

'Then I don't think you can quite understand. I wasn't just brought in for questioning, I was kept in a tiny room, with two police officers asking me the same questions over and over, until I honestly couldn't think straight any more.' His voice cracks and he takes a moment, reaching out for his whisky tumbler and draining it, before pushing it towards me to refill it. 'There was a moment in there that I thought about confessing.'

'You . . . what?' The words slug me in the stomach, a visceral gut punch. My head starts to spin as I top up Seb's glass.

'I didn't do it, but they questioned me for so long that I almost believed them when they said it must have been me who caused Lola's head injury. They thought it was an accident before, you see.' His voice has taken on a faraway quality as he relives those days in his mind. 'Lola was . . . wild, I suppose. And they thought at first she'd just overdone it . . . but then when they found the wound on the back of her head it seemed someone hurt her deliberately. It wasn't me, and eventually the police let me go.'

'Plenty of people get arrested, they don't change their names though.' I refuse to feel any sympathy for this man, when I still don't know where my husband is and what part Seb had to play in his disappearance.

Seb stares at me with undisguised contempt. 'You have no idea what it was like, Hayley. I left the police station to paparazzi and people shouting my name. I was spat at on the street . . . Lola might have only been a first year at the university, but she'd already made sure people knew who she was. People liked her, were fond of her, thought she was a brilliant laugh. And I was the guy who had possibly killed her.' He pauses. 'And besides, it wasn't my idea.'

'It wasn't?'

'It was Tamsin's idea. Obviously we stayed together — she knew I could never have hurt Lola . . . I barely even knew her.

Tamsin thought it might be easier for us to start over if I changed my name. I was trying to get started in TV after I graduated and the moment I mentioned my name doors were slammed shut in my face. Tamsin thought if I took my mother's maiden name and used my middle name things might get easier. And they did.'

Seb makes everything sound so reasonable. So believable. I find myself wanting to test him, wanting to force him to tell me who else was there that night, testing his loyalty to see if I can push him into revealing what I already know.

'It wasn't just you though, was it? Someone else was taken in by the police over Lola's disappearance too.'

When Seb raises his eyes to mine, I can't read his expression. It's almost apologetic, as if he knows that what he's about to say will hurt me.

'I'm so sorry, Hayley,' he says. 'There was someone else the police wanted to speak to about that night. It was Nate.'

* * *

The look on Seb's face is priceless when I tell him he hasn't dropped some giant bombshell on me, that I already knew that Nate was there at the party that night.

'You . . . *knew*? You knew Nate was there? So, what's with all the interrogation?' A flash of something ugly crosses his face and I instinctively draw back, out of arm's reach.

'I told you I knew what happened to Lola,' I say defensively. 'I saw Nate's name tied up in that same article as your real name. How do you think that made me feel, Seb? Knowing that Nate has been keeping something this big from me? Knowing that you all knew each other and no one told me?' I pause, my pulse skittering under my skin. It's exhausting, living in a constant state of fear and uncertainty. 'Nate and Tamsin leaving together . . . this all has to be connected to Lola. None of this is a coincidence.'

Seb shoves his chair back and I flinch at the sudden scraping of his chair legs over the tiled floor. 'So you don't know everything?' He begins to pace the kitchen, the stink of charred tomatoes and garlic still filling the air.

Unsettled by his agitation I push my own chair back, not wanting to look up at him as he paces. 'What do you mean? I know Nate was there. At the party.'

Seb pauses and turns on me so fast I stumble backwards. 'I didn't know him, Hayls. I promise you. I didn't know Nate at all — I never met him at the party, after the party, at all. But Tamsin did. Tamsin knew him.'

I shouldn't be shocked, but I am. Of course Tamsin knew him — she must have known who he was after the police picked him up. If it had been my sister who died then I'd want to know everything about the person who might have been the last person to see her alive. The back of my neck prickles and reflexively I turn to stare out of the patio doors, towards the tree line. The sun has drifted below the tops of the trees and the light is gloomy and unsettling, much like the mood in my kitchen.

'Wait a minute. Are you saying Tamsin knew him *before* Lola died? Oh, my God.' I blink rapidly, my eyes smarting. 'Lola was dating him.' As I speak, puzzle pieces seem to fall into place. The look on Nate's face as he walked into Tamsin's kitchen to see Lola's face staring out at him from the fridge. Nate would have been the year above Lola. I knew Nate had almost dropped out of uni at the end of his second year, that Pauline had somehow persuaded him to carry on. I knew he'd had a girlfriend at university, but he never spoke about her, and when I had tentatively raised the subject with Pauline she had shut me down fiercely. I had assumed Pauline just really liked the girl in a way she had never liked me, and didn't press the matter. I never knew that it was *Lola*.

Seb nods. 'They went out a few times apparently. It wasn't serious — not for Lola, at least, that's what Tamsin said.' He reaches out to me, wrapping his hands around mine. His palms are warm while mine are like ice and I want to pull away but I don't think I have the strength.

'I thought all of this was about you,' I say, my voice cracking. 'All of this . . .' I wave a hand. 'The swap. Tamsin and Nate leaving together, I thought it was all because of you.' I think of the obituary, the photographs and the life insurance and I shake my head, not knowing what is right and real any more. 'I thought you were . . . I don't know, obsessed?'

'Obsessed? With who? With you?' Seb lets out a laugh, before he looks sheepish. I feel my face fall. 'Oh God, Hayley. I never meant it like that. You're beautiful, I told you that before. But Tamsin . . . you see how she is? She doesn't leave room for anyone else.'

'You took out a life insurance policy on her,' I say, finally finding the strength to pull my hands out of his. I take a step back, my mouth dry. 'And there was a clipping of my nan's obituary in your office. You must have known that she would have left the house to me.' Things are slowly dropping into place, and the picture that is emerging is far more terrifying than the idea that Seb might have abused his wife.

Seb looks taken aback. 'Those things have nothing to do with me. I never took out a life insurance policy on Tamsin. You know how she is — she doesn't believe in stuff like that, even though most grown adults know it's the sensible thing to do. She would have laughed in my face if I'd ever even suggested it. And trust me, Hayley, it was never my idea to move out here. We had a nice flat in Notting Hill. It wasn't me who wanted to move out to Southeast London.'

It was Tamsin. All of this was engineered by Tamsin. She is the one who is obsessed, not Seb. The photographs . . . I thought they were of me, but Nate is in the background of every one of them. It was *Nate* she was photographing. It was nothing to do with Seb at all.

'Do you think she could have taken out the life insurance policy herself?' My brain is working overtime now, trying to piece everything together. All this time I had thought Seb was the only threat . . . although I still don't feel as if he is entirely innocent. Changing your name is a drastic measure, and I am sure he wasn't just in the bathroom the night of the swap when I woke up alone.

'She could have,' Seb shrugs, an air of defeat about him. 'She's shown me this past week that I don't know her as well as I thought I did. Obviously.'

You and me both, pal. 'Do you think . . .' I want to ask if Nate is in danger, but the words stick in my throat, too big and unwieldy to be spoken aloud.

'I don't know what to think about anything,' Seb says harshly, and once again he is that brittle, abrupt Seb, the one I am leery of. 'But what I do know is that Tamsin was jealous of Lola. Not just your usual sibling rivalry, I mean disgustingly, sickeningly jealous of her. I don't know if it's because Lola was the youngest, a surprise baby who their parents doted on, or what. But whatever Lola had, Tamsin wanted.'

Sour saliva spurts into my mouth, my stomach lurching like an old washing machine. Tamsin was the one who clipped the newspaper obituary about my grandmother's passing. She knew Nate and I were married . . . and I was never the one she really wanted to befriend when she moved in next door, knowing who Nate and I were before we ever knew she existed.

'She's obsessed with Nate,' I whisper. 'This was all about Nate, all along.' Somewhere far away I hear the sound of something smashing. I think it might be my heart.

CHAPTER 35

I'm shattered. Broken into tiny pieces, quite literally gutted, as though my insides have been ripped from my body. My friendship with Tamsin was something I never thought someone like me could achieve. She is so bright, so bubbly, her energy a burning hot blaze of sunshine bringing joy to everyone she meets. I am not that. I am capable, efficient Hayley, a ghost who people walk past every day without seeing. At school Tamsin would have been the girl everyone fought to sit next to at lunch, and I would be — I *was* — the girl who no one saw. Who was never invited. Who didn't matter. Once I met Nate and I finally stopped pinching myself that this man — himself a shiny, glittery male version of the person I wanted to be — wanted me back, I embraced the proficient, methodical version of myself, letting myself bask in the glow that he so effortlessly gave off. I felt myself walk a little taller, smile a little brighter, live a little harder. I'm not sure when Nate's light stopped shining on me — when it shifted, subtly, and then almost completely, casting his golden glow elsewhere. Maybe it was the everyday routine of married life, of work, domestic chores, dinner in front of the TV. Or maybe it was me. Maybe it was my fault he chose to shine in other places.

I should have realised that there was another, unseen layer to the hand Tamsin held out. All this time, every shopping trip we took, every time I laid myself bare, confessing my feelings about Nate and the dissatisfaction I felt in my marriage, she wasn't there because of me. She was there because of Nate.

And Nate. *Nate.* The double betrayal slams into my chest, a bullet direct to my heart. I hear a keening, the low moan of an animal in pain, and it takes Seb's face contorting with concern for me to realise that the sound is coming from me. The idea that Nate lay beside me in bed, keeping another secret from me is almost too much for my heart to bear and I am pretty sure it has snapped in two.

'Hayley? Hayley, just breathe. Take a deep breath, come on, I'll do it with you.' Seb takes my hands the way he did before, and with his help I get myself under control.

'I'm sorry,' I gasp, a few moments later. 'I just . . . the *betrayal*, you know? I never thought anything could hurt as much as this.' Is this how Tamsin felt, when they found Lola's body? When she realised that someone she might have known, someone at that party who she might have interacted with before had stolen her sister's life before it had ever really begun? Grief washes over me, grief for a friendship that never existed, and for the love I thought Nate and I shared.

'I do understand.' Seb's tone is soothing, in a way I've never heard him speak before. 'But you can't fall apart, Hayley.'

'They were having an affair.' My voice cracks, my throat raw from the pain I've let out. 'Tamsin was obsessed with Nate for all this time, wanting him because Lola had him first, and she engineered this whole thing to take him from me.' I tug my hands away, shoving them through my hair as the pain turns to anger. 'They reconnected, they used me and then they left me behind.'

'Hayley—'

'No, Seb, *listen.* I found something.' My breathing has slowed now, but I still feel jittery, my blood seeming to fizz as it flows through my veins, my heart jumping. 'Wait here.'

Leaving Seb in the kitchen I hurry upstairs and dig out the two burner phones from where I have hidden them in an old handbag in the back of the wardrobe. I feel a flash of hesitancy as I reach for the bag and slide the zipper open, a brief second when I wonder if I am doing the right thing by showing this to Seb. *He might not be as innocent as he's making out,* a voice whispers in the back of my mind. *Remember the way his face changed when you challenged him? Remember the fear that spiked in your veins when you thought he might react badly to what you were saying?* My fingers falter as they close around the boxy plastic casing of the phones, before I realise the voice I am hearing in my head belongs to Tamsin.

'Fuck you, Tamsin,' I whisper under my breath, just as Seb calls up the stairs to me, asking if I'm OK. 'Just coming! Wait there!'

Sliding the phones into my back pockets I hurry back downstairs, to where Seb is pacing the kitchen impatiently.

'Before I show you what I found I need to know I can trust you.' I stand behind a kitchen chair, my hands gripping the top of it, a barrier between myself and Seb if things don't go the way I want them to.

'You can trust me, Hayley. I think we've established that I am the only one you can trust.'

'Not yet.' I flash him a smile tinged with sadness. 'The night of the swap I woke up and you weren't there.'

Seb smiles, confusion drawing his brows into a deep V. 'Didn't we talk about this already? I probably went to use the bathroom, or get a glass of water or something.' His voice takes on a harder note. 'To be honest, Hayley, I'm not sure what you're asking me.'

As he speaks, I realise what was bothering me so much about that night, when I woke up with a jolt, my mouth dry and my heart racing. 'You didn't use the bathroom, Seb, or go to get water. The en-suite door was open, the light was off. But the security light was on in my back garden.' The security light, activated by motion. The light Seb had complained about — in a joking way — the light that had nearly been my undoing on the evening I heard him on the phone in his garden.

Seb runs a hand over the stubble on his chin, and anxiety flares, making my stomach cramp. I'm not sure if I'm ready to hear what he's going to say.

'OK,' he says eventually. 'I lied. I didn't go to the bathroom, I sneaked next door to your place through the broken fence panel. But it's not what you think.'

'You don't know what I think.'

'I went over there to try and persuade Tamsin to come back home, that's all,' Seb says, his shoulders slumping. 'I told you — she's done this kind of thing before, dallied with other men — but this time I knew it was different. I was trying to tell her to come back, that it wasn't too late for us to take it all back and stay friends with you guys.' He gives me a long look. 'Believe it or not, Hayley, I've really enjoyed spending time with you.'

Maybe before that might have tugged on my heartstrings but it's not working now and I stare back at him impassively. 'Just tell me what happened.'

'I went over there and . . .' he looks at me, sheepish. 'I got in through the patio doors at the back. I was going to get her to come home, call the whole thing off but . . . they were already gone.'

His words hit me in the gut and I let out a wheezy breath, my throat closing over. 'They were gone? That early?' I suppose I had assumed that they left in the early hours, just as the sun was rising. Not in the dead of night. That stinks of planning, and judging by the look on Seb's face it wasn't what he was expecting either. 'And you just came back and went back to sleep beside me, like nothing had happened?'

'I *didn't know*,' Seb roars now, banging a fist on the table so hard the whisky tumblers jump, as do I. 'I didn't know,' he says again, more quietly now. 'I had no idea that things were going to go as far as they have.'

I believe you, I think, pushing aside everything Tamsin wrote in her diary, the way Seb snapped at her. Any man would lose patience if their wife behaved the way Tamsin did. Right now, I wouldn't blame him at all if he'd had something to do with her leaving.

* * *

Tugging the burner phones from my back pockets I slide them across the table towards him.

'What are these?' Seb picks one up, pressing down on a button to power up the screen, the dim green glow making his face look washed out and eerie. 'Burner phones?'

I nod, feeling nauseous. 'I found one in Tamsin's bag and the other hidden away in Nate's stuff. He bought them both.' I pick up the other phone, my hands shaking. 'Seb, these phones were in use by the two of them before you guys even moved in next door.' I pause, watching as my words hit him the way his hit me minutes earlier, trying not to feel satisfaction as he winces. 'Look at the messages.'

Seb scrolls, his eyes running over the screen as he taps from one message to the next. 'This was going on for weeks before we even set eyes on the house.' He looks ghostly in the feeble glow of the old phone, his eyes ringed by dark circles. 'She was so dead set on moving here, even when I found a place in Chislehurst that was far bigger and less expensive. Tamsin would only consider living here.'

'Well, now you know why.' It's hard to disguise the bitterness that laces my words, coating my teeth and tongue in something unpalatable. 'She told me awful things about you, Seb. Terrible things. And I believed her.'

When Seb raises his eyes from the phone to meet my gaze, the devastation is written all over his face. 'Like what?'

Squirming now, I wish I'd never mentioned it, but I have to get Seb fired up enough again that he'll want to track Tamsin down and confront her. 'That you were manipulative. Bullying, violent. I saw you grab her arm with my own eyes. She had a burn from cooking — but we both know she never cooked.'

Seb's eyes widen. 'I never . . . she did get it from cooking, that wasn't a lie. At least I don't think it was . . . I do know I never hurt her, not deliberately. Hayley, you've got this all wrong.'

'I know,' I say hastily, still debating whether to offer up the diary. 'I know now that Nate and Tamsin have been having an affair, for months at least. I know that Tamsin has probably been obsessed with Nate since he first started seeing Lola.' Her diary entry comes to me on a wave of pain.

I remember him standing in the kitchen, a beer in his hand, and thinking, 'Oh, that's you, is it?' Now though, he might look the same but he's not, not on the inside.

I'd thought she'd been speaking about Seb, but maybe it was Nate after all. 'I know that she used me—'

'*No*,' Seb says, tossing the phone onto the table and moving towards me. He grips me by the upper arms and a surge of fear runs through me, leaving an icy trail in my veins. 'You've got it *all* wrong.'

'Wh—?'

Seb stares into my eyes, not letting me look away. 'They're not having an affair — Nate is as smitten with you as he was the day he met you, believe me he told me often enough when he caught me looking at you. Tamsin is obsessed with Nate, has been since the day they found Lola's body . . . she hasn't done this because she's in love with him, Hayley. She's done this for revenge.'

CHAPTER 36

Revenge. I don't know whether part of me is relieved or devastated by this news, all I do know is my legs won't hold me up much longer and I somehow manage to pull out the kitchen chair and sink into it, before I fall. If Tamsin did this for revenge then Nate really is in danger. But that also means that they aren't having an affair. Nate hasn't left me intentionally, despite what he might have said about our marriage to his mother, although it still doesn't explain why he agreed so readily to the swap. Seb is still talking and I try to block the thoughts that are drowning him out.

'Sorry.' I press my hands to my temples, trying to re-engage myself. 'Say that again.'

Seb runs his eyes over me, before pushing the whisky bottle towards me. 'Take a shot of this, you're as white as a sheet.' He waits as I pour a small finger into the tumbler and shoot it, wincing as it burns its way down. 'I told you Tamsin was obsessed with Lola and she was — she was . . . *bitter*, almost, about the attention Lola received. Lola was sick a lot as a teenager so she was always the main focus of their parents' attention. Tamsin was mostly left to fend for herself.'

'What does this have to do with Nate?' Right now I couldn't give a shit about how neglected Tamsin felt as a child.

'When Lola disappeared . . .' Seb lets out a sigh, as if it hurts to relive the memory. I can understand that. I have my own memories that I prefer not to revisit if I can help it. 'There was some media attention, as I'm sure you can imagine. Tamsin revelled in it, it felt like, even when the paps were shouting at her about staying with someone who might have hurt her sister.'

'That's . . .' *sick*, I want to say, but don't because Seb is here in front of me, opening up and clearly struggling. I never thought I would feel sympathy for this man, but here we are.

'Once Lola was found, and they cleared both me and Nate, everything just . . . went away. For everyone else, that is, not for Tamsin. I tried to tell her for years that it was over, that she should let things lie but she became obsessed with finding Nate, with proving that he was responsible for Lola's death. It took me a while to realise that it wasn't all about finding Nate and proving he was the one who did it. It was also about the attention it would garner. If Tamsin could prove that what happened to Lola wasn't just a tragic accident — which is what the inquest stated, they said the wound to the back of her head was where she had fallen—'

'The newspaper said it was murder,' I say, the words sour tasting in my mouth, even as relief floods my veins at the idea of Lola's death eventually being ruled an accident.

Seb shakes his head. 'Murder sells papers, Hayley. If Tamsin could prove that Nate had murdered Lola, the spotlight would be back on the case. And on Tamsin.' His mouth twists, and I realise he is as horrified by this as I am.

I've always known Tamsin is a show boater — her job makes that clear enough, as does the way she dresses and the way she is so outspoken, her laugh the loudest in the room at all times, but I never believed she was unhinged.

'And you didn't think to tell me any of this before? When I came to you, crying, saying I was worried about Nate?' I can't look at him, sure that if I do my fury will spill out, drowning him in a white-hot lava. 'You let this happen, and you didn't think for one moment to tell me that Nate was in danger?'

Seb shifts, his discomfort evident. 'You don't understand—'

'No, I don't!' I snarl, shoving my chair back and pushing my face in his. 'You let her do this, Seb! You let her take Nate, you were complicit in everything. If Nate is . . .' my throat closes over, not wanting to speak aloud the fate Tamsin has written for him, 'if Nate is hurt . . . or worse, then I'll never forgive you for this. I'll make sure both of you rot in hell.'

'Hayls, please—'

I turn on him, throwing a fist in the direction of his chest. 'Don't call me that! I mean it, Seb, if Nate is hurt I'll kill you both.'

Seb reaches out and snags my wrists in his hands, pulling me towards him. 'She won't hurt him.' He wraps his arms around me, almost swaddling me, my arms pinned to my sides as I struggle to push him off. 'She's not . . . she's not a *bad* person, Hayley. She just wants the truth about that night.'

As Seb hugs me tighter sobs erupt from my chest, ragged and brutal, clawing at my throat until it is red raw. I want to believe Seb so badly, I want to believe that Nate will come back to me, but if Tamsin is so hellbent on the truth that might never happen. Then I really don't know what I'll do.

* * *

'I think you should stay with me tonight,' Seb says, I don't know how much later.

'What?' I squint up at Seb in confusion from the kitchen chair as he looms over me, blocking the last dying rays of the sunset streaming in from the garden. The kitchen is almost dark now, Seb's shadow disappeared from the back wall, and I feel drained.

'Stay at mine.' Seb holds out a hand and pulls me into a standing position. My legs still feel wobbly, the shock of learning that this isn't simply a case of two people running off together not completely faded yet. 'You look like shit, no offence.'

I try to smile. 'None taken.'

Seb lets out a tiny huff of laughter. 'You need a good night's sleep and then maybe tomorrow the two of us can really dig in to finding where Tamsin might have taken Nate. I have a couple of ideas. Please believe me when I say I never expected things to go this far. You haven't slept properly for days . . . and I know you haven't eaten because you massacred the tomatoes. Stay with me at mine tonight — in the spare room, obviously. I don't like the idea of you here, all alone, with that broken fence panel meaning anyone can let themselves into your back garden.' He has the good grace to flush a little at this. 'At least you'll be able to sleep, knowing that I'm in the room down the hall. You'll be safe.'

Will I? The voice that echoes in my mind is still Tamsin's and I shake it off. She is the manipulative one. I believed the things she had written in her diary about Seb, had believed her when she said she was unhappy. In all honesty, the idea of sleeping in Seb's spare bedroom doesn't necessarily make me feel any safer . . . but if it means that I get access to Tamsin's things again then I'm all for it because one way or another I *am* going to find her and get Nate back.

'Sure. OK. I'll stay.' Ignoring the flutter of butterflies in my stomach, I take Seb's hand and follow him to the house next door.

* * *

Seb seems to take an age to fall asleep. I hear him moving around long after he has deposited me at the door to the spare room after a few bites of homemade quiche and salad, washed down with Diet Coke, because I want to keep my wits about me and

I've already drunk more whisky than I should have. The toilet flushes in the en suite and then finally, almost an hour after we have both retired, there is silence from the room down the hall. I wait another half hour before creeping from the four-poster bed, pulling my cardigan around my body as I slip silently towards the stairs. Light snoring comes from Seb's room and my shoulders lower, relief that he is finally out for the count washing over me. I thought he'd never fall asleep.

Despite my own exhaustion, I make my way downstairs to the study, hoping Seb has left the door unlocked. I'm not sure what I'm looking for — I suppose I just want to see everything with fresh eyes, knowing what I know now. The door opens, the hinges creaking. I pause, my heart pounding in my chest so hard I can barely breathe, and when no movement comes from upstairs, I slip inside the study.

It's tidier than it was before, that's the first thing I notice. The books are all stacked neatly in place on the bookshelves and the teetering piles of scripts on the desk have all disappeared. Is Seb not working at the moment? Or has he just cleaned house? It's almost *too* tidy, as if he's had a huge clear out and disposed of all the evidence. I catch myself at that thought. *Evidence of what?* Seb made it clear in our conversation earlier that Tamsin was behind all of this, and the whole wife swap *was* her suggestion.

The desk is clear, save for Seb's laptop, the screen dark. I swipe a finger over the keyboard and it bursts into life, the password box blinking at me. I have no chance at guessing that, so I leave it to go dark again and turn my attention to the desk drawers instead. The photographs of me are gone, as is the photograph of Lola, the life insurance document and the obituary for my grandmother. I pause in my rummaging. Why would Seb throw these things away? It's almost as if . . . a shiver runs down my spine. It's almost as if he's got rid of anything that could tie back to me and Nate.

Anything that could give any weight to what has happened over the past few days, anything that could associate Nate and I with the Coopers if we were to, I don't know . . . disappear. I feel it again, that instinctive roll in my gut that Seb isn't being one hundred percent truthful with me.

The bookshelves are neat and tidy, double stacked, and I move towards them. It's easy to hide documents in books, to slip them between the pages where no one would think to look and I pull a copy of *One Hundred Years of Solitude* from the shelf, flicking through the pages. I've never read it even though I think of myself as an avid reader, but Seb clearly has more than once, the page corners folded down and the spine cracked. More literary tomes line the shelves, all things far more highbrow than the John Grisham and Harlen Coben novels I devour. The row of books behind look more promising. They are hard covers, all larger than average, and seem to run more towards Tamsin's tastes than Seb's. They're coffee table books; mostly interior design tomes, and they are perfect to hide documents in. Pushing the paperbacks in front to one side, I run my fingers over the spines of the hardbacks, stifling a gasp as my hand rests on a navy-blue leather-bound spine. The title, printed along the spine in gold lettering says, *YEARBOOK UNIVERSITY OF BRIGHTON 2014*. Jackpot.

Anticipation buzzes through me as I pull the yearbook out, a flush of surprise heating my cheeks. This is the last thing I was expecting to find — in all honesty, I no longer know what I am looking for — but this . . . this is perfect. I realise now that my best bet is to find someone Tamsin was close to at university, someone who may even have been at the party. If all of this goes back to then, to the night Lola died, then perhaps that's my best lead to finding where Tamsin might have taken Nate.

The spine cracks as I open the cover, my eyes flicking over each page searching for Tamsin's face. I flick the pages, faster and faster, until I see something that makes my stomach drop away. Nate's face, grinning out at me, a beer in one hand and his other arm around a boy I don't recognise. It's as if someone has punched me in the gut. I should have known that Nate would pop up in here. In the photo he is grinning madly, his blond hair flopping over his forehead and I feel a wrench in my heart. He is so familiar, this Nate. He is the Nate who asked me on a date and never realised how much I'd longed for him to ask, the Nate who would sit up talking with me about everything and nothing until dawn, the Nate who remembered the tiniest details about me, things that no one had ever paid attention to before. There is no sign of the Nate that comes home to me on a Friday night, who is too busy to stop and talk, who has plans for every minute of the weekend, who barely hears a word I say. And this Nate, 2014 Nate, has no idea what's coming. Resisting the urge to tear the photo from the book, I force myself to turn the page, flicking on until finally towards the back I find Tamsin. This photo too is a gut punch. Tamsin pouts at the camera, a feathered fascinator in her hair and a long cigarette holder delicately balanced between two fingers. Lola is smiling in the background of the photo, her long hair falling over one eye, half obscuring her face, but it is the other girl in the picture, standing beside Tamsin, looking up at her with an adoring grin, who piques my interest.

According to the caption the picture shows *Tamsin Goode and Floss Barker, stars of The Drama Society, our own Roxie and Velma.* Flicking further on through the yearbook I don't find any more pictures of Nate, only one or two of a skinny, wide-eyed Lola, all of them with her hair half hiding her face, but there are many of Tamsin and Floss Barker together. At a picnic on the beach, on stage together, laughing at some sort of formal, Floss's eyes on Tamsin instead of the photographer in every picture. There is something sickening about the way Floss gazes at Tamsin and horror seeps in through my pores as I realise this is the way I must have looked at her, that day when she came to the office to take me shopping. I remember looking at her and thinking she was so perfect, I was so lucky to be her friend, and now . . . now, I wonder if Floss Barker is still enthralled with Tamsin. If they are still in contact or if Tamsin broke her heart the way she has broken mine.

There is only one way to find out. Floss is the only person from that time that I have uncovered who might still be in contact with Tamsin. *Florence*. Could Floss be short for Florence? Tamsin wrote in her diary that she met with Florence, an old friend, for coffee. Gently easing the page with the photo of Tamsin and Floss on the beach together from the yearbook, I close it and replace it on the bookshelf, arranging the other books as they were before I sneak back upstairs to the spare room. Climbing into the four-poster, I hear Seb moving around and the flush of the en-suite toilet again, before footsteps move along the hall. Switching out the lamp, I lie dead still, the duvet pulled up my chin and my breathing heavy as I hear the doorhandle turn. I can feel his eyes on me in the darkness, my heart clattering, my pulse sounding in my ears like rolls of thunder. After what feels like an hour, Seb pulls the door closed and his footsteps retreat, the faint sound of his bedroom door closing coming seconds later. I let out a long breath, my lungs burning, and reach for my phone. It takes only a few minutes for me to find Floss Barker on Facebook, her profile picture showing her standing on a beach — maybe even the same beach she sat on for a picnic with Tamsin years ago — and even less time for me to send her a friend request and a short message.

Five hours later, I wake to sunlight streaming in through the windows and a new message in my inbox.

I'd love to talk to you, Floss has written, *can you meet me today? 2 p.m., Brighton, on the pier.*

CHAPTER 37

'I was thinking we could try her yoga class today,' Seb says as he tips granola into a bowl. 'Although I'm not sure she'll actually still attend given that . . . you know.'

She's holding my husband against his will? Yeah, I kind of think that's her priority right now. I resist the urge to roll my eyes in Seb's direction — I can't believe I ever thought Tamsin would carry on her life like usual. I might have only slept for a few hours but it's more sleep than I've had all week and given my discovery about Floss Barker, I feel like a new woman.

'I don't think she'll be there, do you?' I try my hardest to keep the sarcasm from my voice, but Seb still looks at me in surprise.

'Don't you think she'll try and keep things semi-normal?' he asks. 'She doesn't need to with me because obviously . . .' he ducks his head, avoiding my eyes, 'I know she's gone off with Nate, but she might want to try and keep things normal elsewhere. She's very friendly with her yoga teacher. She might want to avoid questions.'

It sounds more to me like Seb is trying to steer me in the wrong direction, if I'm brutally honest, trying to buy Tamsin some time. I swallow down the bile that burns the back of my throat, wishing I'd trusted my gut all along.

'Why don't you go?' I say brightly, forcing a smile onto my face. There is no way in hell I'm telling him where I'm really off to today. 'If she sees me there it might spook her . . . and whatever is happening with Nate, she'll be more likely to speak to you alone.'

'What will you do while I'm gone?' Seb frowns, and I wonder if he realises that his eyes flick towards the study door.

'I'm going to go home and freshen up,' I say, my mind whirring frantically as I try to think up an excuse. 'And then I might do some digging online. See if I can't get some idea of where Tamsin might be holed up.' Not strictly a lie.

Seb takes a moment and I half think he's going to try and persuade me otherwise as he chews on his bottom lip. 'OK, well, I guess, if you're sure.' He doesn't look convinced and I don't blame him, given the fury I displayed last night. If I were him, I would be expecting me to jump at the chance to try and track Tamsin down, to confront her to her face.

'I just think . . .' I say slowly as if I am mulling things over. 'I need some time to compose myself. To think rationally about things. If I see her now I'm scared of how I might react . . . and if Nate isn't with her, I don't want to jeopardise my chances of finding him.'

Seb nods as if what I've said makes sense and I slide my sweaty palms over my trousers under the table. 'OK. Maybe I'll see you back here this evening.' He catches himself. 'Unless I find Tamsin at her yoga class. I'll text you.'

I nod in agreement, but it isn't until I am safely back in my house, watching Seb hurry in the direction of the tube station that I let out a long sigh of relief. I don't think he believes for a second that Tamsin is going to be at her yoga class, but that's fine by me. Because I want to make sure I find her first.

* * *

Brighton Pier is just as I remember it, and I breathe in the scent of salty sea air as I approach. I didn't realise how much I'd missed it. When you grow up by the sea you tend to take it for granted, assume it'll always be there, but now as I inhale the briny air, tainted with the smell of popcorn from the end of the pier my heart aches, and I wish we'd never had to leave. I'm hit with a dizzying sense of déjà vu, images flashing before my eyes one after the other — begging my mum to let me go on the rides at the end of the pier, sticky candyfloss melting on to my fingers, piping hot doughnuts, kissing Nate in the pouring rain, my hair plastered to my head as we ran, laughing, back to the car.

The pier is busy thanks to the school holidays even though the weather is the worst it's been in weeks. The sky is grey and overcast, a brisk wind riding in from the channel, and the sea is squally, white-crested waves smashing over one another. I walk along the east side of the pier, towards the arcade at the far end. Floss hadn't said where on the pier to meet, and I check my phone. It's five minutes to two. As I reach the middle of the pier where it widens out, a restaurant sitting in the centre, I see a woman leaning against the railing, looking out over the water. Her face is turned to the side so I can only make out her profile, but her hair is the same rich shade of auburn that Floss Barker's is in the yearbook photos.

'Floss?' She jumps at the sound of my voice, and I smile as she turns to face me.

'Sorry, I was miles away, off down Memory Lane.' She smiles back at me and I see a glimpse of the old Floss, the teenaged Floss, despite the weight she's put on and the silver strands that glint at the front of her hair. 'You must be Hayley.'

I wonder if I should have given her a fake name as I shake the hand she holds out. 'Thanks for agreeing to meet with me. I know it's been a long time—'

'I'm not sure I'll be able to help,' Floss stares up at me — she's a tiny little thing, five foot if she's even that — in a way not dissimilar to the way she looked at Tamsin in the photos and I shift from one foot to the other. As she pushes her hair away from her face I notice her nails are bitten to the quick.

'Let me buy you a coffee,' I say. 'It's freezing out here, and I don't know about you but I could do with some carbs with that coffee.'

Floss hesitates for a fraction of a second before she nods and we head into the pier restaurant. Impatience makes my smile a little sharper and my tone a little brisker as I order tea and a cake for myself, waiting as Floss orders coffee, cake and then a portion of fish and chips.

'Sorry,' she says sheepishly, 'I'm on a diet but today it feels like winter out there and I'm *starving*.' She gives me a sidewards glance. 'Sorry. Again. This is for Lola, isn't it?'

My brows knit together.

'The story you're writing or whatever it is. It's about Lola, trying to find out what really happened? I'm not sure I ever really figured out for myself what happened that night. Initially they thought it was an accident, a horrible tragedy, but . . .' She trails off with a shrug of her shoulders.

'Err . . . yes, that's right. I'm hoping to put together a podcast episode about what happened to Lola the night of the party.' I had told Floss in my Facebook message that I was a true crime podcaster, unsure if she would talk to me if she knew I was married to Nate. 'You were friends with Tamsin Goode, right?'

Floss frowns, waiting until the waiter has delivered our coffee before she speaks. 'Tamsin? Well, I knew her. But we weren't friends. Not really.' Her mouth twists slightly, as if she's smelled something unpleasant.

'But . . . the yearbook photos . . . the two of you look thick as thieves.'

Floss lets out a laugh, a sharp *ha*. 'We were in the drama society together, and I guess I did look up to her . . . She was just so . . . vibrant, I suppose. A talented actor. I always thought I'd see her on the television someday.'

Disappointment washes over me. 'Sorry, I guess I jumped to conclusions after seeing the pictures.'

'I was in awe of Tamsin,' Floss goes on as the waiter delivers her fish and chips, which she then precedes to salt to the point where I'm half expecting her to have a heart attack. 'Half in love with her I suppose in that platonic way some girls have crushes on other girls. Most of the Drama Society girls were. But she wasn't always a very nice person. Lola though . . . Lola was my friend. My best friend, really.'

The disappointment fades to be replaced by something deliciously bubbly. *Excitement*. 'Lola was your friend? Sorry, I assumed . . . Lola doesn't seem to be a part of things in the photos. She always seems to be hanging back.'

Talking about her dead best friend doesn't seem to have dulled Floss's appetite as she shovels a huge chunk of cod into her mouth. 'Lo never wanted to be in pictures, and that suited Tamsin down to the ground. She was always a bit jealous of Lola. Lo got offered some TV work when we were teenagers, but she turned them down after Tamsin told her the camera adds ten pounds.' She pauses. 'Lola had an eating disorder,' she explains. 'She had it under control by the time she came to uni but I think that was part of the reason why she wanted to be at the same place as Tamsin. So she would have support when she was feeling . . . you know.'

This must be the reason Lola was 'sick' as a teenager. I can imagine Tamsin — this new, brittle, spiteful Tamsin who I never knew existed — being horribly jealous of her thinner, prettier, younger sister, of the attention their parents must have poured over Lola as they tried to persuade her to want to live.

'That's why Lo never wanted to be photographed . . . why she never would have made it in show business even though she was a far better actor than Tamsin.' Floss pushes her empty plate to one side, her eyes narrowing. 'You look *really* familiar. Do I know you from somewhere?'

Wishing I had given a fake name I shake my head. 'No, I get that a lot. I just have one of those faces.' Casting my mind back over Nate's Facebook account I wonder if that's where she recognises me from, if he posted one or two photos of us together back in the day. Maybe she knows exactly who I am. My heart jumps as I speak again. 'What about Nate Turner?'

Floss looks at me with wide eyes as she takes a forkful of her cake. 'Nate Turner? There's a blast from the past.'

'You knew him?'

Floss rolls her eyes. 'Everyone knew Nate Turner. He was the star of the hockey team, went to all the parties. He was usually the last one to leave too.'

'I'd heard that he and Lola were a thing when she disappeared. They were dating?' I make it sound like a question even though I know the answer. Floss lets out a laugh, coughing as cake crumbs get stuck in her throat.

'Hardly dating,' she manages to croak out after a slurp of coffee. 'Although Nate would beg to differ, I'm sure.'

A prickle of unease makes its way down my spine, an icy raindrop of something warning me something isn't right. 'What do you mean?'

'Lola went on a couple of dates with Nate, but she wasn't *dating* him. She said he was too intense. It was all or nothing with Nate, nothing casual about it.'

Her words are like a shard of glass, piercing my skin. I don't think Nate has ever been all in like that with me, although I have been with him since the day I first laid eyes on him.

'She was going to tell him after the party that she didn't want to see him any more,' Floss goes on, her face darkening, 'but then she argued with Alex and well . . . you know the rest.'

'Alex Small? Alex who was dating Tamsin at the time?'

Floss nods, her hand going to her mouth as she nibbles at her nails. 'They had a pretty hefty argument, although I couldn't tell you what it was about. Lola was shouting at Alex and someone said he had pushed her, but I don't know how true it was. They were both drunk, but Alex was always volatile, even if he hadn't had a drink. He could be touchy-feely too, you know? Hand on your arm, around your waist, kissing you hello . . . not everyone liked it. I know Lola hated it, she thought it was disrespectful to Tamsin.'

That is Seb to a tee, and I suppress a shudder. I can't believe I ever thought he was attractive. 'Do you know who Lola left the party with that night? I know the inquest said it was an accident, her death, but it would be good to know the last person who saw her. Was it Nate?' Time seems to slow as I wait for Floss to answer.

'It wasn't Nate,' Floss says with a frown, 'at least I don't think so. I'm pretty sure Alex was the one who followed her after she left.'

'Excellent.' The word slips out before I can catch it and I carry on speaking as Floss opens her mouth, as my heart crashes hard against my rib cage. 'I mean, it's nice to have some clarity — everyone else I've spoken to has been very vague. Now, to go back to Tamsin . . . is there anywhere around here that meant something to her? Somewhere she might have holed up after everything happened with Lola?'

Floss frowns. 'Hole up? Has something happened now? To Tamsin?'

Shit. 'No, nothing has happened to her,' I lie smoothly, 'I'm just trying to piece things together. I wondered if there was somewhere that was special to Tamsin and Lola . . . a place they spent time together?' I've never been the best at thinking on my feet, and I fumble for what to say next. 'Somewhere Tamsin might have gone after to get her head together.'

Floss taps her fingers on the table as she thinks, the skin around her thumb nail red and sore, and I'm not sure she's buying what I've said. 'She didn't really hole up anywhere, she was too . . . outgoing for that.' I get the feeling *outgoing* is not the word Floss really wants to use here. 'The family did have a cottage though. Tamsin and Lola spent a lot of time there in the summer. More money than sense, that family, a cottage down here — even a tiny one like theirs — costs a fortune.'

'Where was the cottage?'

Floss cocks her head, thinking. 'Stanmer Park. It's tucked away though, hidden down a little track off the main path through the nature reserve. It's a tiny place, all crooked and old with a cute little picket fence at the front. The Goode girls used to love it there because it was so isolated — no neighbours for miles to complain about the noise. A whole bunch of us would go, Tamsin always invited as many people as she could, even though Lola would have preferred it to be just us. We'd take bottles of wine and crisps and spend entire weekends there when it was summer.'

'Where is it exactly?'

Floss pulls a biro out of her bag and scrawls a map on the back of a napkin. 'I don't know how overgrown it'll be now or if anyone has been there lately, but that should get you to the cottage.'

Excitement sparks and I push my chair back, keen to get going. 'Thank you, Floss. You've been even more helpful than I could have imagined.'

Floss gets to her feet too, looking slightly bemused by my abrupt decision to leave. 'No problem. You will credit me, won't you?' She flushes slightly. 'In the podcast?'

'Of course.' I sling my bag over my shoulder, keen to get away. I'm at the door of the restaurant before I hear Floss call out to me.

'Hayley! Just one thing . . .' She almost looks sly as she weaves between the tables to catch me up. 'I'm not sure who told you that Lola's death was ruled an accident at the inquest. That wasn't what happened at all. It's a cold case now, but the police are still looking for whoever killed Lola.'

CHAPTER 38

I don't know how I manage to thank Floss and get to the end of the pier without breaking down. *Seb lied to me. Lola's death was never deemed an accident.* If I was ever in any doubt that Seb was not to be trusted I'm not any more. Back at the car, I pound a fist against the steering wheel, glad of the cool darkness of the underground car park. I am one step closer to finding Tamsin though, and a surge of hope powers through me as I start the engine.

The satnav directs me the short distance from Brighton to Stanmer Park, the journey lengthened by the stop-start traffic of people escaping the beach before the forecasted storm rolls in. As I squeeze the car into a parking space, that is clearly marked for permit holders only, rain splatters the windscreen, the storm moving faster than I had thought. My raincoat is rolled into a ball on the backseat, along with a beanie hat and I reach round and grab them both, stuffing my hair inside the hat before getting out of the car. The wind is strong, carrying the scent of decaying sea life with it even this far inland, and a dark sense of foreboding washes over me, as if the smell of death on the air is an omen. For the briefest of moments, I think about getting back in the car and driving home, before I shake it off.

Following Floss's map I make my way through the nature reserve, the ground already starting to grow soggy with the rain, my trainers sliding on my feet as water seeps in through the fabric. Squinting as the wind buffets me from the side, I think I can spot the thin track from the path on the edge of the woodland that Floss says leads to the Goode cottage, the thick line of trees along the path swaying abruptly in the wind.

It's barely four o'clock and the sun should be high above the horizon, but thick black clouds darken the sky making it feel later than it really is. The nature reserve is empty, the dog walkers and joggers already headed home to the warm and dry, and I stride ahead, the rain stinging my face.

Reaching the winding dirt track I pause for a moment, catching my breath and checking my bearings against the map Floss has drawn, the napkin damp and beginning to disintegrate at the edges. The wind is picking up, the branches of an elderly oak tree creaking ominously as I take a minute to check out my surroundings, alert to the possibility that Tamsin could be here right now, could appear at any moment. I pull back off the path, suddenly paranoid that she will materialise in front of me and I'll lose the element of surprise. A couple run past on the tarmac path behind me, holding hands and laughing as the rain plasters their hair to their heads. I feel a pang deep in my chest, the memory of Nate and I doing the same thing all those years ago bright in my mind. It's enough to get my feet moving again, and I step out and plunge deeper into the woods, my eyes scanning the path ahead for the first glimpse of the cottage.

I spot the dark outline of a crooked chimney when I am still several feet away, bramble bushes thickening on either side of the path to encroach onto the dirt track as I head towards it. As I get closer, I hear twigs snapping and a figure that looks familiar approaches from deep within the trees, a dog bounding beside him. The man wears a Barbour, a hat pulled down low over his eyes to protect him from the weather, but he is the right height and build for Seb, the dark curls escaping from the edge of hat a dead giveaway. My heart threatens to burst out of my chest as he lopes towards me, his gaze focused on the ground in front of him.

'Shit. *Shit.*' Every limb shaking with adrenaline, I squeeze behind the thick trunk of an ancient elm tree, pressing myself against the rough, weathered bark, rain dripping insistently onto my head and down my collar. My chest feels as if a rubber band has been placed around it, too tight to allow me to breathe and I feel the familiar sensation of a panic attack tugging at the edges of my mind. *Five things*, I whisper under my breath, *five things I can see, hear, touch, smell*. Rubbing my fingers over the bark until I feel the sharp prick of a splinter, I breathe in deeply as I listen to the rustle and crunch of footsteps in the brush until I feel more myself. Risking a peek from behind the tree, I step out on to the dirt path only to almost bump straight into the man in the Barbour.

'Sorry,' he tuts, as he sidesteps me, whistling to his dog — a Dobermann, not a rottweiler at all — and carries on towards the nature reserve without a backwards glance.

It's not Seb. A harsh bark of laughter escapes my throat and I press my lips together, feeling weak with relief.

'Get it together,' I whisper to myself, pinching the back of my own hand as the wind gusts another avalanche of rain into my face. Seb lied to me about Lola's death being found an accident, and that means if Tamsin knows that too then Nate is definitely in danger. I can't afford to lose my shit, not when I'm so close to tracking them down. Head down, the woods empty now the weather has driven anyone else inside, I make my way towards the cottage.

The paint on the window frames is weathered and peeling, and the small picket fence that Floss remembered is barely standing. The door is tightly closed, the wood cracked and aged, a gnarly, untamed knot of roses winding their way around the frame. This has to be the place. There isn't another cottage around, and Floss said it was isolated. Steeling myself for confrontation, I knock sharply on the front door, shifting from foot to foot as I wait for someone to answer. No one comes, and there is no sound of movement from within, so I peer in through the tiny window at the front of the house. There is a yellowing net curtain across the filthy glass, but if I press my face to it I can just about see inside, although the lighting makes everything gloomy and dark.

There is a tiny sink over a cupboard at the rear of the room, a small worksurface beside it. There is a sofa, barely big enough to seat two people and leaving the tiniest of walkways between the sofa and the open fireplace, the cushions covered with a blue blanket, the pattern on it vaguely familiar. The cushions are piled at one end, as if someone has lain down to nap and I feel the first flicker of suspicion. What looks like empty takeaway cartons sit on the floor space beside the sofa, along with empty Haribo sweet wrappers. *Nate loves Haribo*. He could easily eat a huge bag entirely to himself in one sitting. My stomach lurches and I press my face harder against the glass, ignoring the cramp in my calves from standing on tiptoe. My instinct lights up like a beacon, my gut telling me this is the place. This is where Nate and Tamsin have been this whole time. The takeaway cartons, the bunched-up cushions, the blanket I now realise is the same as the patterned blanket on Tamsin's sofa back at the house, it all points to her.

Something sitting on a tiny coffee table beside the sofa catches my eye, and I pull away from the window. *A phone*. It's an iPhone, a bright white skull etched into the case. *It can't be*. With shaking fingers, the sour taste of bile on my tongue, I pull out my phone and dial Nate's number, my heart beating faster when the phone on the coffee table begins to buzz.

Tamsin and Nate have been here. Fury flares in my veins replacing the panic I felt earlier and I turn to the trees almost daring Tamsin to be walking towards me, but there's no one there. The woods are empty, a lone, brave crow picking at something dead and bony on the path.

'Hello!' I hammer on the door again, showers of paint chips littering the doorstep as I pound my fist against the wood. 'Tamsin! I know you're in there!' Pulling back I call up at the upstairs window, but there is no response, the only movement the crow taking flight with an anguished caw.

Stepping around the side of the cottage, I try to push my way through the thick brambles that have grown over the path until it is impossible to pass, thorns snagging on my clothes and on my hands. I call out to Nate, my voice hoarse, but there is no response. If they were here before, they aren't here now.

Heading back around to the front of the cottage, I slide my hand into my raincoat pocket, my fingers closing around a business card. Harry had them made for me at Wendy's suggestion a couple of years ago and I think I've only ever given out two or three. For some reason Wendy thought it was important for people to know my title and office phone number, I never saw the point before, but now I am grateful for it. Pulling the business card free, I tuck it into the doorjamb of the cottage, pushing it right in so the wind can't take it. Tamsin will know I've been here, will know I'm not going to rest until she tells me where Nate is, and it's with a renewed sense of determination that I turn and head back towards the car, the wind fighting me every step of the way.

The determination runs through me, firing me up as I drive, right up until I hit the M23. My phone rings, the car play announcing the caller as Seb. Squinting against the rain that sheets down the windscreen faster than the wipers can clear it, I jab at the button to answer.

'Hello?'

Seb's voice is tinny and I turn up the volume. 'Hayley? Where are you?'

Shit. I'd forgotten I had told him I was going home. 'Out in the car at the moment,' I say, deliberately vague. I clench the steering wheel, my knuckles turning white. 'I'll be back in an hour or so.'

'Call me when you're back. I'll come straight over.'

That's the last thing I want. I want a long, hot bath, and then I'm going to call Tamsin via Nate's phone and leave a voicemail to tell her to meet me.

'Hayley? Are you still there?' Before I can reply, Seb's voice comes down the line as clear as if he was in the car beside me. 'I've heard from Tamsin. She's told me she knows everything now. She knows the truth about what happened to Lola.'

CHAPTER 39

I am still shaking when I pull up outside the house, Seb's face peering out at me from his front room window as if he has been pacing there the entire time I've been driving home.

'Where have you been?' He's at the driver's door, yanking it open before I even have a chance to unclip my seatbelt. 'You look like a drowned rat. Let's get you inside and get you a hot drink. Or better yet, a brandy.'

Resisting the urge to shudder, I shake my head. 'I just need to change into something warmer, that's all.' Pushing past him I shove my key in the door and step inside, half hoping he'll take the hint and go back next door. No such luck. Seb follows me inside, standing too close to me as I pull off my damp raincoat.

'I need a shower,' I say, taking a step back, my shoulder blade hitting the newel post behind me. I know I should be jumping at the chance to find out what exactly Seb knows, but there is a part of me that is overcome by dread, by the idea that once I hear what it is he has to say, nothing will ever be the same again. 'I can come over to yours after.' Even though the thought of it makes my stomach roll, a leaden ball of anxiety sitting in my guts.

'I'll wait here. Make you tea and something to eat.' There is a steeliness to his tone that brooks no argument, so wearily I nod and head upstairs.

Once the shower is running, I sit on the closed toilet seat, my head in my hands, Seb's words echoing in my mind. *Tamsin knows the truth about what happened to Lola.* Does she, really? Can I believe a word that comes out of Seb's mouth, given that he's lied about his name, and pretended he was as clueless as I was over Nate and Tamsin's disappearance? If Seb isn't lying, and Tamsin really does know what happened that night, then I don't know what this means for Nate, for me. Hot tears spring to my eyes and I let them fall, safe in the knowledge Seb won't be able to hear me over the running of the shower. I wish, more than anything, I could go back to the beginning of the summer. I would never have watched the Coopers move in, would never have longed to be a part of what they have if I'd known. A deeper, darker part of me wishes I could go back even further, to the night Lola disappeared and undo everything. I wish I could have stopped Nate from ever going to that party, have him never have met Lola in the first place.

'Hayley? Are you all right in there?'

Glancing down at my phone I realise I've been sitting here, crying blankly, for almost twenty minutes. 'Yep,' I call back, my voice more wobbly that I would have liked. 'Won't be a sec.'

I shower as quickly as I can bear, not sure if it's the soothing thud of hot water hitting my shoulders that keeps me under the steam or the thought of going downstairs to face Seb and hear what Tamsin has had to say. Eventually, I step out, throw on a tracksuit and head downstairs.

'Here.' Seb pushes a bowl of soup towards me as I enter the kitchen, the chicken-scented steam rising from the bowl making my stomach growl, but I don't lift the spoon.

'Tell me what Tamsin said,' I say, crossing my arms over my chest. Finally, I feel ready to hear it, although the tightness in my chest and the ache at the back of my throat say otherwise.

'Just what I told you — that Tamsin says she knows what really happened that night. The night Lola died.'

I swallow, uncertain for a moment if I am going to be able to hold back the nausea that sweeps over me in a hot wave. 'She must have said more than that. You're her husband, you were a part of it all. You can't tell me she didn't explain anything.'

'I swear to you that's all she said. It was a bad line, it sounded like she was outside, in the storm.'

Was she at the cottage? Did I miss her by mere minutes? My hand creeps to my mouth, the way Floss's did in the restaurant, and Seb's eyes rake over me almost as if he is trying to gauge my reaction. 'Is she coming here? Did she say anything about me?'

'You?' Seb frowns and shakes his head. 'I don't know. She didn't say anything about coming here, but who knows with her?'

'What about Nate? Did she mention him? Was he there with her?'

'She didn't say anything about Nate—'

'How did she sound?' My mouth is dry, as if I've woken up after a night of drinking, and the smell of the soup that was so appetising moments ago now turns my stomach. 'Did she sound . . . ?' I don't know how best to express it, but *vengeful* is the word on my lips.

Seb frowns, his eyes never leaving my face. 'She sounded . . . upset, I guess. I mean, it's hardly surprising. But, Hayley, this might be for the best—'

'Aren't you worried?' I snap. 'You were there that night, aren't you worried she's found something out about your part in it all?' I think of Floss telling me how Seb was over-friendly, too tactile, how the girls — and Lola — felt uncomfortable around him.

Seb's eyes narrow and a sharp dart of fear makes me take a step backwards, but before I can process it his face softens. 'No, I'm not worried for me — but I am worried for *you*, Hayley. I think maybe you should stay with me again tonight, or if you want I can stay here. Just in case.'

Absolutely fucking not. 'That's not a good idea.' The last thing I want is for Tamsin to come home and find me ensconced in her house like the wife swap was a good idea. And even more, I don't want Nate to come back and find me in Seb's house. I don't want Nate to think I ever gave up on him for even a second.

'I can keep you safe.' Seb edges around the table, closing the distance between us. His eyes are fixed on my face, and he reaches for me. I step back, my heart clattering in my chest, as he continues to loom over me.

'I don't need to be kept safe,' I manage, skirting around the other side of the table and out into the hall. He follows and I open the front door, ushering him out. 'I'll be fine. I'll keep my phone by the bed and if anything happens, I'll call you.'

Reluctantly Seb nods, and as I close the door on his retreating back that leaden ball of anxiety returns. I hope I haven't just made a terrible mistake.

* * *

Reheating the soup I manage to eat half the bowl, the greasy chicken stock coating my tongue making me regret picking up the spoon, before I rinse the rest down the sink and shove the bowl in the dishwasher. I tour the house, checking the doors and windows to make sure everything is locked up tight and closing the blinds in the sitting room to shut the world out, a thin layer of dread humming under my skin as I move from room to room. The storm that hit the seafront seems to have followed me home, rain lashes against the window as I stand in the bedroom and my phone pings with a weather alert, advising people not to travel unless absolutely necessary. I am about to close the curtains when lightning flashes across the sky, but it's not the rumble of thunder that follows that makes me jump.

There's someone in the trees. Pressing my face to the glass I look out over the dark garden. Rain is pouring down, splattering the patio in a steady stream from a hole in the ancient guttering. The moon is gone, covered by storm clouds and the trees sway in the wind, the leaves hissing. *Maybe I imagined it.* Seb's bombshell that Tamsin has been in contact has left me unsettled and uneasy, unsurprisingly, and I wonder if I am jumping at ghosts, shadows in the trees.

'Just go to bed,' I whisper to myself, checking my pocket to make sure my phone is there. No one in their right mind — not even Tamsin — would be outside on a night as filthy as this, and I force myself to yank the curtains closed. *It's just the storm*, I tell myself, *the wind riling up the branches of the trees.* Even so, as I move towards the bed I pick up a pair of scissors from the dressing table, the weight of them reassuring in my hand as I slide them under my pillow.

I don't remember falling asleep until I jolt awake. It took me ages to drop off, lying awake until my eyes were gritty and sore, but I must have eventually slept as now I sit bolt upright, my heart pounding in my chest. Reaching for my phone, I check the time. *2.13 a.m.* I've been asleep for a couple of hours, at least, but I don't know what tugged me awake so rudely.

A noise. There was a noise downstairs. My hands shake as I lay my phone on the bedside table, straining to hear any movement from below. An insistent tapping comes from the landing, and for a moment I think I might pass out with fright before I remember the cherry tree in the front garden. When it's windy the branches scrape against the landing window, the sound of bony fingers tapping against the glass.

'Idiot,' I mutter under my breath, turning on to my side and tugging the duvet up to my chin. My phone screen is black, and the last thing I remember before I let sleep drag me under again is the thought that if I haven't heard from Tamsin by the morning then I'll call Nate's phone over and over until she answers. I'll challenge her to tell me where my husband is, and to come and tell me face to face exactly what she thinks she knows about the night Lola died. Because there is no way I'm letting this go on for any longer than it already has.

I don't know how much longer it is when I jolt awake again, my breath stuck in a wheezing gasp as if someone has gripped me by the throat, but it can't be longer than half an hour or so. Foggy and disorientated, I roll onto my back, wondering if it's the tapping of the branches against the window again that woke up me up. But it's not the branches. Fear paralyses me, a scream desperately trying to tear free as a shadow looms in the corner of the bedroom. A figure moves across the bedroom towards me.

'Hello, Hayley,' a voice rasps, and horror turns the blood in my veins to ice.

CHAPTER 40

A hand clamps over my mouth before I can scream, the pressure of cold metal — a wedding band? — pressing against my lips, and I thrash from side to side, the duvet twisting and tangling around my body as I try to get free.

'Hayley, stop. *Stop!* Jesus Christ, just lie still. I'm not going to hurt you.'

Eyes wide, my nostrils flaring as I struggle to breathe with my mouth sealed shut, I stop struggling, my body going limp. A faint floral scent reaches my nostrils and I close my eyes, willing my heart rate to slow before a full panic attack drags me under.

'Good girl,' the voice says. 'Are you going to scream?'

I shake my head, my eyes still closed.

'OK. Open your eyes. Look at me.'

I open my eyes as the hand is removed from my mouth, and I make out Tamsin's silhouette in the gloomy darkness. '*You.*' I struggle into a sitting position, but Tamsin sits on the edge of the bed, pressing her hand against my chest, pushing me back against the pillows.

'You said you wouldn't scream, remember?' There is an edge to her voice, something that isn't anger or rage but more like . . . *fear*. 'Listen to me, Hayley, I don't have much time to explain—'

'*Don't have much time?* You've had over a fucking *week*.' Anger isn't a strong enough word to describe the emotion washing over me as I push myself up the pillows. 'Where is my husband, Tamsin? Where the hell have the two of you been, don't you understand—'

'*You* don't understand,' she hisses. 'Now shut the fuck up and let me speak.'

I snap my mouth closed, suddenly noticing the small baton she holds in one hand. For a moment I don't think I'll be able to hear her over the pounding of my own heart.

'I'm sorry,' is the first thing she says and I frown, an apology the last thing I was expecting. 'This whole thing . . . I fucked up, I got everything wrong.'

'You don't need to apologise,' I lie, my mouth dry. Tamsin holds up a hand to shush me, peering over her shoulder towards the bedroom door. When she turns back to face me, she gives me a brisk nod, but her eyes are wide and her breathing is erratic. *She's terrified*, I think, something inside me softening. Maybe Tamsin isn't here to hurt me, she's here to warn me. 'Tamsin, where is Nate? Won't you tell me where he is? I need to see him, to know he's OK.'

'Hayley, all of this . . . it was never meant to go this far, I thought it would be easy to . . . I don't know, get to the truth.' Tamsin swallows and I gently snake out a hand to turn on the bedside lamp. The bedroom is washed in a soft, golden glow and I feel my heart rate slow a little, feeling more at ease now I can see her face — and more importantly, if she moves to lift the baton. On the pretence of shifting to get more comfortable I slide my right hand under the pillow to grip the scissors. My fingers close around the reassuringly solid handles and I inch them into a better position before I snake my hand back out.

'I don't know where to start.' Tamsin's chest hitches and she blinks hard. 'At the beginning, I suppose. I had a sister,' she says, her eyes welling up.

'I know about Lola,' I say, ignoring her sharp intake of breath. 'I know she went to a student party and didn't go home that night . . . I know she died. I'm sorry.' My own voice thickens, a lump forming in my throat.

'Not as sorry as me,' Tamsin says, a harsh note creeping into her voice. 'I should have been there too that night, but I was being fucking childish. I went home instead, annoyed because my little sister was crashing a party with my friends, and I didn't want her there.' There is a pause, thick with tension and I feel it again, a sensation that has become so familiar over the past week or so. The sensation that I am about to fall and everything around me will shatter into tiny pieces.

'Nate was there that night,' she goes on, tapping the small baton against the palm of her other hand. It's small and black, the extendable kind that I imagine police officers might use. 'At the party, did you know that?'

I sit motionless, not sure how to respond. Tamsin has lost that air of fear surrounding her and seems more on edge, more volatile, in a way that I would connect more with Seb than with her.

'That's why I engineered the wife swap,' Tamsin goes on, the baton still thudding against her palm. 'I had to get him on his own, away from you and Seb. I wanted the truth, that's all. All he had to do was tell me the truth.' Her voice cracks and a fear slices through me. 'I kept messaging him — we had phones that you didn't know about — and I was pushing and pushing for answers, but he just kept cutting me off.'

'Where is he, Tamsin?' Images of Nate lying bloodied and bruised in the cottage flicker through my mind, a showreel of horror and violence. Tamsin doesn't reply. 'I knew about the burner phones,' I say. 'I found them after you both disappeared, saw the text messages between the two of you.' Even now, the betrayal stings like vinegar in a paper cut.

'You thought he was so perfect,' Tamsin says, 'I never look at Seb the way you looked at Nate, and all I could think was how *dare* he have this wonderful life with someone as beautiful and kind as you, when Lola had hers ripped away from her? And then you started to tell me that things weren't that perfect between you.' She gives me a look I can't interpret, but if I had to, I would say was smug. 'I knew Nate would agree to the swap even if you didn't. He was afraid of what I might say to you if he refused.' The branches of the cherry tree tap against the landing window again and Tamsin jumps, her face paling. 'We don't have much time,' she says again. 'We have to get you out of here.'

'No.' I grope under the pillow, sliding the scissors down under the duvet to my side. 'I'm not leaving until you tell me where Nate is. I want to know it all, Tamsin. I want to know the truth about what happened to Lola the night she died.'

* * *

Tamsin's leg jiggles as she shoves a hand through her hair. 'You don't understand, Hayley. We have to leave. I know what really happened that night and I need you to come with me. He knows I know everything and he's coming for me. For us.'

Black spots dance at the edges of my vision as I battle to keep my breathing under control. *What does she know? Who is coming for us?* Forcing myself to draw in a long breath, I try to keep my voice steady. 'I can't come with you, Tamsin. Not until you tell me everything.'

She shakes her head. 'We don't have time.'

'I'm not leaving,' I say, pressing myself against the headboard. I don't know where she'll take me, what she'll do to me. I am not leaving, not with her. 'If you don't tell me, I'm going to call the police.' I whip my hand out and grab my phone from the nightstand. 'But if you tell, me we can fix all of this together.'

There is a long, drawn-out silence, and I'm scared I'll pass out with fear before Tamsin speaks. 'OK. But then you need to do exactly what I tell you.' She stares at me, the baton still gripped tightly in her fist, and panic licks at my insides. I know now, whatever she says, one way or another this is all going to end tonight.

'Nate knew exactly who I was and what I wanted the moment he laid eyes on me,' Tamsin says. 'Do you remember that first night the two of you came to dinner together? I thought he was going to pass out, the way his face lost all colour. I'd tried for weeks to talk to him, but he refused, he just shut me down every time.' I think of the two of them standing too close together in the wine cellar that night, the way suspicion had trickled down my spine. 'In the end I told him to get two burner phones so we could talk privately, and that if he didn't do it, I'd tell you everything.' Something drifts across her face at the memory, as if she enjoyed that brief moment of power over him. 'The night of the swap I put something in his drink, just enough so that I could manage him on my own.'

'You took him to the cottage in Stanmer Park.' I feel sick, imagining the fear Nate must have felt when he realised what Tamsin had done.

'I must have given him too much, because he all but passed out and I needed Seb to come and help me get him out through the back garden, to the car. We had to sneak him out through the broken fence panel . . . I didn't want you to see us leaving on the Ring camera. I needed you to think Seb was your ally.' She blinks, before turning to me with a small smile. 'You were out for the count after what you and Seb did together.'

I swallow, nausea sending sour bile into my mouth. 'Just tell me what happened to Nate.'

'I thought I knew what happened at the party — I told Nate I knew he was seeing Lola, knew that she wasn't as keen and that he was there the night of the party. I was so sure . . .' A sob creeps up her throat and she presses a hand to her mouth to contain it. 'And then Nate told me something that turned my whole world upside down.' She stares me dead in the eyes. 'He told me he saw what happened that night.'

My stomach lurches, and my fingers tighten on the handle of the scissors.

'He told me Seb was the one who killed Lola. Seb pushed her, made her hit her head. He left her there to die. There was a brace-let found at the site, on the ground beside her body. It was one of those woven types, like a friendship bracelet. Seb was wearing one that night. They all had them, a bunch of lads and girls who were . . . the popular crowd, I suppose. If we lived in the US, it would have been like a fraternity/sorority type thing.'

I hardly dare to breathe. I didn't know any of this. Didn't know about the bracelet being found beside Lola's body. The only thing I was ever really sure of was that Nate didn't kill Lola. 'It was definitely Seb's?'

A sound comes from downstairs, and Tamsin gets to her feet, her eyes wild. 'We have to get out of here.'

'It's just the wind,' I say, pushing back the duvet but keeping the scissors hidden. 'That's all. It causes the house to make all kind of moans and groans. Please, Tamsin, you have to tell me everything and then I promise we can leave. It'll all be over.'

'Nate knew about the friendship bracelet,' she says, 'the moment I mentioned it he told me Seb was wearing one. That Seb and Lola had argued, even though Seb swore blind to me that they didn't. He said she was drunk and he told her to calm down a bit so she yelled at him. But Nate said it wasn't that at all.' She gazes somewhere over my shoulder as if reliving that moment.

'They argued because Seb tried it on with her,' I say quietly. 'Floss Barker told me.'

'Floss?' Tamsin looks at me sharply. 'Everything Nate said about that night . . . it told me Seb was dangerous. He's not the man you think he is.'

I beg to differ. I think I've had Seb's number from the moment Tamsin and Nate disappeared. 'He hurt you.'

'We all know I don't cook,' Tamsin says, glancing down at the stripe of burnt scar tissue on her arm. There is a creak from somewhere downstairs again and Tamsin yelps, dragging me from the bed. 'We have to go, you're not safe here.'

Tamsin's grip on my arm is tight enough to leave a bruise and panic flutters in my stomach. Fear has her in a stronghold and where she seemed almost rational a moment ago, now, the wildness has returned to her eyes.

'Wait, let me grab something warm to wear.' Yanking myself free I pull on a hoody from the end of the bed and manage to slide the scissors up inside the sleeve. If Seb believes Tamsin thinks he killed Lola, if he knows she's here, he's going to try and kill us both to stop the truth from coming out, then I am prepared to do anything to defend myself.

'Come on,' Tamsin grabs my hand, crushing the tiny bones and it's as if her panic is transferred between our palms, black spots dancing at the corner of my vision as the creak comes again, closer this time.

'That's the stair at the top of the landing,' I whisper, gripping Tamsin's hand tightly as a wave of dizziness washes over me. 'He's inside the house. He's fucking here, in my house.' *Did Seb want me to stay with him tonight, knowing Tamsin would come here and tell me she thought he was a murderer?* The thought makes the dizziness worse and I press a hand against the wall, so afraid I can hardly stand. 'Tamsin, wait.' I grab her arm before she can reach out to open the bedroom door, her baton raised. 'Where is Nate? You need to tell me, in case . . .' I break off, not wanting to voice it out loud. *In case Seb kills you.*

The creak of the floorboard outside the bedroom floor seems to fill the room and Tamsin yanks me around to face her, her eyes wide and her face a sickly shade of cream.

'That's what I'm trying to tell you,' she hisses, as fear grips my heart in its icy fist. 'I thought it was Seb, and then I realised it couldn't be him after all.'

CHAPTER 41

I can't breathe. My throat closes over and as I try to pull myself free from Tamsin's iron fist she pulls me ever tighter, her grip like a vice.

'Let me go!' The words are a strangled sob as her fingers crush the tiny bones in my hand and then the bedroom door flies open and I stumble, feeling punch-drunk as my legs try to give way.

'Nate!'

Tamsin reels back with a gasp, finally losing her grip on me and I fly past her, almost knocking her to the ground in my haste to get to Nate, to make sure he's OK and he's really, actually here.

'Nate, oh, my God, thank God you're here!' Sobs tear from my throat as I reach for him, but Nate sidesteps me, his eyes on Tamsin.

'You're OK? She didn't hurt you?' He keeps his eyes on Tamsin as he asks me this. 'Tamsin, you need to—'

'You're a fucking *murderer*,' Tamsin hisses, her fingers tightening on the baton in her hand. She is staring at us both, and for one horrifying, dizzying moment I don't know which of us she is talking to.

Nate holds up a hand in a peace gesture and I realise he is wearing gloves. *Why is he wearing gloves?* I don't have time to process the thought properly before Tamsin is speaking again.

'Tell her, Nate,' she says, her voice ragged and her breathing harsh. 'Tell your wife how you killed my sister.'

'I didn't kill her,' Nate says wearily. He looks exhausted, the dark circles under his eyes making him look haunted and sickly. 'I already told—'

'It was the bracelet.' Tamsin turns to me now, and my heart crashes against my rib cage. 'That was meant to be the thing that convinced me, wasn't it, Nate? That was meant to be your proof that you didn't kill her, only it backfired on you.'

Nate says nothing and that flicker of fear grows stronger in my veins. I tuck my hand up into the cuff of my hoody, my fingers pressing against the reassuringly sharp blade of the scissors.

'What is she talking about, Nate?' He doesn't answer and I turn back to Tamsin. 'What do you mean? You told me yourself Seb was wearing the bracelet that night before they found it beside Lola's body.' Nate looks at me sharply, but Tamsin goes on, her voice cracking as she waves the baton about.

'The friendship bracelet,' she says again. 'Nate tried to tell me it was proof that Seb was there when Lola died, but it isn't proof at all. Something just didn't sit right with me, you know? There was something niggling away at the back of my mind, and I remembered how I knew Seb wasn't wearing the bracelet the night of the party.' She pauses, the air around us thick and heavy. 'I had the proof all along that Seb wasn't wearing it. Thank God for Floss and her obsession with her digital camera.'

Like a bus rear-ending me, I suddenly know what she's talking about. 'The photo of Lola in Seb's office. It was taken that night, at the party. Seb is in the photograph, in the background.' It's like all the air has left my lungs and I struggle to draw in enough oxygen. 'You sneaked back into the house and took it. It was you, lurking in the trees, watching me.'

Tamsin swallows, before she steps forward with a determined look on her face. 'I have looked at that photograph every day since

Lola died. I could tell you the position of every leaf on the trees, every blade of grass, every freckle and mole on Lola's body. Seb's hand is shading his eyes in that photo . . . and there's no bracelet on his wrist. He'd already lost it by then.'

My mouth is dry and I look up at Nate, who shakes his head. 'I don't know what you're trying to say but I never had one of those bracelets. I wasn't in that crowd, I barely knew Lola.'

Something cracks inside my chest. *He's lying. I know for certain that he's lying. Floss Barker told me herself he was dating Lola.* As if she can read my mind, Tamsin echoes my thoughts.

'You're lying,' she snarls. The air thickens and Nate's hand slides behind him, towards the fireplace. 'Lola had one of those bracelets — she was in that crowd, because of *me*.' Her lips curl as she flexes her fingers around the baton. 'She lost hers . . . and I called her out on it, two days before the party. Do you know what she told me? She told me that she'd *given it away to a boy*.' She laughs, high-pitched and oddly jarring, the tension almost palpable. 'She gave it to you, Nate! She brought you home, to our house. The only boy she ever brought back. Just that one time, but I saw you in the kitchen and I knew then you were going to be the end of her.'

'None of this is true.' Nate looks at me as if begging me to believe him, but I can't meet his eyes. I know he was seeing Lola, and it stands to reason that he was the boy Lola gave the bracelet to, if they were serious enough for her to bring him home for the weekend. I remember the diary entry, Tamsin talking about a boy standing in the kitchen. I thought it had been Seb. 'When I left Lola she was fine . . . or at least . . .' He swallows, and I realise he doesn't even believe himself. He doesn't believe for a second that Lola was fine when he left her, and a crevice inside me cracks wide open.

'*She wasn't fine*,' Tamsin roars, her cheeks an alarming shade of puce as spittle flies out of her mouth, hitting Nate in the face.

'You *killed* her, you shoved her so hard against that tree that you gave her a head injury and she *died, all because of you!*' Without warning, Tamsin launches herself in Nate's direction, the baton connecting with the side of his head with a bone-cracking thump. She shrieks as Nate crumples to the ground, the baton striking him over and over as Tamsin screams Lola's name.

'Nate . . . Nate!' His name is a wild shriek on my lips, as I rush at Tamsin with all my strength. I don't remember pulling the scissors out. Don't remember them sliding from beneath my cuff into my hand. All I remember is the way it felt when they slipped between Tamsin's ribs. *You can tell when the meat is a good cut,* I hear Seb's voice in my ear, the first night I went to the Coopers' for dinner. *The knife goes through it like butter.*

CHAPTER 42

'Tamsin!' Her name like a war cry on the air snaps me out of the daze I am in, standing over a bleeding Tamsin and a groggy Nate. 'Tamsin? Hayley!'

Fuck. It's Seb's voice and immediately the fog surrounding me clears and I press a hand to my mouth. 'Nate?' I whisper, snatching at his arm. 'Get up, we have to get out of here. Seb's here, he's in the house. He thinks Tamsin thinks he killed Lola — he's going to kill us to stop the truth coming out.'

Nate gets to his feet with a groan, one hand going to the back of his head. It comes away bloody, but the wound doesn't seem to be gushing which is hopefully a good sign. He staggers slightly, stumbling back against the fireplace and I right him, resisting the urge to slap him awake.

'Seb is coming and he's going to hurt us, Nate, just like he hurt Lola.' I stare into his eyes until he nods, although I'm still not sure he fully understands what I'm saying.

'Tamsin? Hayley?' Seb's voice is a roar, filling the hallway outside the bedroom as his footsteps crash along the landing, pain and anger lacing his words. The door flies open, bouncing on its hinges with a crash that rumbles through my entire body. It takes only a second for Seb's eyes to land on Tamsin, a crumpled, crimson ball on the floor. The sound he lets out is like nothing I've ever heard before. An animalistic, broken wail that shatters the air before he turns on Nate.

'You!' Venom leeches out of him and I see his face darken, the way I've seen happen before.

'Nate, run!' I shout from behind Seb but Nate wavers, his hand going to the companion set on the hearth, his fingers wrapping around the cast-iron poker as he tugs it free. Before he can raise his hand, Seb is on him, his hands going to Nate's throat.

'You killed her.' Seb's voice is a ragged wheeze as he squeezes Nate's throat, Nate's eyes bulging and his face a shocking crimson as he struggles beneath Seb's weight, the poker still in his hand.

'No!' I scream, launching myself onto Seb's back. I wrap my arms around his neck, trying to pull him off but he's too strong. 'Stop!' Seb bucks beneath me, trying to shake me off but I cling on tighter, the sounds of Nate's ragged attempts to breathe slicing into my skin. I manage to get an arm around Seb's neck and I crook my elbow, tightening up my hold and I hear Seb gurgle. If I can just hold on for long enough . . . Seb releases Nate and he manages to draw in a breath, but Seb only lets go long enough to flip me off of his back and shove me hard enough that I go flying, crashing against the bed frame.

Slumped against the oak legs of the bed I retch, unable to draw a breath. Tamsin still lies on the floor, the carmine pool spreading from her rib cage telling me she won't be getting up. I retch again, the image of her smiling on the doorstep, welcoming me inside as she invited me for dinner playing like a movie. *I just wanted to be her friend*, I think vaguely, for the short time we were friends, before all of this happened, she was one of the most important people in my life. I don't have time to process things before movement from across the room catches my eye. Seb is on top of Nate again, his hands squeezing tightly and Nate is no longer thrashing beneath him.

'No.' The word is barely a whisper as I struggle to sit up, pressure on my chest making it difficult to breathe. Tears run down my cheeks as I make it on to my hands and knees and begin to crawl across the floor towards the poker, which has fallen from Nate's hand. I am inches away when a hand reaches down and scoops it up, and then there is a crack and Seb falls to the side.

'Nate?' Sobbing, I crawl over to him as he draws in a gasping breath, the colour fading from his cheeks as he opens bloodshot eyes.

'Hayley? Oh, my God, Hayley, are you all right? I knew it, I knew I was right to keep an eye on you.' Raising my eyes, I wonder if I am imagining things, but no. There is Wendy, standing over Seb's unconscious body, one hand pressed to her mouth, the other hand holding the poker.

CHAPTER 43

Six Months Later

Nate links his fingers through mine as we walk along the pebbled beach, the chilly February wind whipping my hair across my face and making me wish I'd worn a hat. As if he's read my mind, Nate tugs the beanie from his own head and shoves it on mine with a grin.

'Told you you'd need a hat,' he says, before leaning in to kiss me. 'Bit different to the beach at Christmas, eh?'

We'd spent Christmas and New Years on a beach in Tenerife, a first for both of us and one that Pauline wasn't terribly pleased about. It turns out Pauline really does hate me and Nate never told her he was unhappy with me at all, although I should have known from the minute she rocked up at our wedding in a dress that was more bridal than my own. I've told Nate that it's OK, and I'll do my best to get along with her, but we'll see how that turns out. Now, we walk along a British beach, breathing in damp winter air, our fingers linked to keep warm. I've never been happier. Or at least, I've not been this happy since Nate and I first got together. It's Deal beach in Kent. Not Brighton. I don't think either of us will ever return to Brighton.

Wendy saved the day, that horrible night back in August, when I thought Nate was lost to me forever. She called the police and they arrived just as Seb came round from being hit on the head with the poker. Tamsin died, on my bedroom floor, bleeding out from the wound I gave her, trying to save Nate. The head injury, combined with the choke marks around Nate's neck were enough for the police to agree it was self-defence. Seb was arrested, and he's now awaiting trial for Lola's murder, as well as attempted murder for Nate. Nate doesn't remember a lot about that night, his memory left hazy and gappy after Seb strangled him. It's my word against Seb's about what happened to Lola that night . . . but I have the diary left by Tamsin, detailing how he treated her as proof of his volatile behaviour.

'Fancy a hot chocolate? With brandy?' Nate turns to me with a grin as we pass a café.

'Brandy for you, maybe, not me. But yes please. Grab us takeaway cups and we can carry on walking.' My heart wants to burst as he kisses me quickly and turns and hurries inside the steamy café. I press a hand against my belly, the baby's foot pressing reassuringly against my skin in response. Add to that the fact that I handed in my resignation at the office days after it all happened, and Nate is fully on board with me starting my own interior design company once the baby is old enough, and things couldn't be better. *Everything I've ever wanted is right here*, I think with a sigh, pushing down the tiniest shred of doubt that presses against my rib cage every now and again. The doubt that this baby will be born with dark eyes, like Seb, instead of Nate's startling blue ones.

A flash of blonde hair catches the corner of my eye and I stand up straight, turning to watch the woman pass by. She looks familiar for a second, and my heart crawls up my throat and into my mouth, before I shake my head. Tamsin is gone for good. I watched them take her away myself, but it doesn't stop me from seeing her ghost at moments when I least expect it. Like the other night, for example. Nate was in the bathroom, I could hear him humming as he brushed his teeth, and I was sitting at the vanity taking my make-up off. The trees were swaying in the wind, and I could have sworn there was movement outside, a dark shadow moving through the trees, just like before. Sometimes, when I step outside into the garden I can feel the prickle of eyes on me, and I glance over the fence at the Coopers' garden, even though the house is empty and has been since that night.

I suppose it's time to think what really happened to Lola, clear my own slate if you like, before the baby comes. I was there that night, at the party. Of course I was. I was wherever Nate was in those days. He'd come into the pub, winked at me when I dropped his change into his hand and I was a goner. It just took him a little longer to notice me, that's all. I followed him, to class, to hockey, to drinks out with his friends. Maybe Floss had been right about Nate being more into Lola than she was into him, because I'd never seen them together when I was following him. If I'd known how seriously he'd felt about her, maybe I would have backed off. Probably not, though. Nate and I were always destined to be together.

At the party, I'd lurked on the fringes, invisible to everybody, watching as they all drank more and more, the 'popular' crowd braying and laughing like the arseholes they all were. Nate was desperately trying to catch some girl's — *Lola's* — attention, and when the red-and-white woven bracelet had slipped from his wrist, no one had noticed when I stooped to pick it up, slipping it over my own wrist before bringing my hand to my nose, able to smell the faintest scent of his aftershave on it. It was a shame for Nate, but Floss was right about Lola, she was more interested in all the other boys. Anyone who would look her way, to be honest.

I missed the argument Lola had with Seb — I never even realised Seb was there, or if I did see him I didn't know who he was. All I could see was Nate. So I watched as Nate ran after Lola as she stormed out into the grounds, hurrying towards the woods. I watched as he tried to comfort her, tried to wrap his arms around her in a way I wished he'd do to me. Lola had shoved him, and from my position behind a thick, old oak tree I'd watched his face change, anger making him ugly for the briefest of seconds before he'd shoved Lola back, her head rebounding off the trunk of the tree behind her. She'd crumpled like a marionette with her strings cut, and the anger on Nate's face was replaced by horror as he leaned over her. Seconds later, the sounds of the party drifting closer on the breeze, Nate had pressed his hand to his mouth and run away, towards the long winding drive where the cars were parked, the roar of an engine following shortly after.

When I approached Lola, leaning down to lift her head, she had groaned, her eyelashes fluttering on her cheeks and the relief I'd felt melted away to leave the bitter taste of disappointment. Her skin was grey, despite the thick make-up she'd piled on in an effort to look more grown-up for the party, and looking back now it was no wonder I hadn't recognised her in the photograph Tamsin kept. I'd barely had the chance to step away before she'd started choking, vomit splattering the hem of her skirt. I didn't know what to do. She was alive, I could see that, but what would happen to Nate? He was the one who left her in this state. Surely she'd tell everyone, report him. I had to protect him. I'd tried to tug her upright, but she was a dead weight, slumping to the side as she continued to choke. So I stepped back and instead I waited. Lola had coughed and gasped and retched until she just . . . stopped. Her eyes were wide, her lips already turning a startling shade of blue when I turned and walked calmly away, already thinking about how I would be brave and comfort Nate when he heard the news. I never even noticed that the friendship bracelet had slipped from my wrist.

EPILOGUE

Wendy moves away from the window as the car pulls into the space behind the removal van, her heart clattering in her chest as she slides the bright gold bangle she wears up and down her arm, the ruby stones catching the light. She doesn't know why she's so nervous — after all, it's not like she hasn't met the new neighbours before. In fact, she feels as though she probably knows them better than they know themselves.

Wendy has been trying to strike up a friendship with Hayley for years, ever since she first started working with her. Hayley is everything Wendy wishes she was — she's kind and professional, capable and efficient, has a lovely home and a lovely husband. Everything Hayley wants, Hayley gets. At least, Nate was lovely until that woman came on the scene. Maybe that's why it hurt so much when Hayley introduced Wendy to her new friend the day she left the office early to go shopping. Because Hayley had held Wendy at arm's length for all this time, and now she was standing there with the woman that Wendy had seen out for an intimate dinner just a few weeks before with Nate.

Wendy tried to tell Hayley. She pretended she'd seen Nate in an upmarket restaurant in Harrogate when he went up north on a fishing trip. She tried to keep an eye on her, just to make she was alright, knowing that it would all come out sooner rather than later. And then Hayley would turn to Wendy for a shoulder to cry on . . . only she didn't. And then Wendy had to make sure she kept an even closer eye on Hayley. Luckily, the fence panel at the bottom of the garden hadn't been fixed. Wendy had tried to give Hayley a hint — texting from another number to tell her that Nate wasn't who she thought he was, and not to trust him, but Hayley didn't respond. She'd even taken Hayley's parcel of pregnancy books into the house, when she stopped by and it was raining all over the package, not wanting them to be spoiled when Hayley came home. She'd made sure to slip in through the fence panel, using the spare key to the back door that Hayley kept hidden under a plant pot. She didn't want to alarm Hayley by appearing on the Ring camera. When Wendy saw Tamsin's flashy husband lean down and slash Hayley's tyres that night, she knew she would be the only one who could take proper care of Hayley when the time came, but she knew she had to bide her time. Especially when Hayley didn't respond to any of her WhatsApp messages.

Now, she watches as Nate and Hayley step out of the car. Nate says something that makes Hayley laugh, and then reaches out and swats her on the bum. Hayley turns her face to his and wraps her arms around his neck for a quick kiss and Wendy smiles. They're back to how they used to be, thank goodness, after all the unpleasantness. Hayley points at the removal van as she tucks her arm through Nate's and Wendy takes that as her cue. Sliding the bangle off her arm — she's not sure if Hayley ever noticed it was gone from her desk drawer — she shoves her feet into her Uggs and marches up the front path, taking care not to get caught in the rose bush. That's the first job she's going to tackle once she and Matt are settled in.

'Hellooo,' Wendy calls out as Hayley's smile falters, surprise etched all over her face.

'Wendy,' she says, her arm tightening on Nate's. 'What are you doing here?'

Wendy beams and gestures towards the removal van, thrilled to finally reveal the secret she's been keeping. She hasn't texted Hayley for months for fear of letting the surprise slip.

'We're moving in! We're going to be neighbours!' She reaches out and squeezes Hayley's arm. 'I've been keeping an eye on things here for months and months and now . . . Well, we got a bargain after what happened. I'm so excited to be neighbours!' She watches Hayley's reaction, thrilled by the widening of her eyes. She knew Hayley would be pleased — after all, neither Hayley nor Nate would still be here if it wasn't for Wendy. Matt calls her relationship with Hayley obsessive, but Wendy knows she just really cares about her. 'We're going to be *such* good friends.'

THE END

ACKNOWLEDGEMENTS

This book has been such a joy to work on and that is in part down to the incredible team I get to work with. Huge thanks to Kate Lyall-Grant and Kate Ballard for your patience and your wisdom! And to Tara Loder, an incredible editor who spots all the things I get wrong in my early drafts and always knows the best way to fix them.

It wouldn't be proper acknowledgements if I didn't give my thanks to the best agent in the business, Lisa Moylett and her amazing team at CMM. I have been so lucky to have you and Zoe on my side for the last decade. Extra double thanks to Lisa and to Izzy for making the book sexy.

To Darren O'Sullivan, Steven Kedie and Annabel Kantaria for all of the usual things. I don't know how many books in we are between us now, but I know that I couldn't do it without you guys on the end of the phone.

To Abi, Caz, Emily and Lisa. What an absolute joy you are — therapists, comedians and FBI agents all rolled into one. I am so grateful to Tedd for bringing us together and I know if ever I go missing, you guys will be the ones to find me (use my Facebook profile picture for the missing posters, ha ha).

To Timothy, for making me laugh my head off on the days when the words are hard to find, and for passing my books around to everyone you know. I am so grateful for your support and friendship. Enjoy your name check — I always said I'd put you in a book!

And, always thanks to Nick, George, Missy and Mo — every time I start a new book I say I'll be less of a psycho, but we all know that's never going to happen. I love you guys.

THE JOFFE BOOKS STORY

We began in 2014 when Jasper agreed to publish his mum's much-rejected romance novel and it became a bestseller.

Since then we've grown into the largest independent publisher in the UK. We're extremely proud to publish some of the very best writers in the world, including Joy Ellis, Faith Martin, Caro Ramsay, Helen Forrester, Simon Brett and Robert Goddard. Everyone at Joffe Books loves reading and we never forget that it all begins with the magic of an author telling a story.

We are proud to publish talented first-time authors, as well as established writers whose books we love introducing to a new generation of readers.

We won Trade Publisher of the Year at the Independent Publishing Awards in 2023 and Best Publisher Award in 2024 at the People's Book Prize. We have been shortlisted for Independent Publisher of the Year at the British Book Awards for the last five years, and were shortlisted for the Diversity and Inclusivity Award at the 2022 Independent Publishing Awards. In 2023 we were shortlisted for Publisher of the Year at the RNA Industry Awards, and in 2024 we were shortlisted at the CWA Daggers for the Best Crime and Mystery Publisher.

We built this company with your help, and we love to hear from you, so please email us about absolutely anything bookish at feedback@joffebooks.com.

If you want to receive free books every Friday and hear about all our new releases, join our mailing list here: www.joffebooks.com/freebooks.

And when you tell your friends about us, just remember: it's pronounced Joffe as in coffee or toffee!